Love and Omissions

A Novel by Neva Bell

For my sister. You're my rock. Lubalu!

Chapter One

No voicemail today.

Kate Marshall is simultaneously relieved and let down when she sees the red light on her office phone is not blinking. Her twinge of disappointment annoys her. It's been ten years for God's sake.

The first voicemail came three days earlier.

"Kate, this is Matt. Matt Sloan." A long pause. "I know this is awkward, but please call me. I have something important to discuss with you." After leaving his cell number, Matt cleared his throat and mumbled, "Well...goodbye."

Kate was so perplexed by the message that her anger didn't hit her for a solid thirty seconds. Once it did, she hit the delete button without writing down Matt's number.

The second voicemail came the next day. Matt still sounded a bit nervous, but was more assertive. "Kate, this is Matt again. I really need to speak with you. I promise it's important. Please call me."

This time, Kate hit the delete button without waiting to hear Matt's number or send off.

By day three, Kate was not at all shocked to see the blinking light on her office phone. She was amused by the third message, but not enough to call Matt back.

"Jesus Christ Kate. I know you're getting my messages. Just call me. It's important."

Sure it is, she thought as she hit the delete button.

Kate's best friend Theresa Miller, or "T" as Kate has called her since they were kids, enjoyed spinning the reasons why Matt could be calling Kate after all these years.

1

"Maybe he's dying. Seeing you is all he needs to pass peacefully," T pondered over dinner last night.

The thought of Matt's untimely death made Kate smile a little.

"Maybe he's in a twelve-step program and you're part of the forgiveness step," T guessed next.

Matt liked to drink, but Kate couldn't imagine him having an addiction problem.

"That man can't commit to anything long enough to be addicted to it," was Kate's response.

T's best guess: "Maybe he has been miserable without you for the last ten years and wants to beg you to give him another chance."

Also highly unlikely.

In the end, the two couldn't come to an agreement about whether Kate should return Matt's calls. T insisted Kate call him, if only to satisfy her own curiosity. Kate refused to call Matt because the thought of talking to him made her dizzy.

When there is no voicemail on the fourth day, the relief of not having to decide whether to call Matt definitely outweighs any disappointment that Matt gave up.

Kate sets her files down on her desk and flops into her chair. She's just given her students the instructions for their Employment Law final. Now she has to sit in her office and wait out the four hour exam period. Kate will eventually have to grade those exams, but she doesn't want to think about it at the moment. She has big things going on this summer and grading exams isn't one of them.

Kate is logging on to the email server when her office door flies open. The door slams against the backstop and the breeze it creates knocks over a stack of papers on the edge of Kate's desk.

"Hey!" Kate yells as she bends down to pick up her papers. She is assuming a crazy law student, flustered by an exam

question, has come barreling into her office. "That is not how…"
Kate stops when she sees who is at the door.

It's not a student.

It's Matt.

Here in her office.

And he looks pissed.

Matt stares back at Kate for a moment before walking into her office and shutting the door.

"So, you are alive," he says simply.

Kate can't catch her breath. She is stupefied Matt is here. Face to face. Kate turns to look at the message light on her phone as if the red light should be flashing now. It isn't.

"Kate, do you really intend to continue ignoring me while I stand here?" Matt asks her.

Kate glances back at him. Matt looks exactly the same as he did ten years ago, except for a bit more salt in his pepper black hair. His eyes glow a hazel brown and cut right through her.

Get it together girl! Kate yells at herself.

She clears her throat. "I thought failing to return your phone calls would be indication enough that I don't wish to speak with you."

Matt smirks. "Yes, I got the subtle hint Kate. Unfortunately, I do have something I need to speak with you about. If you would have returned my calls, I wouldn't have been forced to fly in from Colorado to visit you in person."

"Colorado?" Kate asks incredulously. "You flew in from Colorado to see me?"

Matt sighs. "I didn't come here for the sole purpose of seeing you Kate. Again, all you had to do was call me back."

Kate stymies her disappointment and hardens her tone. "Then why are you here?"

3

"I got a phone call from Phil Harmon. Judge's lawyer."

Kate is puzzled and a bit thrown that Judge is somehow involved in Matt's visit. "Phil called you? About what?"

As Matt sits in the chair across from her desk, Kate can't help but notice how his crisp blue dress shirt sets off so well against his black dress pants.

Must have left his blazer in the car, she thinks to herself.

Matt always favored a black suit. He sometimes dabbled in grays, but never brown or olive. Of course, that was ten years ago. He could wear purple suits now for all she knows.

"Apparently, Judge has something in his Will requiring the both of us to speak with Phil."

"What?" She's genuinely shocked. "Phil hasn't even spoken with my family about Judge's Will yet. We're supposed to have a meeting with him later this week."

Matt nods his head. "I know. Phil told me the same thing when he called me the other day. Phil also asked your mother to have you call him to discuss this."

Kate sighs. Her mother is the most forgetful person on the planet.

"My mom didn't pass along the message. What could Phil possibly want to talk with us about?"

Matt shrugs his shoulders. "No idea. Phil won't give me the slightest clue. When I told him you won't return my calls, he said I need to get my butt to Columbus and figure it out. He told me not to bother coming to his office unless you are with me."

"Why do we need to go together?" Kate whines. She knows she sounds like a child, but she's still dazed by Matt's presence.

Matt's face hardens. "I don't want to do this anymore than you do Kate. If I didn't love Judge as much as I did, I wouldn't be here."

4

Kate snorts. "Oh, you loved Judge, huh?"

"Yes, I did," Matt answers, his tone icy.

"Enough to skip his funeral?"

Matt shifts his weight. "I didn't think you would want me there. Don't act like you would have welcomed me with open arms."

He has her there.

"Fair enough," Kate concedes.

Kate was happy when Matt didn't show up to her grandfather's funeral. She knew Judge kept in touch with Matt over the years and worried Matt would make an appearance. Kate spent most of the visitation peeking at the door to make sure Matt wasn't walking in.

They both sit in silence for a minute. Neither knowing what to say.

Shaking off images of Judge in his wooden casket with powder blue lining, Kate breaks the silence.

"Do you have Phil's number?"

Matt takes his cell phone out of his back pocket and reads the number to Kate. Dialing it on her office phone (message light still unblinking), Kate feels her heart racing.

Matt is here. Right here in her office.

She's fantasized over the years about what she would do if she ever saw Matt again. The various things she would say. Sometimes the words are hateful and the daydream ends with her slapping Matt across the face. In others, he apologizes profusely and the fantasy has a much tawdrier ending.

Kate hears a low ticking sound and realizes she is clicking her pen over and over again. The point of the pen shooting in and out like a deranged cuckoo bird. Kate sets her pen down and sneaks a peek at Matt. Thankfully, he is looking down at his cell phone.

A memory floods Kate's mind. A younger version of herself standing outside the door of Matt's old apartment. She's in a tight dress with her high heels in her right hand. Should she knock? Should she go home?

Before the memory can go any further, a peppy female voice chirps in her ear. "Law Office."

That's an awfully brief greeting, Kate thinks.

"Hi. This is Kate Marshall. I'm calling for Phil."

"Phil is with a client at the moment Ms. Marshall. But he's expecting your call. He wants to schedule an appointment with you and the gentleman from Colorado."

"Okay." Kate shifts her glance to Matt.

He puts his cell phone in his pocket and looks at her with his hands clasped in his lap.

Kate asks the receptionist, "When is the soonest we can see him?"

"Are you and Mr. Sloan both available tomorrow morning around 10 a.m.?"

Kate wonders how much this secretary knows and whether it is worth her time to beg the receptionist for information.

Without asking Matt, Kate answers. "Yes. We can be there tomorrow at ten."

Kate sees Matt smirk out of the corner of her eye.

"Okay then. We'll see you tomorrow morning."

After muttering a "thank you," Kate hangs up the phone.

Matt stands up and walks toward Kate's door. "I'll see you tomorrow at Phil's office."

"I guess so," Kate responds.

Before Matt walks out the door he threw open a few minutes earlier, Kate stops him. "Matt…."

6

Matt stops in the doorway and glances over his shoulder.

"This isn't going to be good, is it?" she asks.

Matt frowns. "I don't know. Judge was full of surprises." With that, Matt walks out the door and shuts it behind him. Gone as quickly as he appeared.

Kate sits rapping her fingernails against the top of her desk for a moment. "Judge, what are you up to?" she asks out loud.

She can only think of one thing to do. Kate picks up her phone and dials Theresa's telephone number.

*   *   *

Matt lets out a breath after he shuts Kate's office door. Standing in the hallway of the law school, he gives himself a minute to gather his composure.

The hallways are empty and quiet. Every professor's door, with their name plates and office hours plastered on the front, are closed. The receptionist downstairs told Matt it's exam week, which explains the church-like quality in the hallways.

Matt turns around and looks at Kate's door again. "Katherine Marshall, Ph.D., J.D." her gold name plate reads.

Judge told Matt a few years ago Kate accepted this position and it made Matt happy. Kate used to say she'd like to be a law school professor. Now here she is, with her very own shiny name plate.

Matt hears Kate chattering on the other side of her door, but can't quite make out what she's saying. His goal was to barge into Kate's office shock and awe style. Get in, get out. Be done with this whole thing.

But seeing Kate's face temporarily stunned him. He sees her face in his dreams every now and then and thinks of her often. Judge's updates ensured Matt knew exactly where Kate was and what she was up to as the years passed.

Still, Matt had naively believed he could keep her at arm's length. Finish whatever business it was Judge left behind and leave Kate in his past forever.

Being in the same room with Kate was almost too much to handle. Her brown hair is longer than she kept it back then, but her green eyes still shine brightly off her pale skin. Kate's complexion and frame indicate she has taken care of herself, but this doesn't surprise Matt. When they were younger, Kate ate healthy and enjoyed running. Matt would tell people Kate only had two vices – booze and him.

Matt smiles remembering this. The memory is bittersweet. It reminds him of a happy time, a time that came to a screeching halt one night ten years ago.

Matt turns away from Kate's door and starts down the hallway toward the steps. Memories he's repressed over the years come back with a vengeance. Kate at the bar smiling over her beer glass. Kate laughing over a stack of books at the Courthouse library. Kate tangled in his bed sheets…

Alright, cut it out! Matt yells at himself. You cannot let this woman get to you.

Matt steps out into the warm sunshine and slips on his sunglasses. This meeting with Phil better go quickly or he is in a lot of trouble.

*   *   *

"Did he look good?" T asks later that night.

Kate and Theresa are sitting at their favorite local bar for happy hour. Kate can't drink like she used to, but she imbibes every now and then.

"I hate to admit it, but he looked good."

Theresa hits her with a string of questions, most of them related to Matt's appearance.

Yes, he was dressed well.

8

No, he didn't gain weight.

Yes, his ass still looks good.

No, he didn't try to feel her up.

"Seriously T, he was in my office for five minutes, if that. There isn't much to tell."

"Yeah, right. You probably banged him on your desk." T winks.

Theresa is what most people would refer to as a "slut." But to Kate, T is just adventurous and a little immature in the relationship department.

Theresa is blessed with a tall, lean body she doesn't work hard to maintain. She has beautiful stick-straight black hair, thanks to a regular visit to her hairdresser. Her eyes are a beautiful sky blue most believe are color contacts. But Kate has known Theresa since they were in the same kindergarten class. She can verify Theresa's eye color is God-given.

Men love Theresa, and she loves them. One of these days Mother Nature and gravity will catch up with Theresa, but until then, she is going to flaunt her assets.

Kate grunts. "Please. Give me a little more credit than that."

Theresa sighs. "I'm disappointed. I thought for once you'd be able to outdo me in the sex story department." Theresa's face turns more serious, "What do you think Judge is up to?"

Kate picks at the napkin under her beer. "I don't know. My family hasn't heard the contents of the Will yet. Phil keeps telling my mom he is going through the preliminary stuff and he'll get back to us."

Kate found the delay a bit strange, but she doesn't know a thing about probate law. Judge and Phil were friends for years. If Judge trusted Phil, so does Kate.

T sits thoughtful for a moment. "Do you think Judge left something for Matt in his Will?"

Kate shrugs her shoulders. "I guess he could have. He talked to Matt fairly regularly. But that doesn't explain why I would have to be there for Matt's meeting with Phil."

"Maybe Judge wants you to hear it for yourself." Theresa pauses before adding, "You know, so you don't try to fight Matt for whatever he's getting."

The same thought had crossed Kate's mind, and it upsets her.

"Do you think Judge thought so little of me?" Kate asks.

T raises an eyebrow. "Come on Kate. He knew how much you despise Matt. We all do."

"Yeah, I know. But there's no way I would fight something Judge wanted."

She wouldn't, would she?

The thought of Matt getting something from Judge hurts her a little. Kate didn't approve of Judge keeping in touch with Matt after their fallout. But she never asked Judge to stop speaking with Matt. Kate's only request was for Judge to stop filling her in on the details of Matt's life. She didn't want to hear it anymore.

Theresa reaches across their high-top table and pats Kate's hand. "I'm sure whatever it is, it's not half as bad as you're imagining. Judge loved you, and he wouldn't do anything to hurt you."

Kate smiles. "You're right. I'm just nervous."

After calling over the waiter for another round, T asks, "What does Scott think about this?"

Kate drinks the last sip of beer in her glass before handing it over to the waiter. "I haven't had the chance to tell him yet. I'll tell him tonight at home."

"Does he know about Matt?" T asks.

Kate nods. "He does."

"All of the details?" T presses.

"Most of them. The important ones."

Kate has told Scott almost everything about her past, including Matt. She left out the details about how crushed she'd been. Scott didn't need to know that part.

*   *   *

The next morning, Kate limits how much time she takes to get ready. Scott will be suspicious if she overdoes it. She's usually a "light make-up and out the door with wet hair" kind of woman.

Scott took the news about Matt in stride. Like Theresa, he is more interested in what will happen at Phil's office than Matt making a cameo in her life. Perhaps the scathing way Kate spoke about Matt reassured Scott he has no reason to be concerned.

Kate puts on an emerald green wrap dress and a pair of nude heels. Simple enough.

Sure people tell her all the time she looks great in the dress and that it makes her green eyes pop. And she hardly ever wears heels anymore. But she is meeting with Phil, one of Judge's dearest friends. She has to look put-together for him, right? The extra time she is taking to get ready has nothing to do with Matt. Not a thing.

Kate breezes into the kitchen and fills a to-go mug with coffee from the Keurig. Scott is sitting at the breakfast bar with a bagel in one hand and the newspaper in the other. His blonde hair is wet from his shower and a blue towel is wrapped around his waist.

Scott lets out a whistle as Kate opens the fridge to grab some milk. "Gonna make Matt eat his heart out today, huh?"

Kate grimaces. Her attempt to look indifferent failed miserably.

Scott smiles. "I get it. You have to look good for the ex. He has to see what he's missing."

Kate puts her coffee cup down. "Okay, I'm changing."

11

Scott stands up from his chair and snags Kate's arm before she can get away. "Absolutely not." He leans in and smells her hair. "You look and smell amazing. I like it."

Kate is relieved. This is Scott. He isn't the jealous type and he isn't the kind to make her feel silly for dressing up for Matt. Scott understands her and all of her craziness. Which is exactly why she agreed to marry him when he proposed five months ago.

"Thanks baby." Kate kisses Scott and smiles as he licks his lips.

"Lip gloss too, huh?"

Kate laughs. "I'm pulling out all the stops today."

"You siren. I kind of feel bad for this guy now." Scott pulls away after giving Kate a quick kiss on the cheek. "You better get going before I mess up that pretty dress of yours."

Kate grabs her purse and car keys. "I'll let you know how the meeting goes. Hopefully it's one, two, three."

As if Judge would ever make it that easy.

*   *   *

Kate pulls into the parking lot of Phil's office and runs her fingers through her hair. She avoids the temptation to put on more lip gloss or to check her reflection in the mirror. She doesn't want Matt to see her primping.

Phil's office is a quaint, one story brick building a block from the Union County Courthouse. Union County is a rural county neighboring the Columbus metro area. It took Kate almost an hour to get here from her condo in the Short North.

Frowning at the wrinkles that formed in her dress during the drive, Kate steps out of her car. There are only three other vehicles in the small parking lot outside Phil's office. Kate guesses the Toyota with the green rental car logo on the back window is Matt's. Kate squares her shoulders and steadies herself before opening the glass door to Phil's office.

The lobby area is tiny. There is a cutout in the wall for a receptionist's window. Next to the receptionist's window is a door Kate presumes leads back to Phil's office. There are four chairs lining the opposite wall and Matt is occupying one of them.

A young woman in her twenties with her hair pulled back in a ponytail sits behind the cutout. She's on the phone, but nods at Kate to acknowledge her.

Matt looks up from a *Car & Driver* magazine. "Good morning." He says it so blandly. Like he's never met Kate before. Like they've never...

Never mind that, Kate thinks to herself.

"Good morning," she responds, hoping she sounds as apathetic as he did.

The receptionist hangs up the phone and Matt turns in her direction. "Cindy, will you let Phil know we're both here?"

Cindy blushes when Matt flashes her a smile. She's nearly giggling when she says, "I sure will."

Kate rolls her eyes, but she can't blame poor Cindy. She remembers what it feels like to be on the receiving end of one of Matt's mega-smiles.

Kate stands near the front door awkwardly. Not really sure if she should take a seat.

Please be fast Phil, Kate silently pleads.

Kate glances at Matt out of the corner of her eye. He is buried in the *Car & Driver* magazine again. He is wearing jeans, a blue t-shirt and a pair of grey running shoes. He probably didn't spend any time this morning thinking about what he should wear, but he still looks good.

Bastard, she thinks.

Just as Kate decides to take the seat furthest from Matt, Phil opens the door to the lobby. His eyes light up when he sees Kate. "Kate! Long time, no see!"

13

Kate is sorry to see time hasn't done Phil any favors. His face is worn and his once black hair is now grey and balding. Phil was one of Judge's law clerks years ago. After leaving the Court, Phil opened his own probate law practice. But he remained close with Judge until his passing. Phil spends half the year in Florida. Most of his contact with Judge had been via telephone the last few years.

Kate walks over and gives Phil a hug. "I know! I was thinking about it last night. The last time I saw you was at one of Judge's barbeques years ago."

Judge held many barbecues over the summer as he considered himself a grill master. He invited anyone and everyone, and most people showed. Judge made sure he invited all of his previous law clerks. He liked staying in touch with them and finding out where life led them.

Phil nods his head. "That sounds about right." Phil frowns. "I'm sorry we couldn't make it up for Judge's funeral."

"Phil, you had back surgery. It's perfectly understandable."

"Still, I feel awful for not being there." Phil frowns a moment longer, then brightens back up. "You look great."

Kate smiles. At least someone appreciates her efforts.

Phil turns to Matt, who is putting down his magazine. Matt extends his hand and Phil shakes it vigorously. "So you're the infamous Matt Sloan."

Matt raises his eyebrows at this, seemingly as surprised as Kate is. What exactly had Judge told Phil about Matt?

As if reading her mind, Phil explains. "Judge talked a lot about you Matt. You were one of his favorites."

Matt smiles. "As were you."

"It's weird we've never ran into each other at one of Judge's functions."

14

Matt clears his throat and throws a glance at Kate. They both know Kate forbade Judge from inviting Matt to any of his barbecues.

Seeing an odd tension between his two visitors, Phil interjects. "Yes, well, I'm sure you're both very curious about why you are here. Let's go talk in my office, shall we?"

Kate steps in line behind Phil as he shows them to his office at the end of the hallway. They walk past two additional offices that appear to be unused, a small kitchenette, and a tiny bathroom. Despite the sunshine outside, the wood paneling makes the hallway feel dark and narrow.

"Do you share office space with anyone?" Matt asks from behind her.

Phil keeps walking. "No. I had another associate working for me, but I'm starting to wrap up my practice. My wife says it's time for me to retire."

Phil steps into his office and waits for Kate and Matt to walk inside before closing the door.

Phil motions to two tattered, black leather chairs sitting in front of his desk. "Please, have a seat."

To Phil's credit, his office is immaculate. Unlike Kate's desk, his desk is organized. Pencil holder, computer and inbox sitting just so. Kate is jealous of organized people; she isn't one of them.

Phil pulls a large file out of a metal filing cabinet before sitting at his desk. As Phil rummages through the file, Kate walks around the office. Phil's diplomas and various accolades cover his walls, along with pictures of his family. Kate smiles as she glances from picture to picture. The young, dark haired boys she recognizes as Phil's sons becoming older and older as she goes along.

She also spots a picture of Judge. He's standing with Phil at one of his infamous parties. Phil has his arm around Judge's shoulder while Judge grins over the grill, a hamburger flipper in one hand and a beer in the other.

Kate touches the black frame of the photograph and slides her fingers down Judge's face, as if she can feel his skin underneath.

"Ah, here it is," Phil says from behind her.

Kate turns around and sees Phil holding a packet of papers he's dug out from the file. Matt is sitting in one of the chairs by Phil's desk. Kate takes the seat next to Matt and puts her purse in her lap. The feeling of dread in her stomach is heightened when Phil sets the paperwork down and clasps his hands in front of him on his desk.

"Now, before I read the pertinent portion of Judge's Will, I want you both to know I advised against this. Please, don't kill the messenger."

Kate and Matt exchange a glance.

Yikes.

Phil clears his throat and puts on his reading glasses.

Chapter Two

Ten Years Ago

It was warm for October. Matt and his friends took an outside patio table at Patrick's, a bar about two blocks from the Courthouse. Patrick's was packed on the weekends, but being a Thursday, there were plenty of open tables.

This was the first time Matt and his law school buddies met at Patrick's. Their usual bar in German Village was shut down, and they were looking for a new spot. Patrick's was different from the hole in the wall they used to go to. But Patrick's had beer, and that was all they really needed.

Everyone arrived on time, except for Alex. Per his usual, Alex was late. Alex always had some excuse for being late, but Matt suspected Alex just wanted to make an entrance.

Not waiting on Alex, the group of three each ordered a beer and lamented their work week.

"Ugh. One of these days, I'm going to tell him to shove it up his ass!" Dan grumbled.

Dan worked for a large firm downtown. His managing partner, who by Dan's description had to be in his nineties, was the meanest bastard you'd ever meet. Matt watched Dan age about twenty years in the two years since they graduated from law school.

Tom laughed. "I keep telling you man, transfer to the litigation department. They don't even check my billable hours."

Tom worked for the same firm, but for a much better partner.

"Fuck that," Dan grunted. "Litigation sucks. I'll stick with wills and probate."

17

"Suit yourself." Tom took a swig of beer and then yelled, "Hey Alex! Glad you could make it man."

Matt turned to look for Alex, who was never hard to find. Alex stood about 6'3" and was often told he looked like Thor come to life. If Thor cut his hair and wore a suit and tie.

Matt fancied himself more the Superman/Clark Kent type. At around six feet tall with black hair, he met the physical requirements.

Of all of his law school friends, Matt met Alex first. They sat next to each other in Constitutional Law and hit it off from day one. Alex kept Matt entertained with stories about his hare-brained adventures, stories Matt suspected were half true. And Matt helped Alex with homework and studying. Alex was the relaxing influence Matt needed in his hectic law school life.

After law school, both Matt and Alex went to work for the public defenders office. Matt left after a year or so to clerk for the Honorable Judge Payne of the United States District Court for the Southern District of Ohio, Columbus Division. Alex was still working at the public defenders office.

Alex came bounding up to the table and put his briefcase in the chair. He fumed as he wrestled his tie off of his neck.

"What's up with you?" Dan asked before Matt could.

Alex huffed and took his seat. "Some bitch at the bar blew me off. Can you believe that shit?"

Alex wasn't rejected often, and he didn't take it well when he was. Alex often made himself feel better by declaring that the girl who blew him off must be a lesbian.

The three of them – Matt, Dan and Tom – all leaned over to look inside the bar.

"The blonde or the brunette?" Tom asked.

"The brunette," Alex grumbled. "Where is the waiter? I need a drink."

18

Matt checked out the brunette. She was talking and laughing with the bartender and stirring the stick in her drink. Matt could see why Alex went for her. She was pretty and Alex had a thing for brunettes. Matt would have thought nothing more about it if the brunette hadn't turned her head to the side, allowing him to see her full profile. Matt wasn't certain, but he was pretty sure it was Katherine Marshall, Judge Penny's law clerk.

Katherine started working at the Courthouse two or three weeks prior and Matt had not spoken with her at length. She already had a reputation for being a hard worker. She never joined the others for lunch in the break room and didn't go out for drinks with them after work. She smiled if she passed Matt in the hall, but she didn't stop to chat.

No one knew much about Katherine. The only thing Matt knew about her was she graduated from Yale's law school. But Matt knew that before her first day of work. It was the talk of the Court.

A Yale grad? Coming to the Southern District of Ohio? Why?

Cora, a fellow law clerk, told Matt the other day she tried talking with Katherine and it was like talking to a wall. Matt knew better than to accept Cora's opinion as gospel. She was the type of girl who talked poorly about everyone.

Matt didn't necessarily enjoy Cora's company, but they hooked up occasionally. His "friends with benefits" relationship with her had been on and off for the last year. He hated to say it was out of desperation, but whenever he'd gone a while without any action, he called Cora.

Matt couldn't be sure from this distance if the girl was Katherine, but decided to go for it. Alex would be pissed if Matt managed to get the brunette's number after she shot him down.

Matt took a drink before setting his beer down. He pushed back from the table and stood up. "Well, let's see if I can make it happen."

"Make what happen?" Tom asked.

19

"I'm going to get her number."

Tom still looked confused. "Whose?"

Dan had a wide grin on his face, all too familiar with how competitive Matt and Alex could be when it came to women. "The brunette, dumbass."

Matt rubbed his hands together. "Yes, that's right. The brunette."

Alex snorted. "Good luck."

"Bet you a round I get her number."

Alex extended his hand and they shook on it. "Deal."

Matt walked away feigning confidence.

What the hell am I going to do if she isn't Katherine? Worse, what if it is Katherine, and she's as snobby as Cora says she is?

Matt weaved through the tables inside the bar and took a deep breath before walking up to the brunette. Her hair was pulled back in a messy bun, with strands falling onto her white sleeveless shirt. There was a hint of a tan on her skin, but she wasn't a girl who baked in the sun or tanning bed.

Her chocolate brown blazer was hanging on the seat behind her and her brown heels were on the floor under the bar stool. She had one leg tucked underneath her, and the other swinging back and forth as she chatted with the bartender.

"Um, excuse me," Matt muttered as he tapped the brunette on the shoulder. When she turned around, Matt was relieved to see it was in fact Katherine.

A smile spread across her face. "Hey, I know you. Matthew, right?"

The bartender huffed as he walked away to check on his other customers. He wasn't happy to lose Katherine's attention.

"Yes, but call me Matt." Matt took the seat next to Katherine and glanced over his shoulder. The guys were all watching him from the patio.

Matt winked at Alex, then held back a laugh when Alex flipped him off. Matt returned his gaze to Katherine. She was much more approachable here than she was at work. She didn't look as cold and closed off.

"So you're *the* Katherine Marshall. Sorry I haven't had the chance to talk to you."

Katherine set her drink down. "No worries. We're both busy people. But please, don't call me Katherine. Only my grandma calls me Katherine. It's Kate."

"Kate. Gotcha."

The bartender made his way back to Kate and asked if she needed a refill.

Kate shook her head. "Two is enough Dean, but thanks." Kate gave Dean a wide smile, which he returned, until he looked at Matt.

"Need anything?" Dean asked gruffly.

"No, I'm good," Matt answered with a grin.

After Dean was out of earshot, Matt asked, "Is he your boyfriend?"

"Dean? No, he's just a friend."

"Is that why you're here? Visiting Dean?"

"No. My roommate hung the metaphorical tie on our front door."

"Huh? The metaphorical tie?" Then he got it. "Ohh...."

Kate grinned. Matt noticed her eyes sparkled under the bar lights. "Yep. Except in these modern times, you don't need a tie. You text your roommate to not come home for the next two hours. Message received."

21

Matt laughed. "Does she do this a lot?"

"Oh, probably once a week."

"Wow, busy girl."

"Theresa fancies herself a younger Samantha Jones." Kate waved her hand. "Sorry, *Sex in the City* reference."

Matt groaned. "No need to explain. One of my exes was addicted to that show. I've seen more episodes than I care to admit."

Kate chuckled. "At least there was a lot of nudity."

"True. It made the show bearable."

There was a brief pause in conversation before Kate said, "I've never seen you here before. Are you meeting someone?"

Matt pointed outside. "I'm here with some of my buddies from law school."

Kate glanced over her shoulder toward the patio and cringed. "You're with the guy who tried to buy me a drink?"

"I am. Out of curiosity, why'd you blow him off? It doesn't happen often."

Kate turned back toward the bar. "I believe it. He's pretty attractive."

"Why the cold shoulder then?"

Kate frowned a bit before responding. "I, um, just got out of a long relationship. I'm not interested in dating right now."

Matt felt bad for bringing up what was obviously a fresh wound. "Hey, sorry. On the bright side, I don't think Alex is looking for a serious relationship."

Dean dropped off a glass of ice water in front of Kate and she gave him an appreciative smile. "Thanks."

"No problem," Dean responded before giving Matt another dirty look.

Kate began swirling the straw around in her new drink. "I'm not interested in a one night stand either. I've had enough of those for one lifetime."

Matt raised an eyebrow. Really? Interesting…

Blushing, she added, "Like one or two."

"Sure," Matt said playfully.

Kate smacked his shoulder. "Whatever."

Matt wondered what kind of man Kate went for. If Alex wasn't her type, who was? Instead of asking her this, Matt changed the subject.

"How are you liking Judge Penny?"

"She's great. Super smart and she runs her courtroom like a drill sergeant."

Matt heard similar things from Judge Penny's prior law clerk Brad. Except Brad didn't seem to appreciate Judge Penny's attitude.

"She can be a ball buster."

Kate smiled. "I don't need to worry about that."

The two laughed.

"How long have you worked for Judge?" Kate asked.

Matt's boss, Judge Payne, was simply known as "Judge." There were six judges at the Courthouse, but if you said "Judge" without adding a last name, everyone knew you were talking about Judge Payne. Judge was also the Chief Judge at the Courthouse. Matt considered it an honor to work for him.

"I've worked for Judge about a year now."

"Do you like him?"

Matt nodded. "Yes. We get along well. He can be a pain in the ass sometimes."

Kate nearly spit out her drink.

"What?" Matt asked.

"Nothing." Kate smiled. "Go on."

"Don't get me wrong, he's a great guy. Don't try talking to him before his coffee though."

Kate laughed. "Judge is definitely not a morning person."

How does she know that, Matt thought.

"Do you run into Judge a lot?" he asked.

Kate smirked as if she knew something Matt didn't. "Just what I've heard. Has he told you the story of how he got his nickname?"

"No." Matt had wondered, but never asked.

"When Judge was young, he would sit in his high chair and slam his spoon against the tray. His mother said he looked like a judge slamming a gavel. So she started calling him 'Baby Judge.' For whatever reason, the nickname stuck. It was almost prophetic, huh?"

Matt rubbed his chin. "Wow. I envisioned a more epic explanation."

Judge put off such a "real man" aura. He was a big, burly man who looked like he could wrestle bears. He loved cars, motorcycles and fished on the weekends. It was hard to imagine a young Judge sitting in a high chair with baby food smeared across his face.

Kate smiled. "Like what?"

Matt shrugged his shoulders. "Oh, I don't know. But something more masculine than a baby name."

Kate chuckled. "Yeah, well, don't let him tell you otherwise. It's the truth."

Matt was curious about Kate's connection to Judge. She'd only worked at the Courthouse for a few weeks. How did she know all this stuff about him?

24

"Are you and Judge close?" Matt asked.

Kate flashed the "I know more than you" grin again. "You could say that."

"Okay…" He was very curious now.

"Can you keep a secret?" Kate asked.

"Of course I can." Matt crossed his heart.

"Judge is my grandfather."

"What?"

"Yep. He's my mom's father," Kate explained.

"Really. I didn't know that."

Kate took another drink of her water. "It's not something I broadcast. Some of Judge's staff and courtroom personnel know me. I've visited Judge at the Courthouse since I was a little girl. But I asked everyone to keep quiet about it."

"Why?" Matt asked.

"I don't want people to think I got this job because I'm Judge's granddaughter. I earned this job. As soon as people hear I'm related to Judge, they'll assume he got me the job."

Matt doubted it. Everyone thought Kate got the job because she was a super-smart Yale grad. But he understood her position and told her so.

Kate bit her lower lip before she continued. "That's one reason I work hard and keep busy. I want to do a good job and let people see I earn my keep, regardless of who I'm related to."

As Kate finished her sentence, her cell phone lit up.

"Excuse me," she said as she flipped open her cell phone. Kate smiled as she read the message. "My roommate's date was brief."

"Oh yeah?"

"Yep. She sent me a message saying, 'Romeo is gone. Bring pizza.'"

They both laughed. Matt felt at ease with Kate. She wasn't at all what he expected. Cora had been off the mark.

"Sounds like your roommate is perfect for Alex," Matt observed.

"Maybe so."

Matt stood up. "Well, I'll let you get home and I'll get back to my buddies."

Kate leaned over and slipped her heels back on. For a second, her silk shirt gapped wide enough for Matt to see her white lace bra. He looked away as Kate stood up. Without her heels, Kate was around 5'5". With them on, she stood at 5'8" and was eye level with Matt's shoulders.

"Thanks for coming over and keeping me company," Kate said as she put on her blazer.

"Sure thing." Matt started to say good-night and remembered he needed a favor. "Can you help me out with something?"

Kate smirked. "Depends on what it is."

"Fair enough. I promise it won't take more than a second of your time."

Matt explained what he needed and Kate willingly agreed. After walking Kate to the door, Matt returned to his table with a grin on his face.

"I got it! I got the brunette's number," he told the guys.

"Bullshit," Alex responded.

Matt took his phone out of his pocket. "Go ahead. Take my phone and call KM."

Alex grabbed Matt's phone and scrolled until he got to the KM listing. Alex hit the speakerphone button so everyone could hear the call.

Kate picked up after the second ring. "Miss me already, baby?"

Alex threw the phone back at Matt. "Asshole."

*   *   *

A week later Matt was sure he imagined his conversation with Kate. No way the woman he saw in the Court hallways was the same chic he talked to at the bar. "Work Kate" still glided right by him with a head nod and a small smile. There was one time she lingered long enough to say, "Hey Matt," but that was it.

Given her recent demeanor, Matt was shocked when he received a text message from a number labeled KM on Wednesday afternoon.

> *Hey Matt. It's Kate. Heads up: Judge's favorite coffee is Dunkin Donuts. He tolerates Starbucks, but you'll win him over with DD. Large, black, two sugars.*

Matt considered this. Judge drank the Starbucks Matt brought him every morning, but now that he thought about it, Judge only drank about half a cup.

> *Thanks for the tip. I'll try it out tomorrow morning.*

Matt waited for a response to his text, but didn't get one.

The next morning, Judge's face lit up when Matt put the Dunkin Donuts coffee cup down on his desk.

"Excellent! I love Dunkin's coffee. Good job my man."

Score!

"You're welcome Judge. Anything else I can do for you this morning?"

Judge took a big sip of coffee and let out an "Ahh" in appreciation. "I don't think so Sloan."

Matt shuffled out of Judge's office before Judge changed his mind. Judge was a much happier version of himself for the rest of the morning.

Matt shot Kate a quick text.

You were right. Judge loved the DD coffee. I owe you one.

To his surprise, he got a response seconds later.

Yes, you do. I've made your life a lot easier. I think a Jack and Coke is in order.

Matt laughed. This was the girl he met at the bar.

I can handle that. When?

Another quick response.

Tomorrow night. 7 o'clock. You know where to find me.

Matt set his phone down. He was sure she meant Patrick's, but it would be busy on a Friday night. Matt called Alex and asked him to be his wingman in case Kate cancelled last minute. Nothing worse than being at a bar by yourself on a Friday night.

Alex agreed to join him with an enthusiastic, "Hell yeah!"

*   *   *

It was Friday afternoon and Kate was exhausted. Judge Penny had her running all over the place today. Despite her long to-do list, Kate finished all of her work and was ready to get the hell out of there.

Kate checked her inbox one more time to be sure Judge Penny hadn't sent another one of her longwinded emails. Kate was relieved to see there weren't any. She did, however, see an email from Matt.

Hey Kate. We still on for tonight? It's not a big deal if you can't make it, Alex agreed to go with me.

Kate bit her bottom lip. She saw two issues with this brief email. One, Alex was coming. She and Alex hadn't exactly hit it off last week. Kate was nice when she brushed him off, but Alex didn't seem like the kind of guy who took rejection lightly. She

28

didn't want to spend the evening on the receiving end of Alex's glares.

Second, did Matt think this was a date? Kate hoped she hadn't given him the wrong impression. She only wanted to grab a drink.

After thinking about her options for a couple of minutes, and making sure T was available for a night out, Kate responded to Matt's email.

I'm good for tonight. My roommate Theresa is coming too. It's been a rough week, and I need a drink with some friends.

There. She inserted the word "friends", but in a subtle way.

Kate was relieved when she got Matt's response:

Cool. A drink with friends is the solution to most problems. Mine anyway. See you there.

Kate shut off her computer and put her heels on. She despised wearing high heels, but they seemed to be an essential part of a female attorney's wardrobe.

Kate zipped home to pick up Theresa and found her friend lounging on the couch with a glass of wine. After some coaxing and a whiny, "but you promised!" from Kate, T finally got up off the couch.

As Matt predicted the day before, Patrick's was busy. Kate found a parking spot on the street a couple blocks away and was proud of herself for successfully parallel parking her Jetta. Walking through the crowd at Patrick's, Kate spotted Matt sitting at a high top table with Alex.

Kate pointed toward the table. "There they are T."

"Damn!" T exclaimed. "You didn't tell me we were meeting up with some hotties! I figured your attorney friends would be dogs. I should have worn my push up bra."

Kate rolled her eyes. T was the manager of a lingerie store and assumed all lawyers were lame.

29

Kate caught Matt's attention and gave a small wave. Matt and Alex stood as she and Theresa approached the table. Kate immediately felt overdressed. The guys were in jeans and t-shirts and she was in her suit. Theresa was, of course, in one of her trademark tight-as-hell dresses. Theresa made Kate feel like a frumpy bank teller.

"Hey," Matt said when Kate and Theresa made it to the table.

"Hey," Kate responded. Turning to Theresa she said, "This is my roommate and best friend Theresa." Then turning back to the boys added, "Theresa, this is my colleague Matt and his friend Alex."

Alex put on a sly grin and extended his hand to T. "Theresa, nice to meet you."

"Likewise," Theresa replied, nearly batting her eyelashes.

Oh brother, Kate thought.

Matt must have been thinking the same thing. He looked amused as he watched Alex pull out Theresa's chair for her.

Kate pulled out her own chair and sat down. They were at a square-top, with a seat in front of each side. Kate pursed her lips as Theresa pulled her chair to the corner near Alex. This was one of Theresa's classic moves. Get in real close to the target so you can "casually" touch his arm, leg, etc.

Alex seemed to enjoy the attention he was getting from Theresa. Kate suspected he was used to getting fawned over by women. But he had his work cut out for him with T. T liked to reel them in, and then make them work for it. Theresa would lavish a man with attention in the beginning, and then quickly lose interest. It drove men nuts.

"Jack and coke, right?" Matt asked as he sat back down.

"Yes, please. That sounds amazing," Kate responded. She turned to ask T what she wanted, but T and Alex were huddled together in a private conversation.

30

It was loud in the bar, but Kate swore she heard Alex ask, "What do you do? I mean, when you're not looking hot as hell?"

A line like this wouldn't work on Kate, but Theresa was eating it up.

Kate tuned them out and scanned her surroundings. The no-smoking ban meant the air wasn't filled with smoke, but it was still warm in the bar. People were jammed in tight. All of the tables were full and every seat at the bar was taken. Dean held up a glass from behind the bar when he saw her and Kate smiled and waved.

"I bet good-ole Dean is pissed you're not sitting at the bar tonight," Matt noted as he followed her gaze.

Kate laughed. "I doubt it. I'm pretty sure he's gay."

Matt appeared skeptical. "Based on the way he was ogling you last week, and the dirty looks he gave me, Dean is not gay."

Kate shrugged. "He's nice to talk to when my roommate over here," she gestured toward Theresa, "has our apartment occupied."

Matt glanced over at Alex and Theresa. T was practically in Alex's lap at this point.

"This might be a record." Matt looked down at his watch. "It's been less than five minutes."

"Yeah, this is quick. Even for T."

Kate and Matt spent the next ten minutes talking about the work week and the cases they were working on. A law clerk's job is to review all pleadings filed with the Court and to make an initial assessment of the case. Kate researched an intellectual property issue all week, and it was boring her to tears.

"The problem is the lingo is beyond me. I've had to google terms because I have no idea what they mean." Kate sighed. "I became a lawyer because I'm terrible at math and science. And here they are, creeping up on me."

31

Matt laughed. "I'm sure Judge had a lot to do with you becoming a lawyer."

Kate sipped her drink. "Yes and no. He never told me, 'Hey Kate, you should be a lawyer.' But growing up with him and being in the courthouse all the time, it was almost a given."

"Is it living up to your expectations?"

Kate smiled. "Too soon to tell."

Kate reached for her glass again, but Theresa swiped it and gulped what was left.

"Hey!" Kate protested.

Theresa put the glass down with no apology. "It's time to leave. It's so freaking loud in this place tonight I can't hear myself think."

"Where should we go?" Alex asked. The question was directed to Theresa, not the rest of the table.

"To our apartment, of course!" Theresa declared.

Kate's stomach dropped. "T, I don't think so."

"Why not?" Theresa pouted.

"Yeah, why not?" Alex mimicked.

Kate looked to Matt for help. His jawline was set and his eyes were boring into Alex. It was easy to see Matt wasn't fond of the idea of going to Kate's apartment either.

"Our apartment is a mess T, and we don't have any drinks there." Kate gave Theresa her pleading eyes, hoping Theresa would get the hint.

Kate hardly knew Matt. She was trying hard to make a good impression at the courthouse and didn't need a co-worker seeing her messy place. Or seeing firsthand how crazy her roommate is.

Matt hung out with Cora Henry, and Cora had the biggest mouth on the planet. Judge's secretary told Kate to keep her distance from Cora because she was "a drama queen and a trouble

32

maker." Kate didn't need Matt running to Cora and spilling her dirt. Rumors would be flying around the Courthouse hallways in no time.

Theresa, per her usual, was thicker than molasses. "Don't be ridiculous Kate. Our apartment is fine."

Kate started to protest again, but Theresa jumped down off her chair and grabbed Alex's hand. "Let's go!"

Matt voiced his objections before Alex stood up. "Alex, I think we should head home. I have some things to work on."

Alex shook his head. "Nah, man. I'm not ready to go home yet. I want to see Theresa's place."

Theresa snuggled into Alex and whispered something in his ear.

Matt frowned and turned to Kate. "I rode with him. And there's little to no chance I can change his mind."

Kate sighed in frustration.

"I'm sorry Kate," Matt apologized. "I can see you don't want us coming over."

"It's nothing personal," Kate explained. "I'm sick of being put in this position. I don't know why I agreed to be roommates with her again."

Kate had many second thoughts about moving in with Theresa when she came back to Columbus. But Theresa begged her. T was in way over her head with the rent and needed someone to split the bills with her. Against her better judgment, Kate gave in. It was moments like these when Kate wished her will was a bit stronger.

*   *   *

Matt tried talking Alex out of going over to the girls' apartment, but it wasn't working. Alex was a man on a mission and nothing Matt said was sinking in.

33

"Seriously Alex! This is my boss's granddaughter! I don't need her telling my boss about us invading her apartment."

Alex smirked. "I'm not banging the granddaughter. I'm banging her roommate."

"Alex, please. Kate doesn't want us there. And how fucked up will this be? You're just going to bang Theresa while Kate and I are in the other room?"

Alex looked over at Matt. "That's the plan."

Alex nearly sideswiped a parked car before jerking the wheel to the left.

"Watch the road doofus," Matt said in frustration.

As they cruised through downtown Columbus following Kate's red Volkswagen, Matt gave up on convincing Alex to go home. It was pointless. He tried another route.

"Can I at least have your car keys so I can go home?"

Alex snorted. "Yeah, right. Then I'll be stranded there. No way."

After a few minutes, they stopped in front of an apartment building in the Arena District. Kate pulled into a marked parking spot reserved for her apartment, and Alex found on-street parking less than a block away.

When they got out of the car, Alex tilted his head back to look up at the apartment building. "Wow, they're right downtown. I bet their place is sweet."

Matt agreed. "I didn't know there were apartments down here."

The old, red brick building stood five stories tall. It looked like it used to be a factory of some kind. While the first and second stories were windowless, the top three floors had ten windows across the front. A few windows were lit up, but most were dark.

34

Beyond the building were the lights of Nationwide Arena. Matt spent a few nights at the arena watching hockey games or attending rock concerts.

As they walked up to the ladies, Kate was fiddling with her car keys. Matt hoped Kate wouldn't tell Judge about this over the weekend. He made a mental note to buy a donut with Judge's coffee Monday morning. Just in case.

Theresa strutted past Matt and linked her arm with Alex's. "Hey baby," she said with a coy smile.

Matt saw Kate roll her eyes before turning toward the building. He wondered how these two women were friends. Kate was the "girl next door" type and Theresa was clearly the "for a good time call" type.

Using a key to open the glass door at the front of the building, Kate pulled the door open and gestured for the three of them to go inside.

Despite its factory appearance from the outside, the inside of the building was well lit. As Matt suspected, the first story was an open floor plan with no apartments. Couches and fake trees filled the lobby space. To the right were silver mailboxes built into the wall. Along the back wall were two elevators and a door marked "Stairs."

Kate hit the button for the elevator and tapped her foot while they waited for the door to open. She looked pissed. Matt desperately tried to come up with something to say, but failed. It didn't help that Theresa and Alex were practically wearing each other and giggling.

When the elevator door opened, Matt followed Kate inside. The elevator was an old industrial style Matt had only seen in movies. It was cool to watch the elevator's parts in motion as they made their way up to the fifth floor.

"Penthouse suite, huh?" Matt asked, trying to lighten the mood.

Kate smirked. "Something like that."

Her smile fell away and her eyes hardened. Matt followed her glare. Theresa and Alex were in full-on make out mode on the other side of the elevator. Paws all over each other and sucking face.

Great, he thought.

The two lovebirds stopped making out long enough to exit the elevator. They held hands and giggled as Kate unlocked the door for her apartment. Kate held the door open for everyone again. Matt gave her a sympathetic smile before going in after Alex and Theresa.

The layout of Kate's apartment was an open floor plan with the kitchen counters immediately to the right when you walked in the front door. The dining room was to the left and a massive living room was straight ahead. The ladies had a wall lined with bookshelves holding several books, photographs and other knickknacks. A long couch and two chairs adorned the living room, along with a big screen TV. The apartment had dark wood floors throughout, with white crown molding and tan paint.

"Holy shit. This is a nice place," Alex said, momentarily giving his attention to something other than Theresa.

"Thanks," Kate responded while grabbing a sweatshirt off the back of the couch and a pair of sneakers from the floor. She disappeared down the hallway off the living room, opened a door, and threw the items inside. When she came back, she looked flustered, but plastered a smile on her face.

"Can I get you guys something to drink?"

Before Matt could ask what the drink options were, Theresa spoke up. "No thanks. I'm going to show Alex my room."

Theresa grabbed Alex's hand and led him down the hallway to the second door on the right.

"This is my room," Theresa said to Alex as she leaned in the doorway.

Alex put his hands on Theresa's hips and led her inside. "I think I need a closer look." Once through the threshold, Alex kicked the door shut with his foot.

Kate looked down the hallway in disbelief.

"That girl is never going to grow up," she said, shaking her head. Kate turned back to Matt. "Want to take a walk for a while?"

Matt smiled. "You don't want to show me your bedroom?"

He meant it as a joke, but Kate shifted her weight awkwardly. "Not really."

Matt grabbed his chest and feigned despair. "Aw Kate, you're breaking my heart!"

Kate laughed. "Don't take it personally. I'm not giving anyone a tour of my room anytime soon."

The sound of a loud crash, likely the two lovebirds landing in bed, put Kate into motion. She jogged down the hallway and came back with the sneakers she just put away.

Kicking off her heels, Kate slipped the sneakers on and tied the laces. "I think we should leave now."

They rushed out the door and toward the elevator before things between Alex and Theresa got too hot and heavy.

As they stepped out into the nearly fall air, Matt heard Kate breathe a sigh of relief.

"I think we got out of there in the nick of time," Matt quipped.

"No doubt," Kate agreed.

"Which way do you want to head?" Matt asked, looking to his left and then his right.

Kate thought about it for a moment. "How about we head toward the arena? It will be well lit down there."

"Sure. Sounds good."

As they started walking, Kate offered to drive him home.

"Nah. I can't leave you alone with those two."

Kate smiled. "Thanks." After a pause she added, "I'm sorry about tonight. I really wanted to grab a drink and unwind. I didn't realize those two would be all over each other."

"Not a problem," Matt said as they got closer to the bright lights of the arena. "I'm used to Alex bailing on me for a girl."

Kate nodded. "Yeah, I'm kind of used to it with Theresa too."

They walked silently for a minute.

Matt breathed in the cool, crisp air and watched Kate out of the corner of his eye. She was still in her work clothes, except for the sneakers. Her hair blowing slightly in the breeze and her green eyes focused on the arena.

She was cute. Super cute.

Matt wanted to find out about this ex of hers, the one who was keeping her from dating. "Can I ask you a personal question?"

Kate looked at him wearily. "You can ask whatever you want. Doesn't mean I'll answer it."

Matt chuckled before asking, "What's the deal with your ex? Did it end badly?"

Kate flinched.

"You mentioned you aren't interested in dating a couple of times. I'm envisioning an epic breakup," Matt explained.

Kate pointed to a park bench. "Care if we sit down?"

Matt shrugged. "Sure."

They sat down on a bench facing Nationwide Arena across the street. There were a few people out and about, but the lack of a large crowd meant there were no events at the arena tonight.

Just when Matt was about to change the subject, Kate answered his question.

"The breakup with my ex was definitely messy. But it was my doing."

"Oh yeah?"

"Yeah. He asked me to marry him, I said 'no.'"

Matt whistled. "Ouch. And that was it, huh?"

"Basically," Kate responded.

"How long were you together?"

"Two years."

"Damn. That's a long time. Why'd you turn him down?"

Kate started to respond but stopped herself.

"Small penis?" Matt asked with a smirk.

Kate threw her head back and laughed. It was the first time Matt heard Kate really laugh. Not a casual laugh, but a full on, from the gut laugh. He liked it.

"No, nothing like that."

"What was it then?"

Kate was gazing out across the street. "Promise not to laugh?"

Matt stuck out his pinky for a pinky promise.

Kate entwined her pinky with his, then put her hand back in her lap.

"You know how everyone says you'll know when you find 'the one'?" Kate used her fingers to make air quotes when she said "the one."

"Yes."

Kate frowned. "I didn't know."

Matt didn't respond immediately in case Kate wanted to elaborate. When she didn't, he said, "That sucks."

"It was awful. Ben is such a good guy. I tried to feel it," Kate looked down at her hands, "but I didn't."

"If it's not right, it's not right."

"I know," she said exasperated. "But if I don't feel it with a great guy like Ben, I don't think I ever will."

Matt put his arm around Kate's shoulder and gave her a quick squeeze. "You will. We're still young. You have plenty of time to find the right guy."

Kate sniffed. "I thought I found the right one once."

"You did?"

"Yes, but he's fucking my roommate right now. I guess it wasn't meant to be."

Matt laughed, relieved Kate was cracking jokes and trying to lighten the mood.

"What happened with *Sex in the City* girl?"

"Who?" Matt asked, a bit confused by the sudden change in conversation.

"*Sex in the City* girl. You told me last week you had a girlfriend who loved *Sex in the City*."

That's right. Matt had mentioned Leslie to Kate.

"She decided one of my frat brothers was 'the one.' Actually, he was my roommate at the time."

Kate gasped. "That's awful."

"It wouldn't have been so bad if I didn't walk in on them having sex in our room."

Kate covered her mouth with her hand. "You didn't!"

"Oh yeah, I did. The looks on their faces," Matt shook his head, "it was classic."

"What did you say?"

40

Matt smiled. "Seen my baseball glove?"

Kate crinkled her nose. "Huh?"

"I played intermural baseball in college. I went back to the room for my glove."

"Oh," Kate said simply.

"I left for a game about fifteen minutes before I walked in on them. They weren't expecting me to be back so soon."

"I see. Sorry I brought it up."

"Eh, it was a long time ago. And they weren't together long anyway. Poetic justice I guess."

Kate was quiet for a moment and then quipped, "At least you didn't have to watch *Sex in the City* anymore."

"That's true," Matt agreed.

"I don't understand people. If you aren't in love anymore, why cheat? Why not break up with the person?"

Matt shrugged. "No clue."

"How did you and your roommate get along after you caught them together?"

"It wasn't ideal, but at least it was close to the end of the year. We ignored each other most of the time."

"Did he apologize?"

Matt shook his head. "Nope. But I didn't want one anyway. It would have been fake."

"I understand. Better to say nothing at all than to lie."

The two smiled at each other before Kate looked away.

"Where did you go to law school Mr. Sloan?" she asked after a moment.

Matt spent the next two hours sitting on the park bench with Kate. They talked about all sorts of things. College. Law school.

More bad breakups. Judge. She was so easy to talk to. He genuinely liked her.

Kate glanced at her watch. "I think it's safe for us to go back now."

Matt was shocked when he saw the time. "Yeah, we're probably good."

As they walked back, Matt asked, "Are you going to start giving me the cold shoulder again?"

Kate tilted her head to the side. "What do you mean?"

"Last week you acted like I didn't exist. I thought maybe after our meeting at the bar you would actually stop and say 'hi' to me."

Kate smiled. "I told you. I want to be taken seriously. I don't want Judge Penny or anyone else catching me in the halls talking with another law clerk."

She purposely bumped into his hip, temporarily throwing him off balance. "But maybe I'll give you a minute or two of my time next week."

Matt gave a huge, over the top grin. "Really? That would be swell."

This made Kate giggle. He felt good when he made her laugh.

Once inside Kate's apartment building, they stood outside her apartment door listening for signs of life on the opposite side.

"I don't hear any loud screams or moans, so they must be done," Kate said matter-of-factly.

Matt turned the door handle and stepped into Kate's apartment. He went in first to scope out the situation. He laughed and motioned for Kate to come inside.

"Look," he said and pointed toward the couch.

Alex and Theresa were both passed out in front of the TV. Alex with his head on the armrest, and Theresa leaning against him. A popcorn bowl was tipped to the side in Theresa's lap. Its contents all over her lap and the floor. The TV was quietly playing an infomercial for a non-stick frying pan in the background.

Kate took in the scene. "At least they have clothes on."

Chapter Three

Kate can't move. She and Matt sit shell-shocked when Phil finishes reading the pertinent portion of the Will to them.

Phil shifts uneasily in his chair as he waits for one of them to break the silence.

"No way," Matt says finally, his tone icy.

Kate finds his indignation a bit offensive. What is he so pissed about? He'll end up with Judge's beloved 1970 Chevelle Super Sport if all goes well.

Phil sighs. "Like I said, this wasn't my idea."

Kate purses her lips. "Phil, you know we can't do this."

"Unfortunately Kate, it can't be changed now," Phil says sympathetically.

"My mom and aunt are going to hit the roof!" Kate protests.

"Hitting the roof" isn't enough of a description for how angry Kate's mom and Aunt Estelle are going to be. How will she ever explain this to them?

And worse, how will she explain that Judge's estate will be in a very long holding pattern if she doesn't follow his directives?

"How could he do this to me Phil?" Kate asks, almost in a whisper.

Phil shakes his head. "He was adamant about this Kate. You know how much he loved scavenger hunts."

Kate knows it all too well. As a child she had to hunt around Judge's house for her birthday or Christmas gifts following a trail of clues. One time it took her four hours to hunt down her gift. Thankfully, the Barbie dream house had been worth it.

45

Evidently, Judge sent Matt on a scavenger hunt of his own.

"Sending me around the Courthouse when I first started working for him was one thing. This is something else entirely Phil. This is ludicrous. I'm not driving all over God's green Earth with *her* for God knows how long."

Kate grimaces.

Does Matt have to be so disgusted at the thought of spending time with her? Kate isn't thrilled by the situation, but she isn't attacking him.

Phil puts up his hands. "There are only six locations. It should take you a week or two."

"A week or two!" Kate exclaims. "I can't Phil. I have exams to grade...a research project this summer...and a wedding to plan."

Matt snorts.

"What?" Kate asks, shooting Matt a nasty look.

Matt rubs his chin. "Are you going to make it to the church this time?"

Kate feels her face flush as fire runs through her veins. She is about to call him every bad word she can think of when Phil intervenes.

"Enough. You two have to figure out how to get along. Judge's Will specifically states that if you two do not complete the scavenger hunt *together*," Phil pauses to look at both of them, "the estate will not be distributed for five years."

Kate sighs. Her Aunt Estelle will be on her ass every day for the next five years if she doesn't do the scavenger hunt. But the thought of spending that much time with Matt makes her want to throw up.

She is screwed. Plain and simple.

"Fine," Kate says. "I'll do it."

46

Phil turns to Matt. "How about you?"

"No," Matt responds, face stern.

Phil's jaw clenches as he strums his fingers on his desktop. "You're willing to make Kate's family wait five years to settle the estate?"

"Yes, I am," Matt answers.

Selfish bastard, Kate thinks. Although, if the situation were reversed, she'd probably flip both men off and walk out.

"And you're willing to give up the beautiful muscle car Judge wants you to have?" Phil presses.

"Yes," Matt answers again.

Phil sits back in his chair and crosses his arms over his chest. "The way Judge talked about you, I thought you would agree to this immediately. It's clear to me now that Judge's feelings toward you were not mutual."

Kate watches as the skin on Matt's neck turns red. Phil has struck a nerve.

Uh oh...

Phil doesn't stop. "Your willingness to leave his family in limbo for five years tells me you aren't the man Judge thought you were."

Matt grips the armrests of his chair, his knuckles white and his eyes filled with rage.

"I don't need you to patronize me," Matt hisses. "I loved that man. He was my mentor, father figure, hero."

Phil leans over his desk. "Then do this. Kate's family will be unable to move on if you don't agree to do the scavenger hunt with her. Judge wouldn't want that for them. It was his last request of you Matt."

While Kate waits for Matt's response, she wonders again what the hell Judge was thinking. Why did he want the two of them

47

going on this scavenger hunt together? He should have sent them on separate hunts.

"You know," Matt says, his tone lighter, "I think we could have avoided all of this if I'd been more truthful with Judge."

"What do you mean?" Phil asks.

Yes, what did he mean? Kate wonders. What had Matt lied to Judge about?

Kate and Phil stare at Matt. He picks at the frayed leather on the chair's armrest.

"I will do this. For Judge. Not for the car. Not for Kate's mom and aunt, but for Judge. But I don't think we'd be here today if I had told Judge an important fact."

"Okay. So what is it?" Kate asks impatiently.

Matt doesn't look up as he says, "I'm married."

*   *   *

Kate and Matt walk out of Phil's office. They agreed Kate will pick Matt up at his hotel and ride into downtown Columbus together. Without saying "good-bye", they get into their own vehicles and head toward Matt's hotel in Hilliard.

Phil gave them a manila envelope containing five thousand dollars in cash and the first clue:

> *My war room. Under the first Christmas gift Matt gave me.*

It is an easy one to solve. Judge commonly referred to his office at the Courthouse as his "war room". Kate also knew Matt gave Judge a football signed by Woody Hayes the first Christmas Matt worked for him. An avid Ohio State fan, Judge loved it. It sits on the right-hand corner of his massive desk.

Kate debates who she should call first on the twenty minute drive to Hilliard. Her mom? Scott? Theresa?

She decides to call T because the conversations with her mom and Scott will need more than twenty minutes. Plus, she wants to put those conversations on the back burner for as long as possible.

"No freaking way!" Theresa yells through the Bluetooth into Kate's car.

"Yep."

"He's married?!"

"Seriously T? That's what you're focusing on? Did you not hear me say I will be stuck with him for at least a week? I won't make it!"

"Sorry, sorry," T says with a sigh. "I'm just thrown off. Married?" T asks again.

Kate hadn't expected the news about Matt's marriage either. When she thought about Matt over the years, she never envisioned him settling down with someone else. In her mind, he was perpetually single.

"I think the fact that he's married is a good thing T. Maybe it will keep Scott from flipping out."

"Maybe so," Theresa agrees. "But it kills the opportunity for one last fling, doesn't it?"

*   *   *

The car ride from Matt's hotel to downtown Columbus is awkward. Kate doesn't know what to say and Matt makes no attempt at conversation.

A few minutes into the trip, Kate asks what she feels is an appropriate question. "What's your wife's name?"

"Naomi."

"How long have you been married?"

"Seven years."

This shocks her. "Seven years? Why didn't you tell Judge?"

"I didn't want to upset him."

"Upset him?" Kate asks as she turns onto High Street.

Matt looks out his window as he responds. "Judge hounded me to reach out to you. I think he envisioned us getting back together some day."

Kate almost yells, "what?!", but she catches herself. To hear that Judge was trying to sneak Matt back into her life pisses her off. Kate fumes silently for a few minutes.

"Have you told Naomi about the scavenger hunt?" she asks after she's calmed down.

Matt nods. "She's not thrilled about me being gone so long."

"That's understandable. I'm sure Scott won't be happy about it either."

"Yeah, but you won't be leaving him alone with two kids while we're gone."

Matt has kids? Did Kate know this man at all? The Matt she knew was single and care free. Not a dad.

"True," Kate answers when the astonishment wears off. "What, um, did you tell her about me?"

"I told her I had to do the scavenger hunt with Judge's granddaughter." Matt is still staring out the window as if he's never seen Columbus before.

"Okay. But what did she say when you told her it was me? Was she upset?"

Matt turns to look at her. "Why would she be upset?"

"Because I'm an ex. Doesn't it make her uncomfortable?"

Matt returns his gaze to the window. "I've never told her about you."

"Oh," Kate mutters.

50

Matt never told his wife about her? Aren't you supposed to tell your future spouse about your exes? Get it all out there before the big day?

Maybe you weren't that important to him, so he didn't bother bringing you up, a tiny voice in the back of her head speculates.

Ouch.

Kate finds on-street parking about a block from the Courthouse. Matt drops a couple quarters in the meter and they head south toward the main entrance of the building.

Kate hasn't been inside the Courthouse since Judge's passing and her stomach does a flip-flop when she sees the building. She has been here so many times throughout her life she can probably walk the hallways with her eyes closed. It used to feel like a second home. Now, it's a grim reminder of her grandfather.

"When was the last time you were here?" Kate asks Matt as they wait for the crossing signal to change.

"Not since my last day. About eight years ago."

Kate nods her head and walks forward when the signal changes. She knew Matt stayed on as Judge's clerk for a couple years after she left. Kate avoided the Courthouse for those two years.

"What about you? When was the last time you were here?" Matt asks.

"About a month before Judge died. He wanted some paperwork from his office. I came here to get it."

Kate thinks back to that day. It seems like forever ago now. Judge insisted she retrieve a manila folder from the top drawer of his desk. Judge was in the hospital bed set up in his living room, overlooking the back yard of his house, when he asked Kate to run the errand.

Kate was hesitant. She didn't want anything to do with Judge's Will or other important documents for fear her Aunt Estelle would assault her with questions later.

Estelle is her mother's only sibling. As the oldest, Estelle believes she should be in charge and know what is happening at all times.

"Grandpa, I don't know," Kate said. "You should have Estelle get it."

Judge shook his head. "No. It has to be you."

"Why? You know how Estelle is."

Judge smiled. "Yes, I do. Which is why I need you to do it. Estelle is too nosey. I need someone I can trust to retrieve it."

Kate was conflicted. She wanted to help Judge, but she didn't want to be in the middle either.

Judge reached out and took Kate's hand. "Please sweetie?"

Kate was unable to refuse Judge on a good day, and in his weakened state, Kate was even more inclined to do anything to make him happy.

In the months prior, Kate watched helplessly as her grandfather shriveled. Things went downhill quickly after his stage four cancer diagnosis. She hardly recognized the man in the hospital bed next to her. But his eyes still shun a bright blue and when he was up to it, he showed his spunky attitude.

"Sure Grandpa. I'll go get it tomorrow."

Judge grinned with approval. "I knew I could count on you." Judge laid his head back down on his pillow and shut his eyes. "Now, tell me about the wedding again."

Kate spent the remainder of the evening talking to Judge about Scott, the wedding and her job at the law school. Judge would occasionally chime in with a comment or question to let her know he was listening.

Around 10 p.m., Kate paused and heard Judge's quiet and steady breathing. He had fallen asleep. Kate quietly stood up and leaned over to kiss Judge on the forehead.

"I love you Grandpa."

The next day, Kate retrieved the envelope as promised and brought it to Judge. After looking through the contents, Judge handed it back.

"It's all there. I need you to write Phil's address on it and mail it."

"Phil? Your lawyer?"

Judge nodded his head. "Yes."

"Would you rather I deliver it in person?"

"No. Phil already has signed copies of the critical documents. This is supplementary instructions."

Kate raised her eyebrow. "Are you sure?"

Judge assured her mailing the documents would be fine.

I should have burned that envelope, Kate thinks as she and Matt ascend the Courthouse steps. The envelope she retrieved and mailed is the same envelope containing the instructions for the scavenger hunt.

"Anyone I know still work here?" Matt asks.

"The judges are all the same. I think they have new clerks though."

Matt holds the door open for Kate and she walks up to the security post. Taking off her purse and putting it in a plastic bin, Kate steps toward the metal detector.

A familiar face greets her. "Well, well, well. Kate Marshall! How are you doing?"

Kate smiles. "Hi Darrell!"

Darrell has worked security at the Courthouse since Kate was a little girl. He is a short, African American man with a shiny bald head and a black mustache. Darrell has to be at least sixty, but he doesn't look a day over forty.

"C'mon through." Darrell waves Kate through the metal detector and gives her a hug on the other side.

"Sure is good to see you!" Darrell looks over Kate's shoulder. "Matt Sloan, I'll be damned!"

Matt walks through the metal detector and shakes Darrell's hand. "Nice to see you Darrell."

Darrell stands back and shakes his head. "It's like a blast from the past seeing you two. Reminds me of good times. What brings you here?"

Kate and Matt exchange a glance. How do you explain this situation?

"It's a long story Darrell," Kate says. "We have to get something from Judge's office."

Darrell frowns. "I'm real sorry about Judge. We all miss him."

Kate smiles sadly. "Thanks Darrell."

"We haven't done anything to his office yet. Everything is as it was. I've been wondering when your family would come to collect his things."

Kate grabs her purse off the conveyor belt. "We're only grabbing one thing today. My mom and aunt will be coming in the next week or two for everything else."

"Alright. Let me know if you need anything. I'll watch the cameras and buzz the door open when you get there."

Kate thanks Darrell and makes her way toward Judge's office. Matt says good-bye to Darrell, but his voice is drowned out by Kate's heart beating in her ears.

Kate has done her fair share of crying, but she hasn't come to terms with Judge's passing. Being in the Courthouse without him seems alien and wrong. As if his absence from this place confirms that he is indeed dead.

Kate approaches the large wooden door labeled, "Chief Judge William H. Payne" and feels a lump building in her throat. Beyond this door is a long hallway leading to the receptionist area. To the right of the receptionist's desk will be another hallway leading to a conference room, a bathroom, Matt's old office, and finally, Judge's office.

A buzzing sound goes off above Kate's head and she hears a faint click as the door unlocks. Kate knows she needs to turn the door handle, but she can't move.

"Kate?" Matt is standing right beside Kate, but she doesn't answer.

The buzzing sound emits again, and Kate hears the familiar click. When she doesn't move, Matt reaches past her and turns the handle. The door opens, revealing the familiar dark blue carpet and cream colored walls.

Kate stands still for a moment trying to get herself together.

"Want me to go in? You can wait out here," Matt offers.

Kate looks up at Matt. His brow is furrowed.

Kate shakes her head. "No. Let's go."

Matt holds the door open for Kate and she shuffles into the hallway leading to the main part of Judge's chambers. Kate doesn't turn on the overhead fluorescent lights, as natural sunlight from the windows is streaming through the office.

Everything in Judge's chambers looks the same as the last time she was here. Except Judy, Judge's secretary for over twenty years, is gone. Her desk now sits empty. Kate briefly wonders what happened to Judy when Judge went on sick leave and never came back.

Probably reassigned to another judge, Kate decides.

Matt makes Kate jump when he speaks. "Not much has changed here."

For a moment, Kate forgot Matt is with her. She is lost in a sea of memories.

"Everything has changed," she whispers.

Matt nods solemnly. "I guess you're right."

Kate turns to her right and starts down the hallway toward Judge's office.

Matt stops when they reach his old office. "Man, this brings back a lot of memories."

Kate is half listening to him. Her gaze is focused on Judge's office. She makes her way down the hall and into the doorway.

Kate inhales deeply. The office smells like Judge. The faint scent of Old Spice and butterscotch candies fill Kate's senses. She didn't realize how much she missed this smell until right now.

Trying to hold back tears, Kate skims her hand along the wall and flips the light switch. Her eyes are filled with Judge's Buckeye memorabilia, photographs of her family, and shelves of legal books.

The autographed football sits exactly where Kate knew it would. Right next to a picture of her holding a giant, rainbow lollipop bigger than her five-year-old face. Kate struggles to keep it together as she imagines all of these things being boxed up and put in storage somewhere.

Then she sees it. Judge's black robe hanging on the back of his closet door, where it always has been. Where it always should be. It hangs solemnly from its wooden hanger, waiting to be worn again.

The thought of Judge never putting on his robe again is too much for Kate to bear. Kate hears an awful sound. It takes her a second to realize the noise is coming from her. She can no longer

56

choke back the sobs that have been fighting to come out since the hospice nurse looked at her with doe eyes and said, "I'm sorry. He's gone."

Kate closes her eyes and feels the tears streaming down her face. As much as she tries, she can no longer hold back her grief.

* * *

Matt stops and stands in the door frame of his old office. The furniture is set up exactly how it had been when he clerked for Judge. The desk chair looks new and there is a different rug in front of the desk, but everything else is the same.

Matt sees Kate walk into Judge's office out of the corner of his eye. Instead of following her, he steps into his old office and takes a moment to reminisce.

He learned a lot from Judge in this office. Put in a lot of long nights, and a handful of weekends, making sure the work he did for Judge was up to par.

Matt loved his job with Judge, but his history with Kate ultimately tarnished his career here. Judge never held his relationship with Kate against Matt. Judge talked frequently of Kate as though nothing had happened between them. But Matt knew the main reason he worked for Judge as long as he did was his feeble hope that Kate would reappear. Judge was her grandfather after all.

After two years went by without a single Kate appearance, Matt realized the situation was hopeless and he needed to move on. Getting over Kate would never be possible if he continued to work for Judge.

Matt shakes his head as he thinks to himself, two years I waited. What a waste.

Matt's self-admonishments are halted when he hears a strange noise coming from down the hall.

"Kate?" Matt calls out as he leaves his old office.

57

Kate doesn't respond, but Matt doesn't need her to. He's already figured out the noise is Kate crying. Matt jogs down the hallway toward Judge's office.

Any ill will Matt has for Kate crumbles when he finds her on her knees in Judge's office, face in her hands as she sobs.

Matt walks over to Kate and kneels down beside her. Without thinking, he reaches out and pulls her into his chest.

Kate leans into Matt, her head on his shoulder and her face buried in the crook of his neck as she continues crying.

You shouldn't have let her come in here, he thinks to himself.

Matt saw the hesitation on Kate's face as she stood outside the main door to Judge's chambers. He noticed the brief pauses in Kate's conversation with Darrell at security. Matt knew this would be hard for her, and yet, he'd let her wander into Judge's office alone.

"He's gone Matt," Kate chokes out. "Really gone."

"I know," Matt whispers as he strokes her hair. It is all he can think to say.

*   *   *

After a few minutes, Kate composes herself and stands up. Grabbing a tissue from the box on Judge's desk, she wipes her eyes and blows her nose.

"I'm sorry. I was blindsided," she explains to Matt.

"There's no need to apologize. I completely understand."

Kate is a little embarrassed by her breakdown. She is also ashamed of herself for finding so much comfort in Matt's arms.

Not wanting to dwell on how well they still fit together, Kate moves past Matt. Kate carefully picks up the acrylic case holding the autographed football. Sitting on the desk underneath it is a white envelope labeled, "Clue #2."

Matt picks up the envelope and opens it as Kate sets the football back down.

"What does it say?"

Matt scans the clue before reading it out loud. "What Kate didn't know, didn't hurt her. But she'll know of your visit now. You're going to a place in Northern Kentucky where they will train you like the contestants on my new favorite show."

Kate stretches out her right hand. "Let me see."

Matt passes her the sheet of paper and sits down in one of the office chairs.

Kate ignores his sigh and reads the letter again. She has no idea what this clue means. Crossing the Ohio River into Kentucky will take two hours from Columbus. But she doesn't know what to make of the rest of the clue.

"What is this about?" Kate asks as she reads the clue again. "What Kate didn't know, didn't hurt her? What does that part mean Matt?"

Matt is rubbing his temples. "I came to visit Judge a month before he died. You and your mom were out of town for the night."

"What?" Kate asks shocked.

"He called and told me I needed to come see him. He wanted to see me one more time."

Kate sits in the office chair next to Matt. She knows exactly what day Matt is talking about. Judge surprised Kate and her mom with an overnight stay at a spa retreat in Granville. The women enjoyed haircuts, mani/pedis and sea salt facials. Judge told the women they needed a night away to pamper themselves. Little did they know Judge had ulterior motives.

"Okay," Kate says processing Judge's deception. "What about the rest? Judge's favorite show was *Forensic Files*. Is he sending us to a CSI lab or something?"

Matt chortles. "I wish."

"What is it then? Do you know his new favorite show?"

Matt smiles. "During my visit with Judge, we watched a marathon of *American Ninja Warrior*. He made a comment that if he didn't have cancer, he'd kick the course's ass."

"What is *American Ninja Warrior*?" Kate asks.

"I don't think I can properly describe it. Google it," Matt responds.

Kate takes her phone out of her purse and types in the show. She clicks on a link for a YouTube video and waits for a car insurance ad to end. Kate watches two minutes of the video and turns her phone off. She has seen enough.

"No," she says in disbelief.

Matt has his phone out too. He turns the screen so Kate can see what he's found. "Northern Kentucky Obstacle Course Camp and Training Center" it reads across the top. Beneath it are pictures of men and women crawling under barb wire, scaling tall walls and walking on balance beams over mud pits.

Kate takes it all in with horror. "Oh…my…God…"

"I'll need some of the money Phil gave us," Matt says.

"For what?" Kate asks.

"A stretcher."

*   *   *

Kate is nervous. She calls Scott as she and Matt walk back to her car.

"Hey babe," Scott answers. "How did the meeting go?"

Kate glances at Matt. "Not so great."

"What's the deal? Why the mystery?"

"It's a long story."

"Okay…"

"How late is your shift tonight?"

Scott works as an ER doctor at the local children's hospital. His job requires crazy shifts and long hours. He's been known to crash for an hour or two in the doctor's lounge before heading back out for another eight hour shift.

"I'm leaving here in a few. It's a quiet night. I'll be on call though."

"Want to meet up at The Cooler for a quick drink?"

"Sure."

"Okay." Kate pauses then adds, "And Scott?"

"Yeah?"

"Matt's coming with me."

*   *   *

The Cooler sits on the corner across the street from Children's Hospital. Kate pulls into the parking lot and cuts off the engine.

The ride over was once again an uncomfortable one.

How are we going to make it through the week, Kate wonders.

Silently, apparently.

Matt and Kate get out of her car and walk up to The Cooler. Kate waves and smiles when she sees Scott standing outside the restaurant. He has changed out of his scrubs into a pair of jeans and an OSU t-shirt.

"Hey lady," Scott says as she gives him a hug and a quick kiss.

She turns and introduces the men.

"Scott, this is Matt Sloan. Matt, this is my fiancé Scott."

"Nice to meet you," Scott says as he shakes Matt's hand.

"Likewise," Matt responds.

Neither man seems fazed by their meeting, but Kate's stomach rolls. She never imagined a scenario in which Scott and Matt would be face to face.

"Let's go in and get a drink," Scott says as he takes Kate's hand. "The food here is decent if you're hungry Matt."

"I'm starving!" Kate exclaims as they walk through the wooden door into the brick building. "I haven't eaten since breakfast."

The three find an open booth near the back of the bar and order a round of beers.

"Are you going to fill me in on the meeting?" Scott asks.

Where to begin? Kate gives Scott a synopsis of their meeting and the clue they found at Judge's office.

Scott grins. "You're telling me you have to get muddy? This I've got to see!"

Matt laughs. "I thought she was going to crap her pants when I showed her the website for the training camp."

"I want to see the website," Scott says.

Matt turns on his phone. After he finds the webpage, he hands his phone over to Scott.

Scott starts laughing, but stops when he sees the look on Kate's face.

"Thanks a lot," she mutters.

Scott bumps his shoulder into her. "Oh c'mon babe. You have to admit this is a little funny. Judge is sending you to do this knowing full well you won't be able to get back at him for it."

"That's the most frustrating part!" Kate pouts. "I don't know why he did this."

Scott's eyes soften. "There has to be more to this than torturing you Kate."

"Like what?" she asks as the waitress puts their salads on the table.

"Maybe he wants you to widen your horizons. Do something you wouldn't ordinarily do. Or maybe he wants to live vicariously through you a little bit. Make you do the things he always wanted to do, but never did."

Kate considers this, crunching a crouton covered in ranch dressing.

"You might be right," Matt says thoughtfully. "There has to be a reason for all of this."

Kate is pretty sure she and Matt both know the reason for the scavenger hunt, but she doesn't say it out loud.

"Matt," Scott says, "please make sure you get pictures of her crawling through the mud pit."

Matt laughs. "Of course."

Kate punches Scott in the arm. "You both suck."

*   *   *

"Matt doesn't seem like a bad guy," Scott says as he walks out of their master bathroom later that night.

Kate has her suitcase on the bed, wondering what the heck you pack for a scavenger hunt. So far she has a few sets of pajamas, underwear, socks and bras. She doesn't know where to go from there.

"You think he's okay because you don't know him," she responds.

Kate hates to admit it, but Matt played nice at dinner. He told them about his new job in Colorado at the prosecutor's office, and talked a lot about his children – Carlie and Noah. He also asked about how Scott and Kate met and listened as they discussed their wedding plans. Matt even cracked a joke about how his invitation must be lost in the mail.

Matt's attitude reverted back to quiet and brooding when Kate drove him back to his hotel. This time, Kate didn't care. She was distracted by her thoughts and didn't try to make conversation.

When she dropped Matt off, he got out of the car and leaned down long enough to say, "See you tomorrow" before shutting the car door.

Scott flops down on the bed next to Kate's suitcase.

"What's the grand plan for tomorrow?"

Kate stuffs three pairs of jeans, some shorts, a couple shirts and a suit into her suitcase. The suit probably isn't necessary, but you never know.

"I'm picking him up at his rental car place. Then I guess it's on to Kentucky. Which reminds me…" Kate walks over to her dresser and opens her workout clothes drawer. She pulls out her oldest pair of shorts, a ratty tank top and a sports bra. The pictures on the website involve people covered in mud, and Kate doesn't want to ruin nice clothes.

Scott lays on their bed and watches Kate pack a few more things.

"Do I need to be worried?" he asks as Kate puts her toothbrush and toothpaste into a tote bag.

"Worried? About what?"

Scott is picking at his nails and avoiding Kate's eyes. "Oh, you know, my fiancée is going on a week long road trip with an ex. An ex who, in my confidently masculine opinion, is very attractive. I think a man with any sense would be worried."

Kate smiles. "Sounds like you want to go on the road trip with him."

The right side of Scott's mouth turns up in a small smile, but it doesn't reach his eyes.

Kate moves the suitcase and sits next to Scott on the bed. "Hey," she says as she snuggles with him. "You don't have a thing to worry about. Nothing is going to happen."

Scott grabs Kate's hand and traces the lines of her palm, giving her goosebumps.

"Good. Because I'd hate to lose you." Scott kisses her palm, making Kate smile.

"You're not going to lose me. I'm coming home. I promise."

Kate leans down and kisses Scott's soft lips.

"What happened between you two anyway?" Scott asks when they pull apart.

Kate stands up and zips her suitcase. "Between me and Matt?"

"Yes. I don't think you've ever told me why you guys broke up."

Kate sighs and thinks for a moment. Her history with Matt flooding her mind. "I found out the hard way I couldn't trust him," she says finally.

"What did he do?"

Kate is desperate to change the subject. "You have one more night with your fiancée before she leaves for a week long scavenger hunt with a man she despises, and all you want to do is talk?"

Scott smirks. "Enquiring minds."

Kate lays down next to Scott and presses her body against his. "We can talk all you want when I get home. But right now, I want to work off the cupcake I had after dinner."

Chapter Four

Kate was late to work because of her annual dentist appointment. She was amazed at how smooth and clean her teeth felt after getting flossed, scraped and cleaned by the dentist. Per the usual, she promised the dentist she would brush twice a day and floss at least every other day. Kate would keep this promise for about a week, then ditch the flossing.

While she waited for her computer to turn on and warm up, Kate reviewed Judge Penny's calendar for the following week. Judge Penny had three criminal sentencings scheduled and a few status conferences, but no big trials.

Kate sighed with relief. Judge Penny's schedule was so busy lately, she hardly had any time to work on motions. Kate turned to her computer when she heard the familiar start up music play. Clicking on her inbox, Kate smiled when she saw an email from Matt.

Playing hooky today?

In the few weeks since their disastrous night with Theresa and Alex, Kate and Matt had become good friends. She did her best to avoid talking to him too much at work, but started eating lunch with him and the other clerks in the break room. It was nice to have people to talk to and vent with when necessary.

Kate typed a quick response:

Nope, dentist appointment.

She shuffled through the papers on her desk and sorted them into case files. She was deciding which case to work on first: the lawsuit against a lawyer for malpractice; or a class action suit against a medical supplier. Kate was opening the file for the class action case when she heard her inbox "ding."

Dentist appointment…sure…

Kate smiled at Matt's email, but didn't respond. Recently, she was getting caught up in twenty-minute conversations via email with Matt and would get nothing accomplished. Kate had to get some work done before Judge Penny started breathing down her neck.

When Kate realized it was 12:30 p.m., she stood up and stretched. She didn't bring in a lunch today, and needed to run down to the local deli to grab a sandwich.

Kate walked by the break room on her way out and stopped in when she saw Matt. He was sitting at a table with a few of the other law clerks. Kate cringed internally when she saw Cora was one of them.

Cora had quickly become Kate's arch nemesis. In group meetings, Cora would negate everything Kate said. Much to Kate's pleasure, Cora often came across as uninformed and a bully. Not many people were a fan of Cora. She was a gossip, and worse than that, most of her stories were either exaggerated or completely false.

Matt looked up and smiled when he saw Kate. "Hey Kate."

Cora didn't seem as happy to see Kate. In fact, she rolled her eyes.

This made Kate grin. "I'm heading out to the deli. Anyone want anything?"

Everyone shook their heads.

"Alright. I'll see you guys later." Kate turned to walk out of the room, but Matt called out to her.

"Want me to go with you?"

Kate glanced over her shoulder and stifled a laugh. Cora's face was so red, steam could come out of her ears at any moment.

"No, I'm good."

Kate nearly skipped to the deli as she replayed the look on Cora's face.

Ha, Kate thought as she made her way along the city sidewalk. Take that you cow!

*   *   *

Matt tried to play it cool when Kate brushed him off, but it hurt a little. She didn't email him back this morning and now she declined his invitation to walk with her to the deli.

Stop being a girl, he scolded himself. She's probably busy.

When Kate focused on work she was unmovable. Unlike Matt, Kate had the ability to shut everything else off and get her work done.

Feeling a bit better as he remembered Kate's work ethic, Matt turned his attention to the rest of the table. The other law clerks were talking about their weekend plans. All except Cora, who was sitting with her eyes narrowed and her arms crossed.

"What's up with you?" Matt asked.

Cora sneered at him. "I can't stand that bitch."

Matt was shocked by the icy tone of Cora's voice. "Who?"

"Kate," Cora responded with a look that said "duh."

"Oh."

"She thinks she's so fucking special."

Matt straightened up in his chair. He suspected Cora was jealous of his new friendship with Kate. He was going to have to tell her, again, that nothing was going on between him and Kate.

Before he could say anything, Cora spoke up again. "The only reason she has this job is because she's fucking a judge."

Matt's heart stopped. He glanced around to see if anyone else heard Cora. Thankfully, everyone was still involved in their own conversations.

69

In a hushed voice, he asked, "What are you talking about?"

Cora sneered. "Come on Matt. Everyone knows it. She's fucking Judge Payne."

Matt almost choked on his water. Of all of Cora's stories, this had to be the funniest.

"Haven't you seen the way they look at each other? She goes into his office all the time. And I've heard he'll stop by to see her."

Matt smiled. "I really don't think they're hooking up."

Cora persisted. "Are you blind? You have to notice how often she goes to visit him. I mean she walks past your freaking office to get to him."

Curious, Matt asked, "Who told you this?"

"All of the secretaries are talking about it. It's disgusting. I thought the days of sleeping your way to the top were over."

Matt screwed the cap of his water bottle back on. "Cora, trust me. Kate and Judge are not sleeping together."

Cora flipped her hair. "Well, I'm sure we'll find out soon enough."

"What do you mean?"

Cora smirked. "I think one of the secretaries will complain about it to her judge. That will get the ball rolling."

Matt was nervous on Kate's behalf. He didn't want the gossip mill to get out of control. Judging by the look on Cora's face, she was going to do whatever she could to slam Kate to whoever would listen.

"Cora," Matt insisted, "whatever you've heard about Kate and Judge isn't true. You should let it go."

Cora pouted. "And why should I? It's not fair. Everyone walks around here thinking Kate is the best worker ever. Like she's smarter than everyone else. It's bullshit and I'm sick of it."

Matt touched Cora's arm. "Please Cora. Let this go."

Cora pulled away. "Stop defending her. I know you're friends, but you're blind to what's going on."

Matt was starting to get pissed. "I am not blind. You are acting like a fool."

"You're the fool. She's fucking your boss and you're too dumb to see it."

"No, she's not."

"What do you think is going on then Matt? She hardly talks to anyone, but she goes out of her way to see a judge she doesn't even work for."

Matt considered his options. Should he keep quiet? If he did, Cora will spout off at the mouth and make a huge deal out of nothing. If Kate found out Matt had the chance to nip this in the bud and didn't, she'll be upset with him.

Matt leaned in toward Cora. "If I tell you something, do you swear not to tell anyone?"

Cora raised an eyebrow. "I'm listening."

"Not good enough Cora. I need to hear you say you'll keep quiet."

Cora pretended to lock her lips and throw away the key.

"I'm serious, you need to promise me."

Cora sighed. "Alright, alright. I promise."

Matt looked over his shoulder to make sure no one was listening. "Judge Payne is Kate's grandfather."

Cora chewed on this a second. "Who told you that?"

"Kate told me. But she doesn't want anyone to know."

Matt's stomach churned as he watched Cora's face go from disappointment to vindication. "I knew it! I knew something was up!"

71

Matt panicked. "Shh!" Matt scanned the room again, but no one was paying any attention to the two of them. "Listen Cora, you can't tell anyone."

Cora stood up and threw out her food. "No worries. The secret is safe with me." Then she sauntered out of the break room.

Matt felt anything but assured.

*　　*　　*

Kate scarfed down her sandwich and bag of chips. She needed to finish her legal research project before their group meeting.

Once a month, all of the judges, magistrates and their clerks got together for a group meeting to discuss court-wide issues. Looking at the clock, she only had about thirty minutes before the meeting.

Should be enough time, she thought to herself as she reviewed the cases she printed out from Westlaw.

Right as she finished reading the last case, the timer on her computer dinged to let her know she had ten minutes until the meeting started.

Perfect timing!

Kate picked up a yellow notepad and a few pens. She grabbed the copy of the meeting agenda from her printer and reviewed it on her walk to the conference room. Kate couldn't help but groan when she saw one of the topics: casual Friday. Hadn't they already discussed this? Cora must have added this to the agenda again. Cora was pissed when the group voted down the idea last time it came up.

Kate walked into the large conference room and was happy to see there were some empty seats at the back half of the table. She hated sitting right next to the judges. How could she doodle if they were watching her every move?

As she continued reading the agenda topics, she was interrupted by a female voice from across the table.

"How was your sandwich?"

Kate looked up and saw Cora peering back at her. Although Cora's question was innocent enough, she looked like the cat who caught the canary.

Kate cleared her throat. "It was fine."

Matt walked in the room with two other clerks and raised his chin to acknowledge Kate. Matt usually sat next to Kate, but the seats on either side of her were already occupied.

Bruce Jones, Judge Worth's clerk, walked in the room and immediately pronounced, "I can only assume that casual Friday is on the agenda again because of you Cora."

Kate tilted her head down toward her agenda so no one would see her smirk.

"I think we should have casual Friday, what's so wrong with that?" Cora retorted.

There was a collective sigh in the room.

"As we discussed last month, the Court does not have a casual day Cora. We're all business every day. It would be unprofessional for us to dress in jeans and t-shirts," Bruce shot back.

Cora huffed. "You're so lame. If you had to wear pantyhose, you'd feel differently. Right, Kate?"

Kate had no idea why Cora was suddenly interested in her opinion, but she didn't like it. Not to be deterred, Kate gave an honest answer. "I think we need to look professional at all times. It helps preserve the Court's image."

Cora crossed her arms. "I don't know why you care. It's not like you're ever going to be fired."

Kate saw Matt shift in his chair.

"I'm glad you think so Cora," Kate responded, trying to get back to the agenda.

Cora snorted. "Yeah, well, if my grandpa was Chief Judge, I'd probably get to wear whatever I want. You should really be taking advantage of that Kate."

Kate felt her face turn red. She shot an accusing eye at Matt, but he wasn't looking at her. He was leaned forward in his seat, glaring at Cora.

"Shut up Cora!" Matt hissed.

All of the clerks, shocked by Matt's tone, turned to look at him. When he sat back in his chair, the clerks turned their attention to Kate. Her heart rate increased as everyone stared at her. Cora had a sickening look of satisfaction on her face.

"You're Judge's granddaughter?" Bruce asked.

Kate sat up straight. She would not let Cora get the best of her. "Yes, I am."

Thankfully, the door opened and the conference room filled with the chatter of the judges and magistrates.

Kate gave Matt an icy scowl, which he returned with puppy dog eyes.

Fucking asshole, she thought before turning her attention to the front of the room.

*   *   *

Matt tried getting Kate's attention for the rest of the meeting without success. He needed to explain himself and why he told Cora about Judge.

But Kate wouldn't even look at him. She maintained a smile on her face and participated in the meeting as if nothing happened.

When the judges dismissed them, Kate left the room without hesitation. Matt wanted to follow her, but Judge stopped him before he could get out of the room.

"Matthew, my office. We need to go over my docket for next week. I'm leaving early today."

Matt was panicking. He struggled to get through his meeting with Judge. His mind was whirling.

How pissed is Kate?

Will she tell Judge?

Will Judge fire me?

Will Kate ever speak to me again?

Matt sent Kate an email after his meeting with Judge asking her to call him. His phone didn't ring. She didn't respond to his email either.

He was reviewing a motion for summary judgment, but kept veering off track. He practiced what he would say to Kate over and over in his mind.

After another hour of no response to his email, Matt was annoyed.

So what if Kate is mad, he thought. Big deal. She'll get over it eventually. And if she doesn't? If she never speaks to me again – oh well. I don't need her

He talked a big game, but not being Kate's friend bothered Matt in a way he didn't want to spend too much time evaluating. He's pissed off a lot of women in his day, but it never concerned him like this.

By 4:45 p.m., Matt was done. He couldn't take it anymore. He pushed back from his desk and headed down the hall to Judge Penny's chambers. After a quick swipe of his badge, the door unlocked and he walked in. His confidence waned with each step he took down the hallway.

He smiled at Judge Penny's receptionist with his best grin. "Hi Betty. I'm here to see Kate."

Betty raised an eyebrow, but didn't say anything.

Kate's office door was closed. Matt stood outside debating whether to knock or to give her more time to blow off steam.

Fuck it, he thought. If I don't talk to her now, I'll never get anything accomplished. And I'm certainly not waiting until Monday. My weekend will be shit if I don't deal with this now.

With this reasoning pounding in his head, Matt knocked. Matt heard a muffled, "come in" from the other side of the door. Matt breathed a sigh of relief. Kate didn't sound pissed anymore. His hope was squashed when he stuck his head in the door and saw anger flash across her face.

"Hey. I wanted…"

Before Matt could finish, Kate put up her hand to stop him. "Not now Matt. Get out."

Ignoring her request, Matt stepped inside her office and shut the door. "Kate, you've got it wrong. I can explain."

Kate pursed her lips. "Matt. Please listen when I tell you this. Not. Now."

Matt couldn't let it go. "Kate, I told Cora about Judge to defend you."

Kate's right eyebrow raised in an arch above her eye. Matt adored this expression, until it was aimed at him. Instead of telling him to get out again, Kate swiveled her chair around and faced her computer.

Matt closed the distance between the door and her desk. "Seriously Kate. She was telling people you and Judge are sleeping together. I only told her to shut her up. I asked that she keep it between us."

Kate didn't turn to look at him as she asked, "Did you really think Cora could keep her mouth shut? I doubt it."

Matt didn't know how to respond. He can't deny he suspected Cora would run her mouth.

Kate kept her gaze on her computer and began clicking on screens with her mouse. "Who has been saying Judge and I are sleeping together?"

Matt stammered. "Cora said all the secretaries are talking about it."

Kate continued to click the mouse. She sighed audibly. "Most of the secretaries have known me my entire life Matt. They know Judge is my grandfather."

Duh! Why hadn't he thought of that before he opened his big mouth? Of course the secretaries would know Kate. Cora was just making shit up.

Matt listened to the movement of Kate's fast fingers as they flew over the keyboard. Was she really able to work while he was trying to make amends? What the hell?! Her calm demeanor disarmed him. He was expecting Kate to be angry, or even tearful. He was not prepared to deal with the iron wall she put up.

Matt's anger was building. "You should be thanking me Kate. I was trying to save your reputation."

Kate finally turned to look at him. Her expression calm, but her eyes penetrating.

"Let me get this straight. In order to defend me from a rumor no one was ever going to believe, you gave Cora, bitch from Hell, a piece of truth she can use against me? Gee, thanks."

When she put it that way…

Kate swiveled her chair back to her computer and began her insistent typing again.

Matt sighed. "Kate. Please. I thought I was helping. I realize I made a mistake. I did it with the best of intentions."

Kate's fingers paused and she turned her head to look at him. "I can't trust you Matt. It's incredibly disappointing." Her eyes softened and he thought he saw a faint glimmer of tears. After giving him the sad eyes for a few seconds, Kate returned her gaze to the computer screen.

She sucker punched him. Kate's disappointment was harder to take than anger.

He turned to walk out, but stopped as his hand reached the door handle. "Kate, I'm so sorry. If it makes a difference, everyone knows you deserve this job more than anyone else here. It won't change the respect they have for you. I'll leave you alone now." As Matt walked out her door, he never felt a silence so heavy.

Matt stayed late working on the summary judgment motions for the Percy matter. It was taking forever and he groaned when he looked up to see it was 8 o'clock.

Needing a temporary distraction, he clicked on his Outlook page. He damn near fell out of his chair when he saw Kate's name in his inbox. She sent him an email at 6:45 p.m.

> *I'm a quick-tempered person who can't hold a grudge for long. I was upset with you and not ready to talk. I appreciate your apology and I understand why you did what you did. Give me some time and I'll be over it.*
>
> *Kate*

Thank God! She wasn't going to hate him forever! Matt was embarrassed by the sudden rush of happiness he felt.

Matt kept his distance for the next few days and didn't approach Kate. He planned to give her the space she wanted. But, as each day passed, he grew more and more concerned that Kate's email was simply telling him she didn't hate his guts. She didn't say in the email she wanted to be friends, or ever wanted to speak to him again. Maybe they were done.

Cora, on the other hand, would not leave him alone. She kept talking to him before and after meetings or in the hallways. They were one-sided conversations for the most part. He would nicely tell her to get lost, but nothing he said would make her go away.

On one of the days, Cora sat next to him at lunch. Matt acted like he was done eating and abruptly got up from the table. As he was throwing out what was left of his lunch, he saw the hurt look on her face.

Good, he thought as he watched her sit down with some of the other clerks. *Maybe she'll feel as crappy as I do.*

Cora also sent him several emails apologizing. Her apologies were laughable.

> *Matt, is this about Kate? If so, I'm sorry. But she deserved it.*

> *Matt, I'm sorry I spilled the beans about Kate. It's not a big deal though, okay?*

> *Matt, whatever I did to upset you, I'm sorry.*

Matt didn't want to say something nasty to a co-worker in writing, so he ignored her and deleted the emails.

Not to be outdone, Cora cornered him where she knew he couldn't retreat – his office. With his office door open, Matt could hear everyone who came and went from Judge's chambers. Late in the afternoon, he heard Judy greet someone. He groaned when he heard Cora's high-pitched voice.

"Is Matt in?"

Please Judy, please lie, he thought desperately.

But she didn't. "Yes. He's in his office."

Why, oh why, hadn't he told Judy no interruptions?

Before he could hide under his desk, Cora was standing in his doorway.

"I need to talk to you," she said matter-of-factly.

Matt tried to maintain a normal tone. "Listen Cora, now's not a good time. I have a ton of work to do."

Cora crossed her arms. "Is that why you're ignoring me?"

"If you know I'm ignoring you, why are you here?" Matt asked through clenched teeth.

Cora took a few steps into his office and shut the door. "I want to talk some sense into you."

79

"What are you talking about Cora? I don't have time for your theatrics."

Cora ran her fingers along the edge of his desk. "I'm sure people would love to hear all about our theatrics. Don't you?"

Matt felt his anger crawl up his neck.

Cora smirked as she continued. "Yep. I'm sure they'd like to know all about you and your, um, preferences..."

"That's enough." Matt stood up from his desk, ready to escort Cora to the door.

She slinked up next to him. "Does Kate know Matt? Does Kate know what makes you tick?" Cora slid her finger up Matt's stomach and tried winding her way up to his neck.

Matt grabbed her hand. "Stop."

Cora pulled her hand free, expression icy. "What's wrong Matt? I'm not good enough for you anymore? I've insulted your new plaything, so we're done?"

"For the hundredth time Cora, Kate and I are just friends."

"Then why are you so mad at me? No one gives a shit about her being Judge's granddaughter. They still think she walks on water."

"You know who gives a shit?" Matt shot back. "Kate. That's who gives a shit. She won't talk to me because of you. You promised me you would keep your mouth shut. And what did you do? You threw it in her face the first chance you got. Because that's the kind of person you are Cora. A mean, spiteful bitch!"

Cora's mouth dropped open and the confidence melted off her face. Matt had never seen Cora look this vulnerable before. Like a little girl who lost her favorite teddy bear.

For the first time, Matt felt bad for her. He could see clear as day now that Cora was never okay with their friends with benefits arrangement.

Matt softened his tone. "Cora, I'm sorry. I thought you understood we were never more than friends."

Cora closed her eyes for a moment, then stood tall with her chin raised. "I know Matt. Doesn't mean I want to watch you and Kate fawn all over each other."

"We don't fawn over each other. We talk to each other. We hang out. It's purely platonic."

Cora chortled. "Keep telling yourself that Matt."

Matt started to object, but Cora turned away.

Before walking out his door, Cora surprised Matt by saying, "I didn't mean to mess up what we had Matt. Call me if you need a *friend*."

Matt breathed a sigh of relief after Cora left. His issues with her appeared to be resolved, at least for the moment. He could never call her again for a hookup. He felt like a shithead for not realizing Cora had feelings for him sooner.

Matt hoped Kate would follow Cora's example and seek him out, but she didn't. Another week rolled by with no improvement. Matt couldn't pinpoint why he cared so much about Kate being mad. He told himself it was the guilt eating away at him, nothing more.

It was a Friday afternoon, and Matt was facing another weekend without Kate's forgiveness. He hated it. When they passed each other in the hallway, she would acknowledge him, but never stopped to speak with him.

No emails.

No texts.

Nothing.

The weekends sucked because he would stew over the situation the whole time. He was angry at himself for trusting Cora, but more upset that he opened his mouth in the first place.

At least he could catch glimpses of Kate during the week. The weekend meant not seeing her at all.

Just when Matt accepted that he would need to drink a lot of beer over the weekend, Kate stopped by his office.

She was juggling a handful of files. "First round on you tonight?"

Matt answered as coolly as possible. "Sure. It's payday."

"Great. I'll see you there." Kate walked away without saying where "there" was, but he knew she meant Patrick's.

A goofy grin crossed Matt's face.

Chapter Five

Now

The drive to Kentucky is uneventful. Matt keeps his quiet demeanor, occasionally taking out his cell phone to check messages.

Kate doesn't have to worry about calls or messages. Everyone who calls her on a regular basis knows what she is up to this morning. Now that the school year is officially over, it's unlikely anyone from the law school will call her. Unless of course, she takes longer than a few weeks to grade exams.

Law students start to get itchy about their grades around the third week after an exam. Their impatience eventually becomes the administration's annoyance. Kate considered bringing the exams with her, but didn't want to risk losing them somewhere along the way.

Kate turns on the radio and flips around until she finds a hip hop station.

Matt snickers from the passenger seat.

"What?" she asks.

"I figured you'd be out of the hip hop phase by now."

Kate smiles. Matt always teased her about her love for rap and hip hop music. "I haven't outgrown it yet. You still listening to classic rock?"

"Hell yeah!" Matt answers enthusiastically.

Kate drives them over the Brent Spence Bridge. The brown water of the Ohio River is moving calmly below them. In the distance, Kate can see The Montgomery Inn Steakhouse, one of Judge's favorite restaurants.

Why couldn't Judge have sent us there instead of boot camp, Kate wonders wistfully.

"How far are we?" Kate asks as they cross into Kentucky.

"It's about an hour from here. We're going to get off the highway in about fifteen minutes and then drive into the middle of nowhere."

"Great," Kate says with zero excitement.

Matt pulls a piece of paper from the pocket of his jeans. "I wrote the directions down. I have a feeling we'll lose navigation."

"Good idea. At least one of us is thinking ahead."

"If you're relying on my judgment, we're in a lot of trouble."

Kate laughs and resists the temptation to make a smartass comment. The two fall back into their usual silence.

Despite the quiet, Kate feels like the tension in the car has eased a bit. She is not ready to make nice with Matt, but she doesn't want to spend the next week perpetually on edge either.

The past is the past, she tells herself as she exits the highway. The sarcastic side of her brain adds, yeah...until the past is sitting next to you in the car...

Kate steals a glance at Matt in the passenger seat. She remembers the days when she would have reached out her right hand and run her fingers through his black hair. Kate can almost feel his left hand on her thigh, where he used to keep it when she drove.

As she drives through the hills of Kentucky, those days seem like another lifetime. Her right hand firmly on the steering wheel and Matt's left hand in his own lap.

Kate's reminiscing is interrupted when Matt reads the next set of directions. They are almost to their destination and the fear in Kate's stomach is growing by the second. What exactly is in store for them when they get there?

Kate hasn't dared go back to the camp's website again. Seeing the different obstacles at the camp was too much for her to process. She hasn't climbed a rope since freshman year in high school and she sure as hell has never crawled under barb wire fencing.

"This is going to be a nightmare," Kate says matter-of-factly.

Matt grunts. "I haven't run a mile in a few years now. I'll probably pass out."

"Did Phil give you any details this morning when you called him?"

Matt shakes his head. "No. He confirmed the camp will be ready for us. That's it."

Kate frowns. They are driving further and further into no-man's-land.

Five minutes later, Matt points out his window. "There it is. There's the sign."

Kate looks toward the sign. In yellow paint, over a camouflage background, are the words "Northern Kentucky Obstacle Course Camp and Training Center." Under the name is a picture of a man climbing over a large wall.

"Ugh," Kate mutters as she turns right onto a dirt road.

If it weren't for the sign, Kate would have never noticed the driveway. There are no buildings or obstacles close to the main road. She drives through a lane of trees as Matt alternates looking through the windshield and his passenger window.

After reaching the top of a hill about a half mile up the dirt road, a white farmhouse and a huge, black barn come into view. When Kate looks to the right, she sees a giant wall made of wooden planks. Kate parks her car on the concrete pad outside the farmhouse.

Great, we made it, she thinks to herself as she opens her car door. Can't wait.

Matt gets out of the car and takes a deep breath. "Ah, gotta love that Kentucky air. A sweet combination of manure and tobacco."

Kate giggles and the two exchange a smile.

"Are you Kate and Matt?" a husky voice calls out from behind Kate.

She turns to see a mountain of a man emerging from the house. He is tall and muscular, the type of man you see on TV, but never in real life. As he approaches, Kate guesses he is about 6'5" with a perfectly shaved head. He has a small scar under his right eye, like a permanent teardrop. There is something oddly familiar about the man, but Kate can't quite place him.

"That's us," Matt responds, coming around Kate's car to shake the man's hand.

Kate marvels at how small Matt looks next to the tall man.

"Thomas Monroe. Welcome," their host tells Matt.

Kate steps up and shakes Thomas's hand. "I'm Kate Marshall. Nice to meet you. I'm also scared to death!"

Thomas grins, softening his imposing face. "I'm sure you are. But I promised Judge I'd look out for you, and I will keep my promise. Him, however," Thomas points at Matt, "I'm supposed to give him hell."

Matt's face pales for a moment. "Great."

Kate laughs. "Good to hear. He deserves a little hell."

Thomas turns toward his house. "Why don't you two follow me inside? I'm sure you're ready for a nice meal. My wife made chicken and dumplings for us."

"How kind. Chicken and dumplings sounds wonderful." Kate follows behind Thomas and is again impressed with what she sees. Thomas's calf muscles flex and move like a well-trained athlete. His movements are fluid and powerful.

Despite her awe, Thomas's physical prowess worries Kate. If this level of athleticism is required to complete the obstacle course, she is royally screwed.

Thomas gives Kate and Matt a brief tour of the first level of his house. Kate is surprised when she hears it was built in the 1850s. Thomas and his wife bought it ten years ago and have been renovating it ever since.

When they walk in the kitchen, Kate is welcomed by the warm smell of biscuits. As promised, the farmhouse table is filled with a giant bowl of chicken and dumplings, a plate of biscuits, a bowl of apple butter, corn, carrots and a pitcher filled with lemonade.

Kate can't hide her awe. "This is amazing!"

"Thank you," a petite woman with red hair says as she sets down the silverware. "I'm Beth."

Kate and Matt shake Beth's hand and introduce themselves.

"We're happy to have you here. I've been curious about the guests Judge was sending our way," Beth says with a smile.

Beth isn't as physically imposing as her husband, but one look at her and you know she is in great shape. Her yoga pants cling in all the right places and her tank top reveals well-toned arms that would make any woman jealous. She has kind eyes and a softness to her face.

"You have outdone yourself Beth! I can't wait to dig in," Kate says.

Beth smiles. "I figured you two need a hearty meal before tomorrow."

Kate grimaces. "Don't remind me."

Thomas laughs as they sit down at the table. "You'll be fine. I've seen many older, and out of shape people, complete the course."

"No added pressure," Matt chimes in as he smooths apple butter over a warm biscuit.

"What will they be doing tomorrow Hon?" Beth asks as she pours everyone a glass of lemonade.

"A team event," Thomas answers.

Kate hands the bowl of corn to Matt. "A team event? Matt and I will be competing against another team?"

"No." Thomas smiles. "You'll be competing against each other. I've called in some of my trainees to help you guys out."

Kate gulps. Great! Now she gets to embarrass herself in front of a large group of people instead of just Matt.

"My friends will be showing up around 6 a.m. tomorrow to meet with you guys and strategize. The event starts at 7:30, so you better get a good night's sleep tonight."

"Is there a hotel close by?" Matt asks.

Beth shakes her head. "No, no hotels. We have two guestrooms upstairs ready and waiting."

"Are you sure?" Kate asks. "We don't want to impose."

"It's no trouble at all," Beth says. "There's no sense in you spending money on a hotel room. Plus, you have to be here so early in the morning. It would be silly for you to travel to town tonight and then right back here at sun up."

"That is so nice of you. Really, it is," Kate tells Beth with a smile.

After she's taken a couple bites of her dinner, Kate looks at Thomas. "Can I ask you a question?"

"You only have one question?"

Kate smiles. "I have a ton of questions, but the one I want to ask you is how you knew my grandfather."

Thomas puts his fork down and sets his elbows on the table, hands clasped in front of him. "You may not remember him, but my brother was Timothy Monroe."

Hearing Timothy's name makes something click in Kate's mind. She instantly remembers how she knows Thomas.

"Oh my gosh! I can't believe I didn't put it together sooner. We've met before, haven't we?"

Matt and Beth both look confused, but Thomas nods his head. "Yes, we have."

"I thought you looked familiar. The hair threw me off."

Thomas chuckles. "Yeah, I don't have the curly blonde hair anymore."

"Care to let me in on the secret?" Matt asks.

"Thomas's brother Tim clerked for Judge a few years before you started working for him," Kate explains.

Beth's eyes widen. "Oh, you two met at Tim's funeral."

"Yes, we did," Thomas confirms with a frown.

"I'm sorry to hear about your loss," Matt says, sincerity in his voice. "I didn't know your brother, but any man who worked for Judge was a good man."

Thomas nods. "Tim was a good guy. Even when we were kids. While I was competitive, he was in it for the fun. He was a talented athlete, played both football and basketball. He cared more about school though. He was my younger brother, but as we got older, I looked up to him in many ways."

Thomas's eyes are lost in the past. "He was smart and articulate. He went to college and law school at OSU on a full ride scholarship. He was clerking for Judge when he got the brain cancer diagnosis."

Kate doesn't have a sibling, so she can't comprehend what it would be like to lose one. But she is no stranger to mourning. Kate wants to say something to ease Thomas's pain.

"Judge talked very highly of Tim. He was devastated when he got the news."

89

"I know. Judge was supportive throughout treatment, and after," Thomas pauses for a second, "after Tim passed."

Beth reaches out her hand and Thomas grabs it. "That's why I owed Judge a favor. For all of the comfort he gave our family in what was the worst time in our lives."

Matt speaks up. "Judge isn't here to say it, so I will. You don't owe him anything. Whatever he did for your family, he did it out of love. Judge saw his clerks as family, and didn't think twice about being there for you."

Thomas smiles. "That's exactly what he said when he called me a couple months ago. He told me he needed a favor, and I told him whatever it was, it was done. I owed him one."

Beth stands up to clear the table and Kate lends a hand. Matt and Thomas follow the women's lead, and soon the table is empty. Beth fills the sink with water and Kate offers to help with the dishes.

"Anything I can help with?" Matt asks.

The area around the sink is crowded. "I'll help her now," Kate says, "and you can help her next time."

Matt nods. "Sounds good to me. Beth, is there a place around here I can get some clothes for tomorrow? I don't think jeans will do the trick."

"Yes. There's a sporting goods store about twenty minutes from here," Beth says as she hands a wet plate to Kate.

Kate dries the plate with a towel. It reminds her of all the times she helped her mom and aunt dry dishes in her grandmother's kitchen.

Thomas pipes up. "I'll go with you Matt. I have to grab a few things myself."

Matt and Thomas take off for the store and Kate stays behind with Beth. She would rather spend time with a total stranger than go out with Matt.

90

"Want to take a tour of the property?" Beth asks. "It will give you the first peek at the course."

Kate grins. "I'll take any advantage I can get!"

It's a nice day outside, if not a bit humid. Beth shows Kate the various obstacles set up on the property. The least daunting of which is the balance beams. Kate isn't too worried about this one. But she's dreading the wall.

"I could never climb the rope in high school," Kate tells Beth.

Beth takes a hold of the thick rope. "This is easier than the rope in gym class because you have the wall for leverage. If you can make it three quarters of the way up, your team can pull you the rest of the way from the top."

Kate still isn't sure. "Can I try it?"

Beth hands the rope to Kate. "Sure. I won't tell the boys you've been practicing."

Kate grips the rope. She tilts her head back and looks at the platform. It seems impossibly far away.

"Don't look at the top," Beth advises. "Focus on where you're putting your feet."

Kate struggles to plant her feet on the wall. Beth comes over and helps Kate get started. Kate is surprised when she makes progress. Before she gets too high, she jumps down.

Beth grins. "See! I knew you could do it!"

"That made one of us," Kate says as she wipes her hands on her jeans. The rope was rough on her soft skin.

"You'll probably be in teams of four tomorrow. Have two of your teammates go up first, and keep someone down here with you to get you started."

They spend the next hour going from obstacle to obstacle. Beth gives Kate a few pointers and she feels better about the whole thing. She can do this with the help of teammates.

91

Once back inside, Beth shows Kate to her room and gives her some privacy. The bedroom is covered in white wallpaper with little blue flowers. The full size bed has a pretty, pale blue comforter and frilly pillow shams. The view from Kate's window is not of the obstacle course, but of the other side of the yard. She smiles as she looks out over the green acreage.

Kate takes a book out of her bag and props herself up against the pillows. It's been a while since she could sit and read anything other than case law. The experience would be wholly pleasant if not for the circumstances that brought her here.

After reading a few chapters, Kate feels her eyelids getting heavy. She decides to put her book down and give in to her sleepiness. Why not? She doesn't have any plans. Kate rolls to her side and falls asleep within minutes.

Kate wakes up to a light knock on the door.

"Come in!" she says in a ragged voice. She clears her throat as she sits up in the bed.

The door cracks open and Beth smiles in at her. "Dinner time sleepy head."

"What time is it?" Kate asks.

"About 6:30."

6:30! That means she napped for a solid two hours.

Kate cleans herself up in the guest bathroom before heading downstairs. Matt and Thomas are already at the table. Kate sees a meatloaf and several side options laid out for them.

Kate isn't a huge fan of meatloaf, but she eats it. She isn't going to complain about her meal when Beth was nice enough to cook for everyone again. She's relatively quiet over dinner. Matt and Thomas do most of the talking.

They must have done some male bonding on their trip, Kate thinks to herself.

When everyone is done eating, Thomas smacks his hands on the table. "What do you two think, should we go outside and check out the obstacle course?"

Kate and Beth exchange a glance, but say nothing.

"That sounds great!" Matt says. "I need to see what I'll be dealing with tomorrow."

Thomas takes them outside and Kate pretends to be seeing everything for the first time. Thomas gives them some pointers here and there, but most are the same as Beth's tips earlier. Kate watches Matt practice on the climbing wall and isn't surprised to see him jet right to the top.

For all his talk about being out of shape, Matt is as agile and strong as he was ten years ago. He tackles most of the obstacles with ease.

Kate's thoughts lead her to a memory of Matt walking around shirtless in his apartment and pretending to be a bodybuilder for her. It was a silly moment, but he looked so damn hot. She remembers how taut his body felt under her fingertips. And how safe she felt in his strong arms. Kate spent a lot of long nights in those arms. Those nights were some of the best nights of her life.

"Want to give it a try?"

"Huh?" Kate shakes the ghosts from her mind.

Thomas is pointing at the mud pit. "Want to give it a try?" he asks again.

Kate crinkles her nose. "No. Not really."

Thomas laughs. "Suit yourself. But you'll be in it tomorrow."

"Can't wait," Kate mutters to herself.

*   *   *

Matt wakes up the next morning at 6:00 a.m. His team members will be here soon and he wants to be up and ready for them. Beth has muffins, scrambled eggs and fruit laid out, but he isn't sure he

93

wants to eat anything. It would be embarrassing if he throws up later.

Kate saunters down a few minutes later and picks up a blueberry muffin. She exchanges pleasantries with Beth as she takes a few bites of her muffin. Her hair is in a ponytail and she's in workout clothes. The outfit makes her look younger, around the age of the girl he was in love with.

"Where's Thomas?" Kate asks Beth.

"He's outside getting everything ready."

No sooner are the words out of Beth's mouth that Thomas comes bounding in.

"Your teams are outside. Let's move!"

Kate drops her muffin like a child who's been caught with cake. The expression on her face is priceless. Matt can't help but chuckle.

Kate narrows her eyes at him, but says nothing. Her contempt for him comes off of her in waves. There are times she lightens up a bit, and they have a pleasant conversation. Inevitably though, her eyes will darken and she'll turn cold again.

Which is why he has been keeping to himself. Why bother being nice when she hates him? There's a big part of him that doesn't want Kate's forgiveness. Civility on her part would be worse. Being able to say Kate hates him makes it easier for Matt to push thoughts of her to the side.

A group of six people is waiting for them when they walk outside. Three women and three men. They are wearing red or blue shirts. All are physical specimens in their own right.

"Matt, this is Hector, Carla and Janet. They are your team," Thomas says as he points to the group in red.

Thomas turns to his left. "Kate, this is Mark, Paul and Ashley."

94

Kate walks over to her team in blue and Matt heads to his red team.

"I'll walk you guys through the course and tell you the order of the obstacles. I've labeled each one with a flag, so you don't have to remember everything I say. The team with the best time wins."

"What do we win?" one of the male members of Kate's team asks.

Thomas smiles. "You don't win anything Mark. If your team wins with Kate, Matt will be punished. If Matt's team wins, Kate will suffer the punishment."

Punishment? No one said anything about a punishment yesterday.

"Um," Kate says, biting her lip, "what is the punishment?"

Thomas laughs. "You'll find out. Just make sure you win, okay?"

Even from a distance, Matt can see Kate gulp. Matt doesn't like the sound of a punishment either. Hard telling what could be done to him out here in the sticks.

Thomas walks them through the course and nothing about it surprises Matt. There will be six obstacles total: the balance beams, the mud pit, the tire flip, the cargo net, the monkey bars, and finally, the climbing wall.

"Take some time to get to know each other," Thomas instructs. "I'll call you to the start line in a little while."

Matt and his team huddle together and discuss strategies for the different obstacles. Luckily, his teammates have done this a hundred times.

"Don't worry," one of his female teammates assures him, "we're gonna win!" She looks like an Olympic hammer thrower, so Matt likes his odds.

95

Thomas calls the groups back together and announces Matt's team will go first. Matt and his team line up at the start line and wait for the air horn. As soon as it blows, Matt and his team take off.

Matt struggles on the balance beams for a second and almost falls into the mud below. Luckily, one of his teammates has his back. Literally. She puts her hands on his waist and steadies him before he can fall.

"Thank you!" he yells to her.

"Move it!" she shouts back at him.

Matt gets down on his stomach and belly crawls through the mud pit. His head is only three inches from barb wire and he does all he can to avoid it. He is much slower than his teammates, but he feels like they're making decent time.

Next up is the tire flip. They each have to flip a tractor tire twenty yards. The first few flips are easy, but Matt feels his strength waning as he goes. His team comes up beside him and eggs him on until he goes the full twenty yards.

Matt gets up the cargo net despite his arms turning to mush. He takes a moment to catch his breath before starting the next obstacle. Matt hasn't done the monkey bars since grade school. And these are monkey bars on crack. There are twenty-five rungs and the apparatus hangs over a pool of muddy water.

Here goes nothing, he thinks as he uses his momentum to swing from the first bar to the second. He makes it across without falling and smiles when he realizes he only has one obstacle left.

Making his way up the climbing wall is a lot harder today than it was yesterday, but he makes it. He and his male teammate pull the girls up to the top and ring the bell.

"Yeah!" Matt exclaims as he high-fives his teammates.

He's covered in mud and will be sore tomorrow morning, but his adrenaline is pumping.

When his team returns to the start line, he asks Thomas, "How'd we do?"

"Pretty well."

"What was our time?" Matt's male teammate asks.

Thomas shakes his head. "You'll find out after Kate's team finishes their run."

Matt and his team groan collectively.

He watches as Kate and her team line up at the start. Kate is still in great shape, but given the issues he had with the course, he wonders how Kate is going to handle it.

The air horn goes off and Kate sprints to the balance beam obstacle. She's like a gymnast on the beams, making them look like a cake walk. She hesitates at the mud pit, but gets down low to crawl under the barb wire.

Matt laughs as Kate tries fruitlessly to wipe mud off of her hands when she's done. There's not a clean spot to wipe them on.

Kate has a hard time with the tire, but her teammates lend a hand. Matt almost objects to Kate getting help flipping the tire, but if Thomas doesn't think it's cheating, Matt won't protest. Plus, he's not sure Kate could have finished the tire flip on her own. He doesn't want Kate to win, but he wants her to finish the course.

Kate struggles through the monkey bars and cargo net, but she completes the obstacles without falling.

"They're making really good time," the thinner of his female teammates says.

When Kate's team reaches the climbing wall, Matt sees her talking with her teammates. She doesn't look happy. The two men climb the wall first. Once atop the wall's platform, they lay on their stomachs and extend their hands down to help the ladies.

97

Kate takes the rope for her turn, but her female teammate makes a grab for it too. The two women go back and forth while the men yell down at them to hurry up.

Kate frowns as her teammate starts climbing the wall. She throws her hands up in exasperation.

"What's going on?" Matt asks Thomas, who is watching the scene with a furrowed brow.

"Ashley is being a pain in the ass again, that's what," Thomas says. "Ashley was supposed to let Kate go first so Ashley could boost her up. Looks like Ashley decided she needs the boost more than Kate does."

Kate helps Ashley with a scowl on her face. Ashley uses the rope to climb up a few feet, then the men grab her arms to pull her the rest of the way up. Kate stands at the bottom of the wall holding the rope and looking up at her teammates. Matt watches as Kate makes an attempt to start climbing. He cringes when she falls.

After three more failed tries, Matt asks Thomas, "Why doesn't one of the guys climb down and help her?"

Thomas shakes his head. "Once you're at the top, you stay at the top." Judging by his tone, Thomas isn't happy about this rule at the moment.

Matt's male teammate claps his back. "You're going to win. She's never going to get up there."

Kate tries a couple more times to climb the wall, but she can't get her feet planted properly. Matt hears her yell to her teammates, "I'm sorry, I can't do it."

The look of defeat on Kate's face puts Matt's feet into motion. Kate cannot fail. Not today. She'll never forgive herself.

Matt jogs up behind Kate. "Need a hand?"

She glares at him. "Don't patronize me, okay? I feel shitty enough already."

Matt stands next to the wall. "You want a boost or not?"

Kate's mouth drops open. "You're going to help me?"

Matt claps his hands together. "Let's go!"

Kate nods and grips the rope. He grabs her waist and boosts her up as high as he can.

"Plant your feet on the wall Kate! Just like that!"

Matt smiles as he watches Kate ascend the wall. She's wobbly, but she's doing it. A minute later, her teammates grab her arms and pull her up. Kate looks down at him and mouths, "thank you" as her team hoots and hollers around her.

Kate's wide grin as she high-fives her teammates warms Matt's heart. All he can do is smile back up at her.

Once everyone is together at the starting line, Thomas announces the winner. "And the winning team is...Kate's team! By ten seconds!"

Kate and her team shout as they jump up and down.

"Way to go man," Matt's burly female teammate whines. "We would have won if you didn't help her out."

Matt is disappointed, but he feels good about what he did. This scavenger hunt Judge has them on is more for Kate than it is for him. Kate would have beat herself up if she didn't finish the course.

"What's my punishment?" Matt asks Thomas when Kate's team calms down.

Thomas grins. "We're going to a honky-tonk in town for karaoke tonight. Kate gets to pick the song you perform in front of the hometown crowd."

Everyone laughs, including Matt.

He's relieved. Karaoke? No big deal.

*   *   *

Kate calls Scott after her shower.

"You have to pick 'Touch Myself' or 'Baby Got Back'," Scott jokes.

"I feel like I should go easy on him. He's the only reason I won."

"True," Scott concedes. "But that doesn't mean you can't mess with him a little."

"I'll think about it," Kate says as she dries her hair with a towel. "How has your day been?"

"Hectic." Scott proceeds with telling Kate about his day at the hospital. Sometimes Scott's work stories are awesome. He improves the life of a child every day. But there are times when they're awful. Not every child can be saved.

Kate tells Scott she loves him before she hangs up. She searches her suitcase for an outfit suitable for a country bar. She ends up picking a pair of jeans and a green shirt. She doesn't have anything remotely cowboyish, so this will have to do.

As she dries her hair, she wonders why Matt helped her. He would have won. There was no way she was getting up that wall. Ashley totally screwed her over. They agreed before they started the course that Ashley would help Kate, but Ashley went rogue. Kate suspects it was because Ashley was afraid she wouldn't be able to get up the wall on her own and didn't want to look stupid in front of the group.

Kate was so relieved when Matt came to her rescue.

But why did he do it?

At least the punishment isn't a big deal. Kate would feel awful if it was something more than karaoke. She isn't surprised by the punishment. Judge loved karaoke and would set up a machine at all of his parties. Judge was a big, imposing man, but he loosened up when the music started. He would even sway his hips and sing in a faux female voice.

Judge always told her, "Karaoke is like bowling. You never know who's good at it."

Kate is happy to see Thomas and Beth dressed in normal, everyday clothes, and not cowboy gear, when she gets downstairs. Like Thomas and Beth, Matt is in jeans and a t-shirt.

Matt looks good, she catches herself thinking.

They all eat a big meal – steak and potatoes – and have some time to kill before leaving for the bar. Kate and Beth walk around the property. Kate isn't sure what Matt and Thomas do while they're gone.

Beth and Kate share stories about their childhood. Beth has a lot of questions about Judge, which Kate happily answers. Beth tells Kate about her days growing up on a farm in a traditional family model.

"I wish my childhood was more like that," Kate admits.

"Really?" Beth asks surprised. "Why?"

"My dad wasn't around growing up. It would have been nice to have a normal, loving family. And maybe a few siblings."

"You can have some of mine," Beth offers. "I have a brother who's in and out of county jail. He's all yours."

Kate laughs. "Thanks."

"You had Judge though, right?"

Kate nods. "I did. He was my father for all intents and purposes. He was very involved in my life." Kate stops to pick a dandelion. "But it's not the same."

Beth and Kate return to the house and find the guys watching a baseball game. After an hour or so, they decide to head out to the bar.

The group gets in Thomas's Jeep, Matt in front with Thomas and Kate in back with Beth. They talk about the race and other events hosted on the property. After a while, Kate's mind starts wandering as she stares out the back window. Thomas and Beth are sharing war stories about their own obstacle course adventures, but Kate is reminiscing.

Matt's act of kindness reminds Kate of how he used to look out for her. How he used to be her best friend. Kate locked away those memories because of the pain they caused. Now, they are starting to leak out.

And it scares her.

The sun is barely visible over the horizon when the Jeep pulls up to the bar. The bar is a small, brick building with a neon sign out front reading, "Jerry's Place." There are a few beer company banners hanging on the exterior of the building and a single metal door with "Entrance" painted above it.

"Classy place," Matt whispers to her as they walk up.

She smiles at him.

"Don't be deceived by the outside guys," Beth says. "It's nice on the inside."

Kate wouldn't choose the word "nice" to describe the inside of the bar, but it's not quite the dive she was expecting. They walk down a narrow hallway covered with cork boards holding various flyers and ads. The place is poorly lit and reminds Kate of some of the questionable bars she went to in college and law school.

The lounge area is a giant square. A large dance floor takes up the bulk of the room. It is surrounded by wooden tables with wooden chairs. All but three of the tables are full. There is a stage at the back of the building with a single microphone and a table holding the karaoke machine. To her left, several patrons fill the stools in front of a long, wooden bar.

There are couples out on the dance floor. A slow song is playing overhead. Kate thinks it's an Alan Jackson song, but she isn't sure.

"I'll grab the song book," Beth tells them. "You guys get a table."

Kate follows Thomas and Matt as they weave through the circular tables. A few people lift their beers or tip their heads to Thomas. Kate feels uncomfortable as all the bar's regulars give her a once over.

Beth walks up behind her with the song book. She senses Kate's nerves. "You're a strange lady in a small town," Beth explains. "They're curious about you, that's all. They'll behave themselves."

"I hope so," Kate says as she takes a seat in between Beth and Matt.

"They will," Beth promises. "If not, Thomas will handle it."

"I'll handle what?" Thomas asks.

"The men checking out Kate," Beth tells him.

Kate feels her face flush. She feels ridiculous. She's in her late thirties for God's sake.

Thomas scans the room. "I know every person in here. They won't mess with you."

A waitress walks up to the table and Thomas orders a pitcher of beer.

"Better make that two," Matt pipes up. "I'm going to need some liquid courage."

"Speaking of," Kate takes the song book from Beth, "let me see what I can pick out for you."

Matt groans. "Please, none of the hip hop stuff. There's no way I'll be able to get through a rap song."

Kate laughs. "I don't think they're going to have a huge Snoop Dogg selection here."

Matt smiles. "You're probably right. I don't think the clientele would appreciate it."

Kate searches through the song book and sees a lot of Garth Brooks and George Strait options. She's not a big fan of country music, but Judge was. He preferred the older singers to the likes of Tim McGraw and Kenny Chesney. The old school singers like Conway Twitty and Merle Haggard.

Remembering Judge's favorite singers gives her an idea.

Kate flips to the "C" page and finds the singer she's looking for. She grins as she writes the song selection down on the pad of paper next to the karaoke machine. Judge would approve.

"You're number five," she tells Matt when she returns to the table.

"At least I'm not first," Matt responds.

"The people here take their karaoke very seriously," Thomas says. "Hopefully you're up to snuff."

Matt shifts in his chair. "Have they ever booed anyone off the stage?"

"Yes," Beth and Thomas answer in unison.

Kate is suddenly very happy she won the challenge today. She would be crapping her pants right now if she had to get up in front of this group. She can't carry a tune to save her life.

"You'll be fine," Kate says to Matt. "You're good in front of a crowd."

"Yeah, but not this crowd. They look like they want to kick my ass already. Wait until they hear me sing."

Kate laughs. "I picked a good one for you."

Matt raises an eyebrow. "I'm sure you did."

"No, really. I did. They'll like it."

"We'll see about that."

Kate scans the room. No one is staring at them anymore. They've gone back to their drinks and conversation.

"Want to dance?" Thomas asks Beth as he stands up.

"Sure," she answers with a smile.

Kate watches them walk out onto the dance floor. Beth puts her left hand on Thomas's tall shoulder as he wraps his arm around her waist. They clasp their free hands and start moving to the music.

Kate tries to remember the last time she slow danced. Her friend Marlie's wedding maybe? That was a few years ago, before she started dating Scott. She can't think of a single time she's slow danced with him. Is it possible their wedding will be their first slow dance together?

"I'd ask you to dance," Matt says, "but you hate my face."

Kate laughs. "I'm not much of a dancer."

"Yeah, I know."

Kate looks at Matt for a moment. He does know. He's seen her awful dance skills first hand. Unlike Scott, Kate has shared many slow dances with Matt.

On the nights Theresa convinced them to go out to a dance club, the deejay would play at least one slow song. T would bitch and moan about it, but Kate loved it. She would press her body against Matt's as they swayed to the music.

A chill runs up her spine as she remembers how Matt used to lean over and whisper in her ear. He would tell her all the things he was going to do to her when they got home.

"You okay?" Matt asks her, interrupting her daydream.

She nods. "Yeah, I'm good."

"You look like you're on another planet."

"I feel like I'm on another planet."

Matt grins. "We're a long way from home."

No kidding, Kate thinks to herself.

The slow song ends and a pudgy man wearing a flannel shirt and a beat up cowboy hat takes the stage.

"Well now, ladies and gentleman. It's time for karaoke!" he announces in an exaggerated Southern drawl.

"Oh God," Matt says under his breath as the bar erupts.

"First up," their emcee says, "is Miss Darla Jenkins. Get your butt up here Darla!"

A petite woman who weighs all of one hundred pounds saunters up to the stage. She is wearing a sleeveless, flannel shirt tucked into her tight jeans. Her cowboy hat is pink and her belt buckle says "Farm Girl" on it. She looks younger than Kate, but not young enough to be considered a "Girl" anymore.

"Hey y'all!" Darla says when she reaches the microphone.

"Hey Darla!" the crowd, including Thomas and Beth, yell back.

"I'm doing Shania Twain tonight," Darla tells the audience. They clap their approval.

The music starts and Kate recognizes the song. It's "Any Man of Mine." To her credit, Darla does a decent Shania Twain. There are times when Kate winces at Darla's attempt to hit a high note, but she does a better job than Kate would have.

The next three performers are men and they all do Garth Brooks' songs.

When Matt's name is called, he tips back what's left of his beer. "It's show time," he says before standing up.

The crowd murmurs as they watch a stranger take the stage.

Matt has a huge smile on his face. "Hi, my name is Matt. I'm not from around here. But you know that already."

The crowd chuckles.

"I'm standing up here because I lost a race at Thomas's obstacle course today."

Thomas waves his hand to everyone as they look his way.

106

"I have no idea what song I'm about to sing," Matt explains. "My apologies in advance."

Matt licks his lips as he waits for the music to start. Soon, a familiar bass line thumps through the room. The crowd cheers with appreciation. They all hum along with Johnny Cash.

Kate knew they'd love "Walk the Line." It was Judge's favorite song to sing on karaoke night. Matt smiles at her before turning his attention back to the lyrics scrolling on the screen. He knows she went easy on him.

When Matt starts singing, he's not alone. Half the crowd is singing along with him. Matt takes the microphone off the stand and walks around the stage with it, really playing it up. The man can fit in anywhere he goes.

Kate sings softly with the crowd. After the second verse though, she feels tears welling in her eyes. Maybe she shouldn't have picked this song. It brings up memories of Judge and all the times he performed it at family gatherings. When a tear spills out onto her cheek, she gets up from the table.

"Are you alright?" Beth calls out to her over the crowd.

Kate nods. "I need to get some air. I'll be right back."

Kate turns away before Beth can ask her any more questions. She makes her way to the exit, avoiding eye contact with the other bar patrons. When she makes it through the exit and into the night, she lets out her breath. Knowing she will never hear Judge sing Johnny Cash again was too much. She walks over to the brick wall and leans up against it. She stares up at the stars.

"I miss you," she whispers to the night sky. "I wish you were here."

Kate stands up straight when the bar door opens. Matt steps outside with a grin on his face.

"You missed it! I got a standing O!"

Kate musters a smile. "I'm not surprised."

107

Matt puts his hands in his pockets as he walks up to Kate. "Was my singing that bad?"

She shakes her head. "No. The song reminds me of Judge, that's all."

Matt leans on the brick wall next to Kate. "He did love the man in black."

"Yes, he did."

They gaze up at the stars together. Each remembering the man who sent them on this journey. Kate is about to suggest they go back inside when Matt turns to her.

"You could have roasted me up there. But you didn't. Why?"

"The only reason I won this morning was because of you. It was my thank you."

Matt smiles. "I appreciate it."

"No problem."

The two stand quietly for a moment.

"Hey, um, I know this is awkward," Matt says. "Maybe we can make the best of it though. Put the past behind us and all that."

Kate considers this a moment. "Sure, why not? We're going to be stuck together for a little while. No point in dwelling on the past, right?"

Matt smiles. "Good. Ready to go back in?"

"I'll be there in a minute."

Matt nods before heading back inside.

"Put the past behind us," Kate whispers.

Can she?

Chapter Six

Ten Years Ago

Matt was about to log out of his computer when his cell phone rang. It was Alex.

"What's up douche?" Alex asked in his typical way.

"Getting ready to leave work. What's up?"

"Are you heading out to the bar tonight? I'm trying to get a couple of guys together."

Matt looked at the clock. It was after six. He needed to get moving.

"Can't man. Kate's having a party at her place tonight."

Alex grunted. "I should have known your ass would be with Kate. You hitting that yet?"

"No dick. I told you. We're just friends." Matt turned his office light off and made his way out of Judge's chambers.

"You spend an awful lot of time with your *friend*. When are you going to tell her you're into her?"

"Who says I am?"

"Screw you dude. You can play the friend game with everyone else, but I know you. You're into that girl or you wouldn't give her the time of day."

Alex had a point.

Matt looked around to make sure no one else was in the hallway. "Okay, fine. I like Kate. A lot. But she isn't ready for a relationship yet. So I'm biding my time."

Alex snickered. "Until when? She grabs your junk?"

Matt sighed. "I don't fucking know." Matt got in his car and started the engine. "She's trying to get over her ex."

"Yeesh. That doesn't sound good. Is she hung up on the guy?"

This was exactly Matt's fear. "I don't know man. He's going to be at her party tonight, so I'll get a good look at him and the situation."

Alex laughed. "The infamous ex is gonna be there? Can I come to this party? I'd love to watch you mean-mug his ass all night long."

It would be hard not to be a jerk to Kate's ex. Ben told Kate he was in town for work, but Matt suspected he was there to win Kate back.

"It's not a big party. I think fifteen to twenty people will be there. Tops. That will make it hard for you to hide from Theresa."

"Ah, Theresa. I should have called her back."

Matt laughed. "No worries man. She's moved on." In fact, from what Matt saw, Theresa moved on with about ten other guys.

"I'm sure. A girl like her doesn't sit at home waiting for the phone to ring."

"Nope." Matt pulled into a parking spot near Kate's place. "I gotta go. Have fun tonight."

"Always do. Don't beat up the ex."

"No promises. Later." Matt hung up his cell phone and pulled his tie off.

Matt didn't have time to run home and change, his suit pants and dress shirt would have to do. He thought about bringing a change of clothes with him this morning, but feared it would look like he was trying too hard.

Matt was second-guessing himself about everything Kate was involved in. He wanted to spend time with her, but didn't want to come on too strong. He was constantly walking the thin line between friend and boyfriend.

As Matt walked up to Kate's building, his chest tightened. What if he walked in to find Ben and Kate warm and cuddly with each other? What if he got to witness their reconciliation up close and personal?

It would be his own fault. The party was his idea.

"Ugh," Kate groaned over her peanut butter and jelly sandwich a few days ago. "Guess who's coming for a visit this Friday?"

"Who?"

Kate rolled her eyes. "Ben."

"Ben?! The ex?"

Kate nodded. "Some work conference. I didn't ask for the details."

Matt took a drink from his water bottle. "And he thought he'd swing by your apartment?"

"Yep. He asked if he could see my new place. I didn't know how to say 'no.'"

"You're too nice. I would have told him to go fly a kite."

"I know, I know. I should have. But I feel a little guilty about how things ended."

"You don't owe him anything Kate. You broke up. Happens every day."

"Yeah, but we were together for a long time. I still care about his feelings, even if we aren't a couple anymore."

Matt considered this. He didn't want Ben and Kate to be alone. He made a suggestion based on his own, selfish interests.

"Why don't you have a dinner party? Then you aren't stuck with him by yourself."

Kate crunched a carrot. "You know, that's a good idea. Now I have to figure out who to invite."

Without thinking, Matt responded, "I'll go."

Kate swept up her trash and stood up. "Alright then, you're in."

In retrospect, Matt had invited himself to this shindig. He was sure the evening would be uncomfortable for everyone in attendance. But he was too curious about Kate's ex. Matt wanted to see Ben for himself.

Matt knocked on Kate's door, a bottle of red wine in his hand. Matt knew nothing about wine. His method was to buy a bottle with a cool label in the median price range.

Theresa answered the door. She poured herself into a yellow dress and black heels. Alex's eyes would have popped out, but Matt was used to seeing Theresa like this. She left nothing to the imagination and Matt was over it.

Matt and Theresa had a rocky relationship. Matt tried to be as nice as possible to Theresa, but in her eyes, he was nothing more than Alex's best friend. According to Kate, Theresa had uncharacteristically sought out a second date with Alex. Except Alex never returned Theresa's call.

Tonight, Theresa had a smile on her face when she opened the door. "Hey Matt. Come on in."

Matt handed Theresa the bottle of wine, which she looked at approvingly, and made his way to the living room. There were a few people standing around with drinks in their hands, and a couple more sitting on the couch chatting with plates of finger foods. But he didn't see Kate.

As if reading his mind, Theresa walked up beside him and whispered, "Kate is in her room with Ben. I'm getting a little worried. They've been back there for ten minutes."

Alarm bells went off in Matt's mind. Ben and Kate are alone in her room?

"Was Kate okay when they walked back there?" Matt asked.

Theresa shifted her weight and bit her bottom lip. "Not really. He showed up early and played Prince Charming with her. When Kate said she wanted to finish getting ready, he followed her in there."

"Have you checked on her?"

"No! What if they're hooking up?"

Matt's stomach flipped. He didn't want to think about Ben and Kate hooking up.

"Think I should interrupt?" Theresa asked.

"If something bad was happening, we'd hear it, right?"

Theresa shrugged her shoulders. "The stereo's on and people are talking." After a pause, Theresa straightened herself up. "You know what? I'll walk up to her door and see if I can hear anything."

Despite the situation, Matt smiled as he watched Theresa tiptoe down the hallway. She looked like a character in the old Looney Tunes cartoons he watched as a kid.

When Theresa approached the door, she leaned in slightly. After a minute or two of listening in, Theresa's expression hardened. Matt walked toward Kate's room when he saw Theresa push the door open. He couldn't hear exactly what she said, but he thought it was, "That's enough!" in a soft hiss.

Matt reached the bedroom door as a male voice answered, "Mind your own business Theresa."

Theresa was standing by Kate, whose face was flushed and stern. Kate was wearing a blue dress with a pearl necklace, and of course, no shoes. She would look pretty if her face wasn't twisted into a snarl.

"Don't talk to her like that Ben," Theresa warned.

Matt turned his attention to the other man in the room. Ben wasn't what Matt expected. Matt pictured Ben as an average guy in a suit and tie. The kind of guy you'd walk by on the street and not remember seeing. But Ben wasn't the average guy at all.

Ben was tall, probably about 6'3", with short blonde hair and brown eyes. He was wearing faded jeans with black Nike Air Force Ones and a black sweater pushed up to his elbows. His watch gleamed when hit by the light and Matt guessed it cost Ben a pretty penny.

Ben gave him a once over as well. "Who are you?"

Matt didn't like the disdain in Ben's voice. "One of Kate's friends."

"A friend. Sure you are." Ben looked at Kate. "Is this the poor bastard you're dating now?"

"Hey!" Matt exclaimed, but Kate interrupted him.

"No. This is my friend Matt from work."

Ben didn't believe Kate. The way he glared at Matt was evidence enough of that. "Let me give you some advice Matt. Stay the hell away from this one," he said, pointing at Kate.

"Ben, please. Leave," Kate pleaded.

A wicked grin spread across Ben's face. "I wasted years of my life on this girl. Treated her like a princess. I loved her like I've never loved anyone else before. And what do I get?" Ben paused as he glanced at Kate, but then returned to Matt. "She breaks up with me after I propose to her."

"Shit happens," Matt responded.

"Ha!" Ben nearly shouted. "What did she tell you about me? Did she say I was an asshole? That I did something to deserve being shit on?"

Matt felt his anger level rising. "Actually, she said you were a good guy."

Ben cocked his head to the side. "And what does that tell you? She says I'm a good guy, who treated her right, yet she runs away when I tell her I love her?"

Matt shrugged.

Ben's eyes widen. "She can't commit. She's incapable of loving anyone."

"Stop it!" Theresa hissed from across the room. Theresa had her arm protectively over Kate's shoulders. "You've said enough Ben. Now go."

"I think she's right. You should leave," Matt added when he saw Kate's eyes tearing up. It was all he could do to keep himself from dragging Ben out of the room.

Ben ignored Matt and Theresa. He stared at Kate as he continued his tirade. "Did she tell you her daddy left when she was three? That she'll never trust anyone because of it? Has she told you she thinks all relationships are doomed to fail?"

"Shut up Ben," Kate whispered.

But Ben continued. "Or how she's ended every relationship she's been in? She finds some silly reason to break up, then blocks the person out of her life like he never existed."

"I said, shut up!" Kate's voice was getting louder, more confident.

Ben smirked. "How about this one? Has she told you the only thing she cares about is her career? She'll throw you to the curb and leave town when an opportunity comes up."

"You're pissed off and saying nasty things. Why don't you leave? It's not getting you anywhere," Matt said as calmly as possible.

"What about Steve?" Ben asked undeterred. "Has she told you about poor Steve?"

Kate's hands were curled into tight fists by her side. "That's enough Ben."

115

Ben turned to Matt. "You see, Steve made the mistake of falling in love with Kate their senior year of college. Steve turned down a full-ride scholarship to Duke's medical school because Kate said she never wanted to move outside of Ohio. It was a great opportunity for Steve. But you know what happened? Kate went off to Yale the second they extended her an offer. Poof! Gone! And poor Steve was left alone in Columbus."

Matt hadn't heard about Steve before. But he couldn't care less at the moment. "Sounds to me like you should have seen it coming then."

Ben laughed. "She's already gotten to you, hasn't she?"

Before Matt could respond, Ben started clapping his hands. "Bravo Kate! Another sucker lined up."

Matt stiffened. "It's time for you to go."

The smile fell from Ben's face. "I'm doing you a favor. I'd hate to see another good man go down."

"Get out," Matt responded, his anger reaching its boiling point.

"Are you going to make me?" Ben asked as he walked toward Matt.

Matt readied himself. Alex's advice about not getting in a fight replayed in Matt's head. It looked like he would have a story to share with Alex in the morning.

Kate pushed herself in between them. "Enough. Ben, you've insulted and embarrassed me in front of my friends. You've accomplished what you came to do. I feel like shit. Congratulations."

Ben's face softened. "This isn't how I want things to end with us Kate."

"Get out asshole!" Theresa scowled.

Kate put her hand up. "Theresa, please."

Theresa swept past Matt in a huff and left the room.

Kate glanced at Matt, but glared at Ben as she spoke. "Matt, you should go too."

Matt stammered. "I can't leave you alone with him," he said pointing at Ben.

Kate sighed as she turned to him. "I don't need you to defend me Matt. I'll be fine."

Matt wanted to protest, especially when he saw the smirk on Ben's face, but he didn't. He walked out of the room and Kate shut the door behind him.

Matt stormed down the hallway and into the kitchen with Theresa. "That guy is a dick!"

Theresa, still angry, slammed the refrigerator door. "Kim! Here's the rest of the cheese!"

A bewildered red head walked into the kitchen and grabbed the container of cheese from Theresa. Matt heard her say, "What am I supposed to do with this?" when she got back into the living room.

"Do you know what he was saying when I walked up to the door?" Theresa asked Matt with fire in her eyes.

"No."

Theresa leaned one hand on the counter and put her other hand on her hip. "He was telling Kate she'll never find anyone like him and she's going to spend the rest of her life regretting her choice."

Matt felt his blood pressure rise. "What an asshole."

"Oh, and he said she didn't deserve him in the first place."

Matt shook his head. "Why did she stay with him for so long?"

Before Theresa could respond, Ben walked past them without a word. Kate stopped at the edge of the hallway and the living room. She flinched when Ben slammed the front door behind him. Everyone in the apartment was silent, no one sure what to say or do.

Kate straightened her shoulders and put a smile on her face. "Well guys, that's the end of the show for the evening."

A few laughed uneasily.

"Please, everyone, enjoy the food." Kate turned and walked back toward her bedroom.

Matt followed behind her. "Kate…"

Kate stood inside her bedroom, left hand on her bedroom door. "Matt, please go."

"Are you okay?" He was concerned about her. She looked deflated.

"No, I'm not. I'm fucked up. You should know that after hearing everything Ben had to say about me."

"I don't believe anything he said. And you shouldn't either."

Kate grimaced. "Ben knows me pretty well Matt. Which is why I can't understand why he wants me back."

Matt moved forward to touch Kate's shoulder, but she pulled away. "I'm tired. I'll talk to you later. Okay?"

Matt was being dismissed and he didn't like it. But he knew Kate needed time to cool off and get her head on straight.

"Okay. Call me if you need anything."

Kate closed the door softly and Matt stood outside of it for a minute before turning away. He only came tonight to get a good look at Ben, and boy, did he get one.

*　　*　　*

Saturday morning, Kate laid on her couch with a carton of ice cream. She didn't care she was acting like the stereotypical, sad woman eating cookie dough ice cream. Ben humiliated her. And some of his comments hit home.

Am I afraid of commitment?

Do I think all men are destined to leave me?

How fucked up am I because my dad bailed out on my mom?

Am I really watching my third Lifetime movie in a row?

The part she felt the worst about was the look on Matt's face. He was stunned as Ben unloaded all of her baggage. Seeing the astonishment on his face was a punch in the stomach. Like he'd been clued in on the fact that she is a psychopath.

Theresa was at work, so Kate had the apartment all to herself. At 5:30 p.m., she was still lounging in her bathrobe and slippers. Her hair was in a lopsided pile on the top of her head.

She didn't care what she looked like. She felt like crap and didn't have the energy to take a shower and get dressed. Sick of Lifetime movies, Kate flipped around the channels. Not finding anything she wanted to watch, she went with her standby, *The Holiday*.

As she debated whether she should eat Oreos or Doritos, her phone beeped. Ben sent her a dozen texts throughout the day apologizing. Wanting to avoid Ben at all costs, she almost didn't bother to look at the message. To her pleasant surprise, it was Matt.

> M: *Whatcha up to?*
>
> K: *Oreos or Doritos?*
>
> M: *Hmmm...that's a tough one. Got milk?*
>
> K: *No*
>
> M: *No brainer then, Doritos. Wait...cool ranch or nacho cheese?*
>
> K: *Cool ranch*
>
> M: *Yuck! What the hell is wrong with you? Everyone knows nacho cheese is the superior Dorito.*

Kate laughed out loud at this. Grabbing a beer and the Doritos, she returned to her spot on the couch.

K: *Doritos and a Sam Adams it is. Thanks for the help. What are you doing?*

M: *Funny, I thought I asked you that first. Nothing. You?*

Kate debated whether she should be honest, but in the end, she always was with Matt.

K: *Wallowing in my own self-pity.*

M: *Seriously? You aren't watching The Holiday again are you?*

Kate nearly spit out her beer. She looked up guiltily at her television. Cameron Diaz was running through the snow-filled English countryside so she could tell Jude Law she was in love with him.

K: *No*

M: *Liar*

K: *Whatever. I don't need your judgment.*

Kate waited for a response, and was disappointed when none came.

Oh well. He's probably getting ready to go out with the guys, she thought.

Kate pictured Matt out with Alex hitting on women. The image was unsettling. Kate saw the way women looked at Matt when they were out. It was only a matter of time before Matt found a girlfriend. Then he would spend all of his free time with the new woman in his life and not Kate.

Kate snuggled further into her bathrobe. Matt tried to defend her last night and what did she do? She sent him away. She felt awful doing it, but she didn't want Matt to see her break down. Kate worried Matt would be mad at her for being rude, but his text messages proved he wasn't upset.

Her bigger fear was Ben's skeleton throwing would send Matt screaming for the hills. Who wanted a woman with the issues Ben

120

brought to light? Then again, she and Matt were just friends. But if she and Matt were just friends, why did it make her sick to think about him with someone else?

Kate realized the movie ended and the title menu was playing over and over again. How long had she been sitting there thinking about Matt?

Shake it off, she scolded herself. This is dangerous territory. He's a friend, nothing more. Leave it alone.

Plus, Matt had never given Kate any indication he was interested in her as anything more than a friend. Wouldn't he have made a move by now if he was?

Sighing, Kate stood up and turned off the DVD player. While debating what to do with herself for the rest of the night, her doorbell rang.

"Did you really forget your key again T?" Kate trudged over to the door, but was shocked when she threw it open.

It was Matt.

Smiling widely, he held up a brown paper bag. "I brought Chinese."

Kate was mortified. She was in her bathrobe for God's sake.

"What are you doing here?" she asked as Matt pushed past her.

"I'm being a good friend and bringing you food. Doritos, especially cool ranch Doritos, are not a meal."

See, she told herself, he's being a "good friend."

Kate closed the door and followed Matt to the kitchen. "I wish you would have told me you were coming. I haven't showered."

Matt took four white containers out of the bag and set them on the kitchen island. "Stop being such a girl. Plus, I like the funky bun you got going on there. You should come into work like that."

Kate punched him in the arm before handing him a plate and a fork. "What did you bring me?"

"We have chicken and broccoli here, beef and broccoli in this one, fried rice in this one, and plain lo mein noodles in this one," he explained, opening each container as he described them. "I wasn't sure what you like, but I figured these were safe options."

Kate scooped plain lo mein noodles onto her plate, then piled chicken and broccoli on top. "This will work. Thank you."

Kate sat down on one of the bar stools, but Matt opted to stand across from her. He didn't bother with a plate and ate straight out of the containers.

After a few minutes of small talk about the weather and how good the food was, Matt asked, "Why the pity party and girly movies?"

Kate pushed the lo mein around her plate. "Just feeling crappy today. That's all."

"Really?" he asked doubtfully. "This isn't about last night, is it?"

Kate looked up at him. "Of course it is. It was awful."

"He's a shitty ex-boyfriend Kate. Don't take anything he says to heart. You hurt him. Bad. Ben wanted to get back at you. He said things he knew would get under your skin."

Kate popped a piece of chicken in her mouth. "I know. But it was …" Kate stopped herself.

"What? It was what?" Matt pressed.

Kate blushed, but responded. "You heard horrible stuff about me. It's embarrassing."

Matt put his food down. "Kate, come on. You don't think I believe a thing that d-bag said, do you?"

Kate didn't answer, she was back to pushing her food around the plate.

Matt leaned over the island and put his hand on hers. "Nothing Ben said changed my opinion of you."

She gazed up at him, tears in her eyes. "Some of the things he said were true. I did pick Yale over Steve after he turned down Duke to stay here with me. What kind of person does that? And my dad did leave us. Maybe I am really messed up because of it."

Matt came around and sat next to her, pulling her into his side. She couldn't help it, she started to cry.

"You didn't want to marry him. Period. It doesn't mean you're afraid to commit. You told me a long time ago it didn't feel right. There's nothing wrong with you."

"But what if it didn't feel right because I was scared? Or because I subconsciously torpedo my relationships?"

Matt tucked her head onto his shoulder and rested his chin on top of it. "You haven't found the right one yet. That's all."

They sat this way until Kate felt composed again. Sitting up, she wiped her tears on her bathrobe. "You're right, I'm such a girl. I can't believe I'm crying."

Matt stood up and went back to his container of Chinese food. "Nah, don't worry about it. I have sisters, remember?"

Kate gave him an appreciative smile. "I have to blow my nose. I'll be right back."

"Please do. I don't want to watch you use your robe like a Kleenex."

Kate chuckled as she walked to her bathroom. She abruptly stopped when she saw her reflection in the mirror. To her horror, she was a hot mess. She looked like a frumpy old lady with Medusa hair.

It's only Matt, she told herself after realizing there was no quick fix to her situation. And he's just your friend, remember?

Despite her better judgment, Kate went back into the kitchen. Matt relocated to the couch and was watching a basketball game. Kate grabbed a container of food and sat down next to him.

"Who's playing?"

"Lakers, Bulls" he answered without turning away from the screen.

"Don't you have better things to do on a Saturday night than listen to a silly girl cry?"

He turned and gave her one of his dazzling smiles. "No, not really."

Kate was momentarily struck by him. When did Matt become so good-looking? She was suddenly even more self-conscious about her appearance.

"I'm sorry about the whole bathrobe thing. I wasn't expecting company."

"I told you, it's no big deal. Plus, you look kinda cute in your robe and bunny slippers."

Kate found herself blushing again.

Get a hold of yourself, she screamed internally.

"They are not bunnies. They're cats."

Matt put his hands up in mock horror. "My bad. You look kinda cute in your *cat* slippers."

They watched the game for a few minutes in silence, but it was a comfortable silence. When a commercial came on, Matt turned his attention back to Kate.

"Where is Theresa? Don't you ladies like to cry in groups?"

"Yes. And then we have pillow fights in our bras and panties."

Matt's eyes lit up.

Before he could comment, Kate answered his original question. "She's at work. She should be home in a little while. If she comes home at all."

"Gotcha." No further explanation was needed. Matt knew Theresa sometimes hit a bar after work and went home with whoever bought her the most drinks.

124

"Do you want a beer?" Kate asked as she stood up and walked toward the kitchen.

"Whatcha got?"

Kate leaned down into the fridge. "I've got Sam Adams of course, but we've also got some Bud Light in here."

"I'll take a Bud Light."

Kate grabbed two bottles and closed the door with her foot. She flopped down on the couch and handed Matt his drink.

"What's Alex and the crew up to tonight? Are they going out?"

Matt took a sip of beer. "They're going to some new bar in the Short North."

"You should go. I don't want you to feel obligated to stay here with me."

Matt looked at her. "I didn't come over here because I felt obligated to. I came over here because I wanted to."

Kate stammered. "Oh." A gentle heat crept up her body. Blinking, she looked down at her hands. "Well, I really appreciate you being here."

"No problem," Matt answered smoothly before turning back to the TV.

Now the silence felt awkward. Kate didn't know what was happening. Was she imagining all of this?

Should she say something?

What would she say? Gee, Matt, I'm kind of into you. Do you like me too?

Her internal struggle must have shown on her face.

"What's up with you?" Matt asked.

"I don't know." It was the most honest answer she could come up with.

Matt sighed. "It's not the Ben shit again is it? Seriously, the guy's a dick Kate."

Kate shook her head. "No, that's not it."

"Then what?"

"It's nothing, really. I'm fine."

"Ugh. Whenever a girl says she's fine, she's anything but fine."

Kate laughed. "True."

Matt smiled. "What is it then?"

Kate took a big swig of her beer.

"I feel like something is going on with us," she blurted out. She immediately wished she could take the words back.

Matt's eyes narrowed. "With us? Like what?"

Now Kate felt stupid. "You know what, just forget it."

Matt leaned in closer. "No, what is it?"

Kate stumbled over her words. "I...I think that I'm starting to..." Kate paused again, desperately wishing she had never started down this road.

But Matt wasn't letting it go. "You're starting to what, Kate?"

Kate peered over at him, flushing as she met his eyes. "Never mind. I'm being a girl again."

Wanting to flee, Kate started to stand up, but Matt grabbed her arm gently.

"Don't walk away. Let's talk about this."

Kate pleaded with her eyes. "Please Matt. I think I was way off and I don't want to say something that will change our friendship."

Matt pulled her closer to him. "That's a shame. Because I do."

Before Kate could respond, Matt closed the distance between them and pressed his mouth to hers. His kiss was firm, then turned tender as he slid his hands onto her hips.

Kate was shocked, but her body moved without hesitation. She wrapped her arms around Matt's neck and opened her mouth to let his tongue inside.

He tasted like Chinese food and beer. She loved it.

As Matt began to move his lips to her neck, the front door crashed open.

"What the hell?" Matt asked as he and Kate both jumped.

"Kate! Your ass better be ready to go!" Theresa yelled as she slammed the door shut.

Kate scrambled to fix her robe and Matt scooted away. They were acting like two teenagers caught making out by one of their parents.

Theresa came into the room, oblivious to what she interrupted.

"Hey Matt," she said as she kicked off her shoes and put her purse on the island next to the remnants of Chinese food.

Matt waved, then acted like he was glued to the TV.

Theresa pouted. "Seriously Kate? Why aren't you ready to go?"

"Ready to go? Go where?" Kate asked confused.

Theresa crossed her arms. "I sent you a text an hour ago. We have a date with the Doublemint Twins."

"The Doublemint Twins?" Matt asked.

"Yes, the Doublemint Twins. We're meeting them in an hour Kate. Chop chop," Theresa said as she clapped her hands together.

Theresa and Kate called Aaron and Robert, who were actual twins, the Doublemint Twins. Despite being in their late twenties, the brothers still dressed alike. Never in identical outfits, but

127

oddly similar ones. If Aaron was wearing a polo and khakis, Robert was too.

Kate groaned. "I don't think so T. I'm not even dressed."

Theresa came over to the couch and pulled Kate up. "Go get your ass in the shower. I'm not missing out on guaranteed booty because you are feeling lazy. You don't have anything else going on."

Kate flopped back down on the couch. "Yes, I do. Matt is here."

Theresa looked over at Matt, who was back to staring at the TV. "Yeah, he's a real bundle of excitement."

"Theresa!" Kate exclaimed.

Matt stood up. "You know what? Theresa is right. You guys have a wonderful time with the Spearmint Twins."

"Doublemint Twins," Theresa corrected him.

Kate followed Matt to the front door. "Matt, please. You don't have to leave."

"Yes he does!" Theresa yelled from the living room.

Matt avoided eye contact. "I'm sorry Kate. I shouldn't have done what I did. You have fun tonight." He paused for a second, then walked away.

Kate stood in the doorway, frozen in place.

He's sorry?

He shouldn't have kissed her?

Have fun tonight?

Kate shut the door and leaned her back against it as she processed everything Matt said. Why had she opened her big mouth? Not only did Matt regret kissing her, he might not even want to be her friend anymore.

128

"Kate! I'm serious!" Theresa hollered. "If you aren't ready to leave in ten minutes, you're going in that ugly ass bathrobe and bunny slippers!"

"They're cats," Kate murmured as she pushed her body forward.

She thought she was down in the dumps before Matt's visit. She felt really crappy now.

*   *   *

It was Matt's turn to sulk on the couch. Images of Kate with one of the Doublemint Twins, whoever the hell they were, kept floating around in his head.

He was pissed at himself. How many times did he say he needed to be patient? Matt knew he had to go slow with Kate, really slow. Did he listen to his own advice? No! He jumped on her the second Kate showed any interest. Literally jumped on her.

The TV lit up his otherwise dark apartment, but Matt wasn't paying any attention to it. In fact, it was on mute.

Matt's cell phone buzzed with a text message. He didn't feel like moving his arm to pick it up. When it buzzed a second time, he sighed and checked to see who it was.

It was Alex.

Still with Kate?

I wish, thought Matt.

No. Home.

Alex responded immediately.

Then get your ass over here! There's a ton of hot chicks out tonight.

Matt didn't care how many women were out. He blew it with the only one he wanted.

No thanks. I'm good.

129

Matt laughed when he got the next message.

Stop being a pussy.

M: *I'm good at home.*

A: *I'm coming to get you.*

M: *Don't bother. I'm not going out.*

Matt didn't get a response from Alex. Which meant Alex was either on his way over, or got distracted by one of the aforementioned hot chicks. Worst case scenario, Alex would show up and they could watch the rest of the game together.

The evening's events played out in his mind again. He thought Kate was about to say she had feelings for him, but his dumbass didn't listen to her. Instead, he jumped the gun and planted one on her.

She kissed you back, the optimistic side of his brain chirped.

Yes, yes she did. Kate was a good kisser too. What threw him off was how quickly she got herself together when Theresa showed up. Like she didn't want to get caught.

The other odd thing was Theresa including Kate in a double date. And what was it Theresa said about Matt? That he wasn't exciting? Matt didn't know a lot about women, but he thought women talked to each other about guys. Theresa wouldn't brush Matt off if she thought Kate was interested in him.

Matt played the scenarios over and over in his head, only vaguely seeing the basketball game.

Alex is right. You are a pussy, he thought as he got up to get a soda. Before he made it to the fridge, there was a knock on his front door.

Alex.

Matt yelled as he walked toward the door, "Alex, I already told you, I'm not…"

Matt stopped short when he opened the door.

It was Kate.

She was wearing a tight black dress and holding her high heels in her hand. Matt guessed the dress was Theresa's. Kate never wore outfits like this.

"Hi," she said as she tucked a piece of hair behind her ear.

Matt got himself together. "Oh, hey. I thought you were going to be Alex."

Kate looked over her shoulder. "Is he on his way? I can go."

Matt's heart was pounding as he shook his head. "I don't think so." Matt stepped to the side. "Come in."

Kate walked past him and into the living room. "Is the game still on?"

"Not the same one I was watching earlier. A different one."

Kate turned back to him awkwardly.

When she didn't say anything, Matt filled the silence. "What happened to the Doublemint Twins?"

Kate smiled. "Boring as usual. They probably haven't realized I'm gone yet."

"Do you want something to drink? I was just about to get myself a soda."

"No thanks. I'm good."

Matt walked into the kitchen in a daze. He couldn't believe Kate was in his apartment. She looked fantastic in her dress. His heart damn near leaped out his chest when he opened the front door.

What is she doing here, Matt marveled.

He was so nervous, he wiped his hands on his jeans before grabbing a can of soda.

131

Matt popped the top on the soda can and walked back into the living room as casually as possible. Kate was standing where he left her next to the couch.

"Want to sit down?" he asked, unsure where to start.

"No." Kate sighed before letting her shoes drop to the floor. She walked closer to him.

"I want to talk to you about tonight Matt. About what happened at my apartment."

Oh God, Matt thought. Kate's going right for the jugular, no beating around the bush. It was so like her to do that.

"Okay." Matt started to apologize again, but Kate cut him off.

"No. It's me who should apologize." She looked down at her feet for a second and then glanced back up at him.

"Don't," Matt said. "Don't apologize. You have nothing to apologize for."

"But I do," Kate pleaded. "I don't know what I was thinking. You're such a good friend to me and I jeopardized that. I don't want to lose our friendship Matt."

"Neither do I," Matt interjected.

"I'm an idiot. I should have kept my mouth shut. I feel like we'll never be the same again."

Matt gave Kate a hug. "You didn't jeopardize anything. We're still friends."

Kate pulled away, a small smile on her lips. "Yeah. Friends."

Except the way she said "friends" felt awkward. Like she wasn't happy with being friends.

"Is it okay if I use your bathroom?" she asked.

"Of course. You know where it is."

Matt watched Kate walk down the hallway. Damn, she looked good in that dress. Especially from this angle. As he stood waiting on her, Matt thought about their conversation.

Why does she feel stupid, he wondered. Wasn't I the one who went too far?

A beam of hope started to shine in his heart. Was Kate saying she has feelings for him?

When Kate came out of the bathroom, he didn't hesitate.

"Let me get this straight. You think I'm upset with you?"

Kate seemed shocked by his bluntness, but then nodded. "Yes. I shouldn't have said anything about my feelings for you. You've never acted like anything other than my friend. This is on me."

Matt couldn't believe what he was hearing. "You have feelings for me? More than friends?"

Kate closed her eyes and shook her head. "I'm so sorry. I don't know what I was thinking. And then you told me you regretted it," she continued, waving her hands, "and I realized my radar was completely off."

Kate has feelings for me! Matt could have jumped over a building he was so happy. But he maintained his composure.

He stepped closer to Kate and wiped a tear from her cheek. "I only said I regretted kissing you because I thought I went too far. Pushed too quickly. I'd do it again if I thought you wanted me to."

Kate's eyes searched his. Matt didn't know what she was thinking. Then suddenly, she wrapped her arms around his neck and pulled his mouth to hers.

Kate's lips were warm and moist, the faint taste of peppermint gum lingering on them. He wrapped his arms around her, pulling her even closer.

Kate broke their kiss and whispered, "Take me to your bed."

Matt couldn't wait that long. He picked Kate up and carried her over to the couch. He laid her down on her back and covered her body with his. He wanted to devour this woman and touch every inch of her body.

While kissing her neck, Matt slid the bottom of Kate's dress up over her waist. Kate gasped.

Fearing he crossed a line, Matt pulled back and asked, "Is this okay?"

"Yes," Kate's response was breathy.

"Tell me to stop if you want me to, okay?"

Kate nodded her head in agreement.

As Matt lived out his fantasies, Kate never told him to stop.

Chapter Seven

Now

After breakfast, Thomas hands Kate an envelope. Kate doesn't need to ask what it is. It's labeled Clue #3. Before she opens it, Thomas speaks up.

"I called the contact person. You need to arrive at the address in the envelope by noon today."

Kate looks at her watch. It is already 8:30 a.m. "Will we make it on time?"

Thomas nods. "Yes. It's thirty to forty minutes north of the Ohio River. You're not supposed to research the address before you get there. You can type it into your navigation, but that's it."

Kate opens the envelope and reads the clue:

*Something I always wanted to do, but didn't. Keep
your eyes open.*

Other than an address, nothing else is on the sheet of paper.

Kate hands the clue to Matt. "I have no idea what this means."

Matt scans the paper. "Me neither."

Thomas helps Kate and Matt load her car. Kate walks over to Beth and gives her a hug.

"Thank you for having us. I had a great time."

"No problem! If you're ever down this way again, stop in and see us," Beth says with a smile.

After saying good-bye to Thomas and typing the address into her GPS, Kate starts the trek down the long driveway.

"Can you think of anything Judge wanted to do that he never got the chance to do?" Matt asks her.

"Other than visiting foreign countries, no."

Matt rubs his chin. "Why would he specifically say, 'Keep your eyes open?'"

"I don't know. What would the average person close their eyes for?"

"A scary movie?"

Kate shakes her head. "Judge hated scary movies. We weren't allowed to watch them at his house."

After a moment of quiet contemplation, Matt sits up straight. "There's an amusement park north of Cincinnati. You think Judge is going to have us ride a roller coaster?"

Kate considers this. Judge loved roller coasters when he was younger. "Could be. Maybe there's a new one he never got the chance to ride."

"That has to be it," Matt concludes.

Except it isn't. They drive right on by the exit for the theme park.

Ten minutes later, they exit the highway and follow the navigation's directions down a series of side roads.

"Your destination is on the right," Kate's GPS tells her as they approach a one-story building.

Kate pulls into a space in the gravel parking lot. "What is this place?"

Matt looks out his window, and then groans. "You don't want to know."

"Oh God," Kate says. "Tell me."

Matt turns to her. "You're not afraid of heights, are you?"

*　　　*　　　*

Kate can't stop her knee from bouncing up and down.

She is sitting in a tiny seat built into the wall of a small plane. She is wearing a blue fabric suit with a parachute she prays will open. Her hair is pulled into a tight bun and she's wearing oversized goggles.

The ride is bumpy and she keeps knocking shoulders with Matt. Their jumping partners are sitting across from them talking about a show they watched on TV last night. As if jumping out of a plane is no big deal.

Kate takes another good look at her jumping partner. His name is Dave and he assured Kate he has skydived "like a hundred times." This should make Kate feel better, but Dave's California surfer dude tone did nothing to quell her nervousness.

The training class she and Matt sat through before jamming themselves into this tin can didn't help much either. Matt is a natural and moves like he's done this many times, not just once.

Kate, on the other hand, was lucky she didn't throw her back out while practicing how to land. None of it matters anyway. All the information she's been given will be thrown out the window once she jumps. Literally.

Kate glances at Matt and scowls when she sees him smiling gleefully out the window. "Are you even nervous?"

He turns to her. "Nope."

"Were you nervous the first time you jumped?"

Matt laughs. "You could say that." He leans in to whisper in Kate's ear, "I thought I was going to pee my pants."

Kate smiles, but her joy doesn't last long.

"It's time folks!" Matt's jumping partner, Jimmy, exclaims.

The three men stand up, but Kate is glued to her seat. Her fingers grip the straps of her parachute.

She pleads with the now standing Matt. "I don't think I can do this."

Matt snaps the chin strap of his helmet into place. "Yes, you can."

Kate shakes her head like a three-year-old. "No, I can't."

Matt crouches down in front of her. She feels tears welling in her eyes. How could Judge do this to her? He knew she is terrified of heights.

Matt reaches up and puts his hands on either side of Kate's helmet, staring straight into her eyes. "You can do this Kate," he says with conviction.

Kate tries to lower her head, but Matt tilts her face back up with his finger.

"I know you Kate Marshall. You have the heart of a lion. You are the fiercest woman I have ever met in my life. I know you can do this."

Something about the way Matt looks at her makes Kate believe everything he is saying.

With her new found courage, Kate squares her shoulders and stands up. She is going to do this. She holds on to the safety line as Matt and his partner stand at the edge of the door. Jimmy tethers himself to Matt and double checks all of the straps. Their blue jumpsuits are blowing wildly in the wind.

Jimmy starts the countdown. "Five...four...three..."

Just before Jimmy gets to one, Matt glances over his shoulder. With a Cheshire cat grin on his face, he gives Kate a thumbs up. Despite feeling less than confident, she returns the gesture.

"Bombs away!" Jimmy yells as he and Matt jump out into the blue sky.

Kate and her partner creep to the open doorway. She musters up her courage and looks down. Matt and his partner are plummeting toward Earth. She lets out a sigh of relief when their red parachute opens up. Matt and his partner are momentarily pulled upwards, then start gliding down again.

"You ready?" Dave asks her as he checks their equipment.

"No!"

He chuckles, then starts the countdown.

Please God, please get me through this, Kate prays. And while you're at it, please punch Judge in the gut for me!

Kate focuses on the clouds and blue sky in front of her. She is so caught up in the beauty of the shifting white clouds, she misses all of the countdown. She realizes with panic that Dave has yelled, "One!"

Before she can protest, Dave jumps out of the plane and propels them out into the sky. Kate's heart is in her throat and she squeezes her eyes tightly.

Despite the wind and Dave yelling, "Woo hoo!!!" in her ear, Kate hears the faintest whisper.

Kate, don't let fears dictate your life...

The voice is a familiar one. It's Judge. If she didn't know any better, Kate would swear Judge was strapped to her back, not surfer dude Dave.

There, thousands of feet in the air, Kate is hit with a memory of Judge. She was at the community pool with Judge one hot July day when she was nine or ten years old. All of her friends were taking turns climbing the steps of the high dive and doing cannonballs. Shrieks of joy and laughter filled the air. But Kate stood paralyzed at the bottom watching her friends with envy.

"Kate!" Judge yelled as he waved his hand for her to come over to his lounge chair. Putting down one of his many Stephen King novels, Judge pulled Kate onto his lap.

"Don't you want to play with your friends?" Judge asked.

Kate nodded in response.

"Why aren't you?"

"I can't Grandpa. I'm too scared."

139

Judge gave Kate a big squeeze. "You have to try new things. Even if they scare you."

Kate bit her lower lip. "Does anything scare you Grandpa?"

Judge puffed out his chest. "Nope. Never!"

Kate giggled at Judge's caveman impression.

Judge dropped the silly face and used his normal voice. "I've been scared many times."

Kate was surprised. Her grandpa? Scared? "Like when?"

Judge thought about it a moment before answering. "When I was twenty years old I went to watch a tennis match with my good buddy John. While there, I meet John's cousin Ann. She was the most beautiful thing I had ever seen. When John introduced us, I could barely say 'hello.'"

Kate interrupted. "My middle name is Ann."

Judge smiled. "That's right. And where did you get your middle name?"

Giggling, Kate answered, "It's Grandma's name silly goose!"

"Right again! Just think what would have happened if I hadn't gathered up my courage to talk to your grandma that day."

"You were afraid of Grandma?" Kate found this to be impossible. Her grandmother was the sweetest woman on the planet.

Judge nodded. "Oh yes. She terrified me."

"Why?"

"I was afraid she wouldn't like me."

"Oh."

"But I faced my fear Kate. And it was the best thing I've ever done. You can't let fear dictate your life."

Kate didn't know what the word "dictate" meant, but she got Judge's message loud and clear. She jumped off the high dive that day, and many days after that.

With Judge's words ringing in her ears, Kate opens her eyes.

What she sees takes her breath away. The wind blows against her as they fall toward the ground, but she is focused on the patchwork of earth below her. The uneven squares of varying shades of green come together like a quilt.

Kate feels the sudden pull of the parachute opening and silently thanks God. She takes in the stunning panoramic view as she slowly descends to the ground, the once tiny specks becoming trees and homes.

When her feet touch the ground she yells, "Thank you Judge!"

Kate will never jump out of a plane again, but she's conquered her fear and feels ten feet tall. Matt and his partner are unhooking from each other about twenty yards away. Matt raises his hand in the air and waves at her.

Kate unhooks from Dave and runs toward Matt. She is laughing as she dashes through the field of wildflowers.

Matt's eyes are wide and he's grinning. "That was amazing!"

Kate's heart is racing and her adrenaline is pumping as she approaches Matt. When she reaches him, she crashes against him, throwing him off balance. He steadies himself and wraps his arms around her back before spinning her in a circle. Kate's laughter is carefree and she feels young again.

When Matt sets her down, Kate's instincts take over. Without thinking, she puts her hand on the back of Matt's neck and tilts his head down toward her. Filled with giddiness and excitement, she pushes up on her tippy toes and plants her mouth against his.

Shocked, Matt hesitates for a moment. But then he falls into sync with her. His hands are on her waist, pulling her in tight. Kate feels a sudden rush of heat as her tongue tangles with his. It feels so right.

141

This is Matt.

Her Matt.

But then, she remembers. This may be Matt, but he is not *her* Matt. Not anymore. This is married with two kids Matt.

Kate drops her hands and pushes away, breathless and embarrassed. Matt looks back at her with hazy eyes. After a second, he blinks a few times and shakes himself out of his stupor.

"Jesus Kate."

Kate struggles to regain her composure. Matt is bent over, hands on his thighs and breathing deeply.

"Matt, I'm so sorry," Kate whispers. "I don't know what came over me."

Before Matt can respond, she turns and jogs back toward Dave and her equipment. Her mind is racing.

What have I done?

Chapter Eight

Ten Years Ago

Things between Matt and Kate were amazing. Kate walked on air these days. Theresa was constantly getting on her for acting like a goofball.

"Would you please stop doing that?!" Theresa yelled one night while they were eating dinner at a restaurant.

"What?" Kate asked.

"Looking at your phone and texting Matt. You're at dinner with me for some roommate time," Theresa huffed.

Kate laughed. "Okay. Okay. I'll put my phone away."

"And can you please stop with the stupid grin all the time? You look like the Joker for crying out loud."

Kate twirled her spaghetti around her fork. "You're just jealous."

"Jealous of what? Being attached at the hip? Walking around like some lovesick puppy? No thank you."

Kate smiled. "No. I know you're not jealous of those things."

Theresa crunched a breadstick. "Then what?"

"The awesome sex I'm having every night."

"Yeah, I guess that would be nice. I mean, I have sex a few times a month, but it's only awesome half the time." Theresa leaned over the table. "Is it that good?"

Kate nodded. "It's the best sex I've ever had."

"Details!"

"You know I don't like talking about sex stuff."

Theresa threw a piece of breadstick at her. "C'mon! Not fair. I share all kinds of details with you."

This was true. More details than Kate would ever want.

Kate pondered how much she should share with T. She hadn't lied about the sex – it was amazing. But talking about her bedroom activities embarrassed her.

"Okay, okay. I'll tell you this much...I had to buy magnums. There. I've shared."

Theresa's eyes widened. "Seriously? Wow, I never would have guessed."

"Why? Do you think you have large dick radar or something?" Kate asked.

"Nope. I've come to learn you can never guess what a guy has going on downstairs unless you see it for yourself."

Kate laughed. "If you say so."

"But does he know how to use it? You can have the biggest wand around, but if you can't do magic with it, it's worthless."

"He's really good. Like, really good."

Theresa was loving the inside information. "Bang your head against the headboard good?"

"Better." Kate thought for a moment. "He is call off work for a week, skip meals, down on your knees begging for it good."

"Damn!" T exclaimed. "I *am* jealous!"

The waiter brought over their tiramisu and left the bill on the table.

Kate grabbed the bill. "It's my turn."

Theresa didn't argue, she was lost in thought.

Kate dug her spoon into the tiramisu and waited for T's next question. She could see the wheels turning in T's mind and hoped T didn't ask anything too humiliating.

Kate laughed when Theresa finally asked, "Does Matt have any brothers?"

"No. Just stepsisters."

Theresa sighed and took a big bite of tiramisu. "Figures."

*   *   *

Matt was sitting at his desk, annoyed with a plaintiff's attorney in a personal injury case. The attorney insisted on using derogatory adjectives when talking about the defendant. The judges told attorneys over and over again to not make nasty, inappropriate comments about each other in pleadings, but it still happened all the time.

Matt's cell phone vibrated on his desk and he took his mind off the motion for a second to see who was texting him. He smiled when he saw it was Kate.

K: *Still at the office?*

M: *Yes. You?*

It was a silly question on both of their parts. They usually left the Courthouse together. On nights when they didn't, whoever left first would say good-bye.

Things were going well with Kate, and Matt couldn't be happier. Even though Kate was right down the hall, he missed her during the day and found himself emailing or texting her every couple of hours.

Kate stayed at his apartment almost every night. The sex was addicting. Matt wanted to make love to her every chance he got. On the nights Kate couldn't come over, Matt craved her like a drug.

He tried explaining it to Alex one night last week when they met up at a bar. Kate was out of town for a family function and Matt was complaining about how he wouldn't get to see her for two nights.

"What's so great about her?" Alex asked between popping peanuts in his mouth.

"What do you mean?"

"What makes Kate different from any other girl?"

"I can't explain it man. She's the best girl I've ever been with. Hands down."

He wasn't shocked when Alex came out the gate with a crude question. Unlike Kate, Matt shared most of his sexual exploits with his best friend.

"Does she give good head?"

Matt shifted in his chair. He didn't want to talk about his sex life with Kate. It felt demeaning to Kate, like he was betraying her in some way.

"Yeah. She does," Matt answered uneasily. Matt hoped Alex would let it drop. Alex being Alex, he didn't.

"What about anal?" Alex asked at a high volume.

Two women sitting at the table next to them turned their heads toward Matt. Their disapproving looks made him blush.

"Would you quiet down please?"

Alex shrugged his shoulders. "What's the big deal?"

"The big deal is the entire bar heard you ask me if my girlfriend is into anal!"

Alex's smirk grew. "So she's your girlfriend now?"

Matt had used the "g" word without thinking.

"We haven't talked about it," Matt admitted.

"Do you think she's your girlfriend?" Alex pressed.

"I don't know. Does it matter?"

"Let me ask you this." Alex scanned the bar. "You see the group of girls over there?"

146

Alex tilted his head toward a group of four women in their mid-to-late twenties. The women were standing together at the bar ordering drinks. All of them were well-dressed and attractive.

"Yeah, I see them."

"If they came over here right now and offered to take us back to one of their places for a party, would you go?"

"No," Matt answered without much thought.

"Why not?" Alex asked.

Matt knew where Alex was going with this.

"Because I don't need to party with those girls. I already have a good girl who will do bad things with me."

Matt took a drink from his glass as he waited for Alex to pounce. But Alex was uncharacteristically quiet, his fingers arched in front of him like a steeple.

"What?" Matt asked when Alex continued to stare at him.

"You love this girl," Alex said matter-of-factly.

"Whatever. Just because I don't want to bang every chick I see doesn't mean I'm in love with Kate."

Alex sat up in his chair. "No, you do. You love her."

Matt tried to come up with a witty response, or at the very least, a believable denial. He came up with nothing.

Alex smiled, Matt's silence an admission.

"You fucking pussy. You really do love her!" Alex laughed out loud.

"Shut up dick," Matt responded as he took another drink.

"At least Kate's a cool girl. You could do worse."

"Gee, thanks."

"And she has a hot roommate." Alex whistled. "That girl damn near broke me."

147

"Theresa seems like a wild one."

"You don't know the half of it." Alex shuddered. "I had claw marks on my back for a week."

"Ouch."

After a pause, Alex asked, "If Kate's gone, Theresa has the apartment to herself tonight, right?"

Matt grinned as he shook the memory of his night with Alex from his mind. His cell phone vibrated again.

> K: *I'm still here, but we may be the last two.*

> M: *I've got an hour of work left. You don't have to wait on me.*

> K: *Okay. I'll stop by your office before I leave.*

Matt sorted through the papers on his desk while he waited. No point in turning his attention back to the motion when Kate was stopping by in a minute. Matt welcomed the break. His brain was fried. He popped a piece of gum in his mouth before Kate got there. Just in case.

Matt didn't mention his "love" conversation with Alex to Kate. Matt didn't want to drop the "L" word too soon and scare Kate off. They'd been pretty hot and heavy for the last few weeks, but it was only a few weeks.

Matt heard the outer chamber door click as Kate scanned her badge. He ran his fingers through his hair and spit his gum into the trash can. He went back to shuffling papers until Kate walked in.

"Look at you, overachiever!" Kate leaned into the door frame of his office and smiled. She was wearing an emerald green shirt with a black skirt and black heels. Her blazer was slung over her arm and her purse was in her hand.

Matt loved when Kate wore green. It made her eyes shine even brighter from her smooth skin. "If I was an overachiever, this would be done already."

Kate walked into his office and set her things down on one of the chairs opposite his desk.

"Working on anything exciting?" she asked, picking up the motion.

Matt snorted. "Yeah right. A motion to compel. A bunch of whining and finger pointing."

Kate set the motion down. "Have any plans later?"

"None that I can think of. What are you up to?"

"Not a thing. I have to run by my mom's to make sure her cat has food. But that's it."

"Where's your mom?"

"She went out of town for a wedding."

"Oh, right. Judge is there too, isn't he?"

Kate nodded. "Yep. That's why he left at noon today."

"Why aren't you there? At the wedding?" Matt asked.

"It's not a family member. The mother of the bride and my mom were friends when they were kids. The invitation was addressed to my mom and Judge. I didn't feel comfortable tagging along."

"Gotcha. Want to come over to my place when you're done with your mom's cat?"

Matt wished he could leave with Kate, but he had to finish reviewing the motion before he left. He promised Judge a draft opinion by the time Judge got back. If he didn't finish up tonight, he would have to come in over the weekend.

"Sure. I'll grab some food and head to your place. What time do you want to meet up?"

Matt looked at his watch. "I think I'll be home around 7 p.m."

Kate shook her head. "No you won't."

"Huh?"

149

"You said you need an hour for the motion, right?"

Matt nodded. "Give or take five minutes."

"What about the time it will take to entertain me?"

Before Matt could ask what the hell she was talking about, Kate stepped around his desk and pushed his chair back.

"I intend to take up some of your time, so it will probably be closer to 8 o'clock," Kate explained in a sex kitten voice.

Matt sat stupefied as Kate pulled her skirt up above her waist. She was wearing an emerald green thong that matched the color of her shirt.

Matt groaned. "I love when you wear green."

"I know."

Kate eased herself onto Matt's lap, straddling him. He was so turned on it was insane. It was all he could do to not bend her over his desk.

Matt pulled back when Kate leaned in to kiss him. "Kate, this is crazy."

Kate started undoing his belt.

"We are at work, there are cameras everywhere."

Matt couldn't believe he was protesting Kate's advances, but he didn't need to get caught fucking his boss's granddaughter.

"Not in here," Kate breathed into his ear. "There are cameras in the main office area, the conference room and Judge's office. But not in here."

"Are you sure?" Matt asked as Kate undid the top button of his pants and unzipped his fly.

"Positive."

Kate slid her hand down Matt's pants and under the top of his boxer briefs. Matt sincerely hoped Kate was right about the cameras because he was going to ravage her if she didn't stop.

"What if Judge comes back?" he asked, keeping his hands to himself.

Kate held his face in her hands. "Judge is four hours away eating shrimp cocktail at a rehearsal dinner. No one else is in the building and we'll hear them if they suddenly show up."

Kate slid her hand down Matt's pants again. She leaned in and whispered in his ear, "This is a fantasy of mine Matthew. I want you to stop worrying and fuck me."

That was all Matt could handle. He lifted Kate up, swept the papers off his desk and laid her down. He stood in-between her open legs and brought his mouth down on hers.

He was passed the point of no return with her. Not just in this moment, but period. He was in love with this woman. No question.

Matt slid his pants and boxer briefs down and pressed his body against Kate's. "Is this what you had in mind?"

*   *   *

A week later, Kate was standing at the copy machine daydreaming about her previous night while her copies printed.

Matt took her to a nice Italian restaurant in Westerville. It was a change up from their usual take out and Kate loved it. After dinner, they walked hand in hand down the sidewalk and enjoyed the evening.

Everything with Matt was special. Even the little things. There's nothing she'd rather do than cuddle up with him on the couch in one of his old t-shirts. She was starting to understand all of his facial expressions and body language. If he was a little cranky he needed a snack or a nap; if the right side of his mouth curled up in a smile, he wanted sex; and if he used the word, "like" a lot, he was drunk.

Kate was head over heels for Matt, but for the first time in her life, she wasn't scared. Matt mentioned the other day that the lease on his apartment was ending soon.

151

She shocked herself when she said, "Maybe we should look for a place together."

She was worried about Matt's reaction, but he smiled and said, "Sure. I'll start looking to see what's available."

Kate's revelry was interrupted by Cora. She suppressed a groan.

Cora was an even bigger bitch than usual lately. She sneered when they passed each other in the hall and she refused to look at Kate if they were sitting at the same table at lunch.

Kate assumed Cora was pissed because her dirt on Kate got her nowhere. Judge being Kate's grandfather was old news and no one seemed to care.

"You done?" Cora asked in an icy tone.

Kate grabbed her stack of documents off the tray. "Almost. I have one more page to copy."

Kate put the last document on the glass and closed the lid. She entered "1-0-0" and hit the green "go" button.

To her chagrin, Cora did not leave. She stood waiting and glaring at Kate. Kate ignored her and pretended to go through her documents.

"You and Matt are getting pretty hot and heavy, huh?"

Kate looked up at Cora. "That's none of your business, is it?"

Cora smirked. "Yeah, I thought so."

Kate didn't respond.

"I'm surprised you and Matt are so compatible. I didn't peg you for his type."

Kate couldn't help herself. "And what does that mean Cora?"

"Oh, you know. I thought you'd be too good for the kinky stuff Matt enjoys."

Kate's eyes narrowed.

Cora feigned shock. "Matt didn't tell you about us?" She chuckled. "I can't believe it."

Kate removed her original from the copy machine. "You and Matt were never an item."

Cora pursed her lips. "Yes we were. Ask him."

"If you two had been a real thing, he would have mentioned it to me."

Cora took a step closer to Kate. "Look on the shelf above the television in his bedroom. Hidden behind a baseball trophy, you'll find a small camera."

"What?" This threw Kate for a loop.

Kate pictured Matt's bedroom in her mind. On the wall opposite his bed was an old, wooden dresser that held six drawers; three drawers high and two across. Above the dresser, centered over a television, was a shelf holding various knickknacks. Among them, a baseball trophy.

How does Cora know what Matt's bedroom looks like, she asked herself.

Cora smirked. "You heard me. I put a small camera on the shelf facing Matt's bed. Matty really likes filming his sexual encounters. There's probably three or four short films starring yours truly on the tape."

Kate's face reddened as anger crept up her neck. Matt never asked to film the two of them having sex. Cora had to be lying.

"Get out of my way Cora. I don't have time for your bullshit."

Cora's face hardened. "Suit yourself Kate. You'll see. Check the shelf."

Kate stormed out of the copy room and down the hallway toward Judge Penny's chambers. She hated Cora. She hated the smug look on Cora's face. And she hated that she let Cora get to her.

153

But something felt wrong. How did Cora know about the shelf in Matt's bedroom? How did she know about that baseball trophy?

Kate spent the rest of the afternoon trying to come up with different ways Cora could know what Matt's bedroom looked like.

Maybe Matt threw a party at his apartment for coworkers and Cora used the bathroom in his room.

Maybe he had a picture of his bedroom on his cell phone and Cora saw it for some reason.

Maybe Matt posted a picture of his bedroom on a social media page and Cora saw it.

None of the explanations Kate came up with made her feel any better. Something about the look in Cora's eyes led Kate to believe she was telling the truth. Cora told a lot of stories, but not all of them were false. Cora had a certain air about her when she had evidence to back up her gossip.

On top of that, Matt and Cora were close when Kate first started at the Courthouse. They used to eat lunch together every day and Kate would see them chatting at meetings. Matt hadn't meant anything to her at the time, so she didn't pay much attention to it.

Now, she wishes she had. She and Matt talked about their exes, but Cora's name never came up. Ever.

Later in the day, Matt called her office phone to see what her plans were for the evening.

"I don't have anything going on," she told him. "What do you have in mind?"

"I'm thinking we'll have dinner at my place and then I'll have you for dessert," Matt cooed into the phone.

Normally, this would make Kate laugh. But she wasn't in the mood.

She faked happiness. "Sounds good to me!"

154

Driving to Matt's, Kate debated whether she should ask Matt flat out about Cora's accusation. Wouldn't that be the best route? Put it out there and see how he responds? On the other hand, asking him about Cora might piss Matt off. She could see Matt being upset she would buy into Cora's bullshit.

When she got to Matt's, Kate gave him a quick kiss.

"I ordered pizza," he told her. "I hope that's okay."

"Sure. I'm good with pizza."

They watched TV while waiting on dinner to arrive. Kate was on edge the entire time. She wanted to run into his bedroom and look on the shelf. It was all she could think about.

"Something going on?" Matt asked her during a commercial break.

"No," she lied.

"Are you sure? Because you're awfully quiet."

She picked at her nail polish. "I ran into Cora today."

Matt groaned. "What did the ice queen say now?"

Kate bit her lower lip. "It's probably nothing, but she has my wheels turning."

"What did she say?" Matt asked again, his eyebrows furrowed this time.

Let's do this, Kate thought to herself.

"She said you…" Before Kate could finish, the doorbell rang.

"Sit tight," Matt instructed her. "I'll be right back."

Kate stayed on the couch as Matt ran to get the pizza.

"What's up? Your total's $15.50," Kate heard the pizza man say.

She was expecting Matt to shut the door, but the two men struck up a conversation.

155

"Don't I know you?" Matt asked.

After a pause, the delivery guy responded, "Matt? Matt Sloan?"

Kate listened halfheartedly as the men bantered back and forth. From the sound of things, they went to college together. While Matt continued talking, Kate's nervousness grew.

Fuck it, she decided. I'm going to look on the shelf while Matt is distracted. If nothing is there, I'll make up some bullshit story to tell Matt. Shouldn't be too hard to pull something from the Cora vault.

But what if there is a camera? What will you do then, her inner voice asked.

Kate was willing to take her chances.

She stood up from the couch and paused to make sure the men were still talking. They were. Kate moved as quickly as she could without making a lot of noise. Her heart was pounding as she walked into Matt's room. The shelf was too high for her to reach on her flat feet. Kate leaned against the dresser. It seemed sturdy enough to hold her.

You're being ridiculous, she told herself as she climbed on top of the dresser.

But she couldn't stop. She had to know.

Once steady on the dresser, Kate slid a couple of steps over to the baseball trophy. The trophy was a gold baseball player holding a bat, ready to hit a pitch. The base was white marble and the gold plate read, "Little League Champions." Kate inhaled and held her breath as her hand touched the cool metal of the baseball figure.

Please, please, please, don't be there.

A dust-free rectangle sat where the trophy used to be. Immediately behind it, a camera. A small, black video camera. Innocent enough, but it sent a shock wave through Kate's body.

What the fuck?!

Kate set the trophy down. Her hands were shaking as she picked up the camera. It fit easily in her hand. She examined it, as if she'd find Cora's name written on it somewhere.

"Kate?" Matt called down the hallway. "Where did you go?"

She was too numb to respond.

"Kate?"

Matt walked into his bedroom holding a pizza box. A puzzled expression settled on his face when he saw Kate standing on his dresser.

"What are you doing?"

Kate held out the camera. "What is this?"

All of the color drained from Matt's face.

Kate's jaw tightened. "What is this?" she repeated.

"How did you know about that?" he asked, frozen in place.

"Lucky guess," Kate sneered. "Why is there a camera on your shelf?"

Matt set the pizza box down on his bed and walked over to her. He extended his hand, "Come down from there before you fall."

Kate jerked away from him. "Don't touch me."

Matt stepped back, hurt. "Please Kate, get down."

Kate glared at him as she got down off the dresser on her own, gripping the camera in her hand.

"Answer my question Matt," she said, ice flowing through her veins.

Matt ran his hand through his hair. "It's a camera. But I swear, I never taped us."

Kate wanted to know how honest Matt would be with her. "Why was it up there?"

"An ex wanted me to put it there. Well," Matt stammered, "she isn't really an ex. We were friends with benefits. She was into that sort of thing," he said as he waved his hand toward the camera. "I forgot it was up there to be honest with you."

"I see," Kate said. "You've told me about all of your exes, right?"

"I think so."

"Which one was it?"

Matt shifted uncomfortably. "Does it matter?"

Kate tilted her head to the side. Matt was definitely being cagey. "I don't know, does it?"

"I don't think it does."

Kate palmed the camera. "I mean, shouldn't you give it back to her? She probably wants it back."

Matt shrugged. "She never asked for it. She's probably forgotten about it too."

Kate smirked. "I doubt it."

Matt mistook Kate's smirk as a sign she was calming down. "A night with me is memorable."

"Especially if it's on tape," Kate countered. "Why don't we watch it?"

Matt's jaw dropped open. "What?"

"Yeah, let's watch it," Kate said. "I want to see what this girl had going for her."

Matt tried to take the camera from Kate. "I don't think that's a good idea. Too creepy."

Kate pulled the camera out of Matt's reach. "What was her name Matt?"

"Why are you acting like this? Are you jealous?"

"Don't try to make this about me. I asked you a simple question. What was her name?"

Matt turned his back to her and walked a few steps away.

He's debating whether to tell me the truth, Kate thought to herself. She prayed he would be honest. All could be forgiven if he was honest.

Matt spun back around, his face a blank slate. "Her name doesn't matter. You don't know her."

I don't know her?!

Kate's fury rose to a fever pitch. She threw the camera as hard as she could across the room. It slammed into the wall with a loud "boom" and broke into several pieces.

"Hey!" Matt protested.

"You lying bastard!" Kate hissed. She stomped toward his bedroom door, but he blocked her way.

"Kate, calm down." Matt put his hands on her shoulders.

"Fuck you Matt! I know it's Cora's camera!"

Matt dropped his hands, but didn't get out of her way. "Then why did you ask?"

"I wanted to see if you would be honest with me. You weren't." Kate glared at him. "Cora? Seriously?"

"It was before you Kate. I haven't been with her since the day I met you. I promise."

Kate snorted. "Your promises aren't worth much. You're a liar."

"I didn't tell you it was Cora's camera because I know how much you hate her."

"So you lied? Do you think that's better?"

Matt shook his head. "No, it's not. I…I didn't know what to say."

Kate stood quietly as the fire burned inside her.

"Come on Kate. It's not a big deal. Cora means nothing to me. She never did."

Kate closed her eyes and took several deep breaths. In through the nose, out through the mouth. When she opened her eyes again, she felt a wall building inside of her. "You fucked her, on camera no less, and she meant nothing to you?"

Matt seemed taken aback by this question. "I, uh, I guess so."

"Nice Matt. Nice. I'm learning a lot about you tonight. And I don't like any of it."

"Kate, what do you want me to say?" Matt asked exasperated. "Cora wasn't my finest moment, okay? I'm fucking ashamed of it. I knew it was wrong, but I didn't stop."

Kate stared at Matt. She didn't know what to say to him. She was hurt. She felt betrayed. But most of all, she felt anger. A fierce, burning rage that scared her a little.

"I need to go now," she told Matt as she moved for his door again.

"Please don't," Matt pleaded. "Don't go."

"I can't even look at you right now. I want to leave."

"Will you call me?" Matt asked, desperation in his eyes.

"Maybe."

Matt stepped to the side, allowing Kate to walk past him. His shoulders were slumped, and his head hung low. Utterly defeated.

She, on the other hand, walked down the hallway with her head held high. She would keep it together until she left. This she promised herself.

"Kate, wait!" Matt called from behind her.

She glanced over her shoulder and saw Matt jogging down his hallway. She stood like a statue as he approached her.

"Before you go, I need to tell you something."

"What?" She didn't want to hear any more excuses. If Matt knew what was good for him, he would let her leave.

Instead, he said the worst thing possible.

"Kate," he took her hand, "I love you."

The anger exploded. Kate could no longer reign in it. She ripped her hand away from Matt.

"You asshole!" she erupted. "How fucking dare you say that to me! You're going to tell me you love me after you lie to my fucking face?"

Matt recoiled.

"Do you think saying that will win me over? Make me forget everything?"

"I didn't mean to make you more upset. I'm sorry."

Kate's hands were balled into fists. "I'm not some dumbass girl who's going to fall all over you because you drop three little words on me Matt."

Kate turned on her heels and grabbed her purse.

Matt stayed close behind her. "I do love you Kate. I'm only telling you now because I want you to forgive me. I want you to call me."

Kate opened Matt's apartment door and without turning around said, "Don't follow me."

She slammed the apartment door behind her and didn't look back when she heard Matt crack it open.

Chapter Nine

Now

Kate's heart is pounding as she approaches the van taking them back to the skydiving school.

What the hell just happened? Why did she kiss Matt?

She climbs into the back row of the van and sits next to her jumping partner Dave. No way she can sit next to Matt right now.

"Did you have fun?" Dave asks her with a wide grin.

"Yes," she answers, still breathless from running away from Matt. "It was beautiful up there."

"Want to do it again?"

"No," she answers without hesitation.

Dave laughs. "Everyone tells me that. It was fun, but never again. I've only had two or three people come back for more."

Kate smiles. "I'm not going to take my chances. God spared me this time, why roll the dice?"

"According to your logic, I should be dead by now. That was my ninety-eighth jump."

"Seriously? Wow! What are you going to do for number one hundred?"

"I'm jumping in my birthday suit." Dave laughs again when he sees the look on Kate's face. "I'm kidding."

Matt climbs into the van and glances back at Kate. His eyes are cold and his jaw is set.

Ugh, Kate thinks, he's pissed at me. I can't blame him. I practically mauled him back there.

Dave talks her ear off on the way to the school. She says, "wow" and "nice" when appropriate, but her thoughts are somewhere else.

When her lips touched Matt's, something in her body woke up. Something that had been lying dormant inside of her for ten years was suddenly springing to life. All the feelings she buried and denied are clawing their way out of the cage she built for them in the deepest, darkest part of her heart.

Kissing Matt had opened Pandora's box. And Kate has no idea how she's going to deal with it.

The van screeches to a halt at the school and Matt slides the van door open. Neither say a word as the group walks back into the building.

Kate takes up residence in the women's locker room and changes back into the jeans and t-shirt she had on earlier. She should be over the moon – she jumped out of a plane and survived! But she's more stressed now than she was before the jump.

When she's done changing, Kate finds Matt and Dave standing in the hallway outside the locker rooms.

"I have something for you," Dave says as he hands Kate an envelope.

Written across the front of the envelope in black ink is, "Clue #4"

Kate exchanges a glance with Matt before opening it. At least he met her eyes this time. A single sheet of paper is inside the envelope.

Kate clears her throat and reads the clue out loud. "Meet my favorite brother at his favorite restaurant."

"That's it?" Matt asks.

Kate nods. "That's it."

"Oh," Dave pipes up, "I also have to give you this." He pulls out two keychains from his back pocket. They are in the shape of blue parachutes and say, "I survived the friendly skies."

Kate chuckles. "Thanks Dave."

"No problem!"

Kate and Matt walk silently to her car. It's not until she takes her cell phone from the console that Matt says something.

"Who is Judge's favorite brother? Doesn't he have three?"

"Yes," Kate confirms. "Only two are living though. His brother Bert died a long time ago in a car accident."

"Which of the remaining two is his favorite?"

"He joked that Jack was his favorite at family gatherings. I think he said it to poke at Ed."

Kate scrolls through her contacts list and finds her great-uncle Jack's number. "I'll call Jack first. Keep your fingers crossed he has no idea what I'm talking about."

"Why?"

"Ed lives in Columbus; Jack lives in Indianapolis."

Matt groans. "It's going to be Jack. Judge is going to make us go as far away as possible."

"Indianapolis isn't too far from here. A couple of hours maybe."

"Yeah, but it's not Columbus."

"True," Kate acknowledges as she hits the "send" button on her phone.

The phone rings three times before Jack picks up.

"Katie, my girl! This is a pleasant surprise."

Jack is one of Kate's favorite relatives. He's funny and quick witted. Jack is a bit bigger than Judge was, which is saying

165

something. He is the youngest of Judge's siblings and never lets them forget it.

"Hi Uncle Jack! How are you?"

"I'm doing pretty good. To what do I owe this honor?"

"What do you know about a scavenger hunt?"

Jack chuckles. "I may know a little something about scavenger hunts."

Kate perks up. "Are you the uncle we're supposed to meet for dinner?"

"Who'd you think it would be? Ed? No one wants to eat with that crusty bugger."

Kate cracks up. "Are you in Indianapolis?"

"I am, but you're not supposed to come here."

"I'm not?"

"We're supposed to meet at my favorite restaurant."

"Okay. Where is that?"

"The oldest inn in Ohio."

"The oldest inn in Ohio?" Kate repeats.

"Yes. Meet me there tomorrow night at 6:30 p.m."

"Tomorrow night? Can you make it tonight?"

"No can do kiddo. I have my bowling league tonight. But I'll be there tomorrow at 6:30 p.m. on the dot."

Kate exchanges good-byes with Jack.

"Where are we heading?" Matt asks.

"The oldest Inn in Ohio."

Matt raises his eyebrow. "Which is?"

Kate shrugs her shoulders. "No idea."

The two research the answer online and find it within minutes.

"The Silver Goat," Kate tells Matt.

"That's quite a name."

Kate scrolls through the website. "They're a restaurant and a full-service hotel. Should we get a room there for the night?"

"How expensive is it?"

Kate turns her car on. "Who cares? We're using Judge's money, remember?"

"Touché."

While driving to the Inn, Kate wonders if she should bring up the kiss. Her guilt is eating away at her. She is engaged, to a wonderful man. And Matt is married. Married!

Does this make her a cheater? She's never cheated on a boyfriend.

"You want to talk about it?" Matt asks her out of the blue.

How does he always know what she's thinking?

"Yes and no."

Matt looks over at her for a second, then out the windshield. "Whatever you want to say, say it."

White-knuckling the steering wheel, Kate says, "I don't know why I kissed you. It was wrong."

Matt is silent.

Kate fumbles to say more. "I hope you're not upset. We were just starting to get along and then I..."

Matt interrupts her. "Your adrenaline was rushing. That's all. Don't make a big deal out of it. Dave's lucky you didn't plant one on him."

Kate giggles, relieved. "So you're not mad at me?"

Matt shakes his head. "Nope. Like I said, no big deal."

"Will you tell Naomi?"

Matt snorts. "Are you crazy? She'd be on the next flight out here."

"Really? Oh God."

"Don't worry. I'm not going to tell her. I'm not going to tell Scott either."

Kate lets out a sigh of relief. "Okay. Good. We'll forget about it then."

"Forget, what?" Matt muses.

The pair exchange a smile before falling silent again.

Thank goodness Matt's not mad at me, Kate thinks to herself. It would have made the rest of the scavenger hunt unbearable. Which reminds her of something she thought about when she read Clue #4.

"Have you noticed how easy the clues are?" Kate asks Matt.

He nods. "I was thinking the same thing myself. The clues for the scavenger hunt he sent me on in the Courthouse were impossible. I had to do internet research to solve them."

"Why is he making it easy on us? Phil said this could take two weeks. We're heading to our fourth destination out of six, and it's only been four days."

"Maybe he worried we'd quit if it was too hard," Matt suggests.

"I guess that could be it," Kate says unconvinced. Judge never went easy on her when it came to his scavenger hunts. She doubts he would now.

"Or maybe these last few are going to be doozies."

Kate frowns. "That's what I'm afraid of."

*　　　*　　　*

They arrive at The Silver Goat twenty minutes later. It is an old, brick building six stories high in the center of a small town. Mom and pop shops line the streets.

"We have two rooms available for tonight," the woman behind the front desk tells them. "How long will you be staying?"

Kate turns to Matt. "Think we should get the rooms for two nights?"

"Probably. We're not meeting your uncle until 6:30. It will be late by the time we're done eating."

The clerk checks them in and shows them their rooms on the third floor.

"All of our rooms are named after famous people or world leaders who have stayed with us," the front desk clerk explains. "Both of your rooms are queen size beds. The only difference is their names."

The clerk stops in the middle of the hallway and points to two neighboring doors on her left. "The room on the left is the Mark Twain room, and the room on the right is the Abraham Lincoln room."

"Was the Beyoncé room booked?" Matt jokes.

Kate snorts, but the clerk looks lost.

"Beyoncé room? We don't have a Beyoncé room."

Kate steps in. "I'll take the Lincoln room."

The clerk smiles as she hands Kate the key. "A great choice."

"I love Lincoln," Kate explains. "I've read at least five or six biographies about him. I've also read most of his speeches word for word several times."

"How lovely," the clerk says before turning to Matt. "Here's your key, Sir," her tone curt. "I hope you have a pleasant stay with us."

"Why do I get the feeling she's going to smother me with a pillow tonight?" Matt asks when the clerk walks away.

Kate unlocks her door. "She'll have to get in line." She winks at Matt before going in her room and closing the door.

Kate takes advantage of her alone time and calls Scott.

"I can't believe you jumped out of a plane!" he says after she tells him about her day.

"Me neither."

"Was it awesome?"

"It was amazing Scott," Kate gushes. "I wish I had a camera up there."

"Did Matt do it too?"

"Yep."

"How are things going with you two?" Scott asks.

Well, we kissed and it was spectacular. Now I can't stop thinking about how good he was in bed...

Kate clears her throat. "It's fine."

"Uh-oh. You only say things are fine when they're not."

Kate winces. She needs to cover her tracks. "It's weird. We're getting along alright, but it's awkward."

"I'm sure it is. I wouldn't want to be stuck in a car with one of my exes either."

Their conversation turns to Scott's day.

Phew, Kate thinks as she hangs up the phone a few minutes later. She got out of that one.

*   *   *

Kate and Matt order take out from a restaurant down the street from the Inn. Matt asked Kate to go out for a sit down meal, but she made up a lame excuse about having to catch up with work emails. Truth is, she wants time and space away from Matt. She needs to clear her head.

While sitting at the bar waiting for their food, Matt offers to buy Kate a drink.

"Nah, I'm good," she tells him.

"Suit yourself."

Matt orders a beer and the bartender sets it in front of him a minute later.

"I don't drink much around my family. I need to indulge while I have the chance," he explains.

Kate puts up her hand. "Hey, no judgment here. I'm just not in the mood tonight."

"How's your Lincoln room?"

Kate smiles. "Good. It's weird to think Lincoln slept in the same space I'm sleeping in."

"I didn't realize you were a Lincoln fangirl."

"You have no idea."

Matt takes a drink, then asks, "Is it the beard or the top hat?"

Kate laughs. "Neither. It's his brain. He was a man before his time."

"Let me guess. Your favorite speech is the Emancipation Proclamation."

"That is one of my favorites. But my favorite quote is actually, 'As a peacemaker, the lawyer has a superior opportunity of being a good man.'"

Matt peaks an eyebrow. "Lawyers? Good men?"

A smile crosses Kate's face. "He said we have the opportunity to be good people. Not that we will be."

Matt changes the subject. "How do you like being a professor? Is it what you thought it would be?"

Kate shrugs. "I like it. It's better than being a law clerk or a litigator. I control my day and I get to choose the research I do for my law articles. It has its pitfalls like anything else."

"Like the students?" Matt asks.

171

"Yes. The students can be a real pain in the ass sometimes. Especially when they think they know more than I do. They've read a textbook filled with cases and they think they can practice law."

A pretty, young waitress brings them two carry out bags. She winks at Matt as she hands over his dinner. Matt doesn't seem to notice.

When the waitress walks away, Kate says, "If you get lonely tonight, I know someone who will keep you company."

Matt looks at her like she has two heads. "What? Who?"

"The waitress you moron. She was practically drooling over you."

"She was?"

"Yes."

Matt drops a few singles on the bar after downing his last sip of beer. "She's a little young for me, don't you think?"

"Yes," Kate answers.

The summer air feels good as they walk back to the Inn. Kate is starving and can't wait to dig into her steak and fries.

"What are you doing tomorrow?" Matt asks. "Before we meet up with Jack?"

"No clue."

"I'm going to walk around town. Maybe hit the library I saw a couple blocks over as we drove in."

Kate nods. "Alright. Just be back here by 6:30."

Matt smirks. "No place I'd rather be."

*　　*　　*

Kate can't sleep. She fluffs the pillows, then beats them into submission. She curls up in the blankets, just to kick them off ten minutes later. She turns on the TV and watches the news for a while, but it makes her sad.

Kate cruises the television stations until she finds reruns of *The Golden Girls*. Of all the women on the show, she relates to Dorothy the most. She doesn't sleep around like Blanche, and she isn't as flighty as Rose. She definitely isn't as funny as Sophia, who makes Kate laugh out loud twice.

After *The Golden Girls* is over, Kate finds herself watching *Frasier*. Before she knows it, it's 2 a.m. She hasn't been up this late in ages.

Kate mutes the TV and rolls onto her side. The lights from the television dance on the walls. Kate closes her eyes, but images of her kiss with Matt whip her eyelids open to full attention.

Dammit! Stop thinking about him, she scolds herself.

After some internal bickering, she falls asleep.

When Kate wakes up in the morning, she takes a long shower and doesn't rush when getting dressed. She's hoping Matt will be gone before she goes down to breakfast. Her goal is to avoid him until their dinner with Jack.

Kate meanders down the stairs and into the dining room with the breakfast buffet. She's relieved to see Matt isn't at one of the tables. Kate fills her plate with scrambled eggs, bacon and fruit. She sits alone at a table next to the window.

Kate watches people walk by as she enjoys breakfast. There isn't a crowd like a large city has, but there are some shoppers out and about. Most of them are women enjoying the local antique and jewelry stores.

Kate joins them after breakfast. She wanders into the various stores and peruses their goods. Kate isn't a huge fan of antiques, but she sees a few items that remind her of her grandparents. They are similar to things Kate's grandmother had in their home.

Kate spends over an hour in a clothing store mixed in with the antique shops. Some of the clothing is equestrian related, with cowboy prints or horseshoe patterns, but Kate finds a necklace and sweater she decides she cannot live without.

Swinging the brown bag holding her new purchases, Kate stops in the local coffee shop to buy an iced coffee. Judge mocked people who drank iced coffee, but Kate loves it.

"What's the point?" Judge asked her one day. "Coffee is supposed to be so hot it burns on the way down."

"Some of us want to taste the coffee Grandpa," she explained.

Judge waved his hand at her. "Your generation is hell bent on ruining everything."

Kate happens upon a park around the corner from the coffee shop and sits on a park bench. She smiles as children run around the playground like maniacs.

Kate wants kids and worries she's missed the boat. Scott wants a family as well, so there's no concern about being on the same page. It's a question of whether her body will cooperate.

Kate wonders what Matt's children are like. He hasn't talked about them much. Which is odd; don't most parents gush over their children? Or is that something only moms do? Maybe Naomi does enough gushing for the both of them.

Kate knows little to nothing about Matt's wife. She's overheard bits and pieces of phone conversations between the two of them, but Matt keeps the calls brief when he's with Kate. One thing Kate has noticed is Matt always tells his wife he loves her when he ends their calls. Kate can't help but remember how she used to be the woman he loved.

Funny how the passing of time dulls heartache. Kate despised Matt for years. But since their reunion, she wonders if she should have given him a second chance.

Water under the bridge now, she thinks to herself as she stands up. Their ship sailed a long time ago.

*   *   *

174

"Katie, my girl!"

Jack pulls Kate in for a hug. He is a big man; probably 6'4" in his day and broad shouldered. He was an offensive lineman in college and is a devoted football fan. Kate notices with some concern that Jack's clothes hang off his body a little and he isn't as imposing as he used to be.

"Jack, this is Matt Sloan. He's my partner in crime for the scavenger hunt."

Jack shakes Matt's hand vigorously. "Nice to meet you young man."

Matt smiles. "I'm not such a young man anymore."

"To me you are," Jack grumbles before taking his seat at the table.

The dining room of The Silver Goat is large and crammed full of small wooden tables. Each has a white vase with a pink rose and traditional doilies as place mats. Pictures of dinner guests at the Inn over the years cover the walls. For its age, the Inn is in great shape. It looks outdated, but in a charming way. More nostalgic than old.

The trio looks over their menus. There aren't a lot of options, but the choices all sound delicious.

"What do you recommend Jack?" Matt asks.

"I get the turkey with mashed potatoes and stuffing. Delicious."

Matt closes his menu. "That's what I'll go with then."

Kate follows suit. "Me too."

Their waitress stops by for their order and to bring them drinks.

Kate thanks the waitress and turns her attention to Jack. "Why is this your favorite restaurant Jack? Judge never mentioned this place to me."

"Our parents used to bring us here as children. We would come and watch a horse drawn carriage parade every year. Then we ate dinner here. It's a tradition I carry on with my own family."

"How lovely," Kate says with a smile.

The group talks small talk for a while. Kate is dying to know why dinner with Jack is a part of the scavenger hunt, but she doesn't bring it up. Jack will tell them in time. For all she knows, Judge wanted her to enjoy a family tradition from his childhood.

As promised, dinner is delicious. Kate eats way too much food and has to tap out with at least a quarter of her meal left.

"You going to finish your food?" Jack asks her, pointing his fork at her plate.

She shakes her head. "Have at it."

Jack picks up her plate and sets it on top of his empty one. Despite his shrinking frame, Jack still has a tremendous appetite. Kate and Matt wait patiently as Jack finishes Kate's dinner. After wiping the corners of his mouth with his cloth napkin, he clears his throat.

"I'm sure you're both wondering why Judge wanted you to meet with me."

"Since you brought it up, we'd love to know," Matt admits.

Jack puts his elbows on the table and leans forward. "Before I tell you this story, I want you to know I advised against it."

Alarm bells go off in Kate's head. Isn't this exactly what Phil said before he revealed the contents of Judge's Will?

Matt must be on the same wave length. "Maybe you shouldn't tell us the story then Jack," he suggests. "If it's bad news, we probably don't want to hear it."

Jack shakes his head. "I promised Judge, and I intend to keep my promise. I don't need that grumpy bastard haunting my house."

176

Kate snickers. She quiets down when she sees Jack rub his chin, a serious expression on his face.

"Let's see, it was about forty years ago now," Jack pauses before he continues. He looks Kate in the eyes. "You know how much your grandparents loved each other, right?"

Kate nods. "Yes."

"I don't want this story to tarnish your image of them as a couple."

Kate's eyes shift to the table, then back up to Jack. "Okay."

"At that time, both your mom and aunt had flown the nest, so to speak. Your grandmother didn't know what to do with herself."

"Understandable," Matt says.

"Everyone is a bit lost when their kids are grown and living their own lives," Jack says. "At any rate, your grandmother became sad. Doctors today would call it depression. Back then, we said a person was sad and waited for them to get over it."

Kate knew her grandmother suffered from a period of mental health issues. Kate can't recall exactly what her mother told her, but Kate remembers thinking it sounded bad. Of course, the grandmother she knew was a cheery woman who never showed an inkling of the blues.

"Judge didn't know what to do. Their family doctor recommended a vacation, which he took her on. They were gone for over a month driving across the country. When they came home, Judge told me your grandmother hardly spoke the entire trip and never cracked a smile."

Kate sighs. "How awful."

Jack nods. "You have no idea. She was like a zombie."

"They didn't have legitimate medication for depression then, did they?" Matt asks.

"None you would want a loved one to take. We didn't openly talk about mental health issues in those days. Taking medications was a huge stigma."

Jack shifts his weight and looks around the restaurant. He doesn't appear happy to continue the story.

"This went on for over a year. Your grandmother locked herself away in the house and we rarely saw or heard from her. She told Judge she wanted to be left alone. My poor brother bent over backwards to help her around the house. He bought her gifts and offered to take her on more vacations. Nothing he did broke the spell."

Kate frowns. "I can't imagine how hard it was on him. Judge was a fixer. He hated when people were upset."

"Exactly. Your grandmother's depression started eating away at him. He was irritable and quick tempered. We all forgave him because we knew what was going on at home." Jack pauses and hesitates before saying, "Then he met someone."

Kate feels the blood drain from her face. "Met someone?"

Jack grimaces. "Yes. He met someone."

"Who?" Kate asks between gritted teeth.

"Her name was Marlene. She worked at the Courthouse."

Kate starts to speak, but no sound comes out.

Matt steps in. "Are you telling us Judge had an affair?"

Kate doesn't want to hear the answer, but she can't compel her body to move either.

"Yes," Jack confirms. "Judge had an affair."

"Why are you telling me this?" Kate asks, her eyes blurring with tears.

Jack puts up his hands. "I didn't want to tell you, remember?"

"How long did it last?" Matt asks.

178

"Long enough," Jack responds. He turns back to Kate. "Your grandmother found a letter Judge intended to give to Marlene. She was furious. Her anger snapped her out of whatever haze she was in."

Kate uses her cloth napkin to wipe her tears. She thought her grandfather was the perfect example of what a man should be. He treated her grandmother like a princess. She never guessed he was making amends all those years.

After a minute of silence, Matt inquires, "Did Judge say why he wanted you to tell us this?"

Kate glares at him. "Don't play dumb Matt. This is all your fault."

Matt widens his eyes. "My fault? What does this have to do with me?"

Jack interjects. "Judge wants you to know that couples have ups and downs. No relationship is perfect. Not even his."

Kate throws her napkin on the table and pushes her chair back. As she stands up, she points a finger at Matt. "If you weren't such a dick, I wouldn't have ever known this story. Thank you so much for ruining the image of who I thought my grandfather was. Now I will always question whether I knew him at all."

Jack stands up and takes Kate's hand. "Good people do bad things Kate. That doesn't make them bad people. Judge will always be the man you thought he was. Don't define him by one indiscretion."

Kate kisses Jack's cheek. "I'm not upset with you. You made a promise and you kept it. We'll get together soon under better circumstances. Okay?"

Jack nods as he lets go of Kate's hand.

Kate throws Matt one more icy glare, then turns her back on him. She has no idea where she's going, but she has to get out of the restaurant before she has an epic meltdown. She makes her way through the lobby and out onto the sidewalk. She walks at a frantic pace.

"Kate!" she hears Matt yell from behind her. "Kate, stop!"

Kate keeps walking. She's in front of the clothing store she was in earlier today when a hand grabs her arm. She's brought to a sudden halt.

Kate tries to wiggle her arm free from Matt's grip. "Let go of me!"

"No," he says firmly. "I've let you walk away too many times in my life and I'm not doing it again."

"Leave me alone Matt. You are the last person I want to see right now."

Matt leans down and gets close to her face. "When are you ever going to admit that it wasn't all my fault?"

"What?" Kate spits back at him.

"You didn't talk to me for weeks Kate. Weeks. Don't act like you didn't play a role in what happened with us."

Kate narrows her eyes. "Fuck you Matt. You are a liar and always will be. I wouldn't be in this mess right now if you were honest with people."

Matt drops Kate's arm. "If you weren't a stuck up bitch who runs away from everyone who loves her, we'd still be together."

Kate's mouth drops open. Stuck up bitch?

"I. Fucking. Hate. You," she hisses.

Matt takes a step back as if Kate punched him. After regaining his composure, he mutters, "Congratulations Kate. You do feel emotion."

Kate straightens up and regains her composure. "I'm going for a walk now."

"Suit yourself," Matt says before turning around and walking back to the Inn.

As soon as he's gone, Kate deflates. For all her posturing, she feels awful for what she said to Matt. He looked genuinely hurt when she said she hates him.

Kate remembers something her mother told her once, "The fires of love and hate both burn brightly, but hate is easier to extinguish. Once love burns, the flame never truly goes out."

Kate didn't understand it at the time, but she does now.

Chapter Ten

Ten Years Ago

It's been two weeks since Kate talked to Matt. There were many times she considered it, but her anger gets the best of her.

Matt has called, texted and emailed her every single day asking for her to call him. She hasn't responded at all. Not even with something nasty. She's had the phone in her hands, but she puts it back down when she can't come up with a single thing to say.

Why did he have to lie? Why didn't he tell her the truth?

If Matt admitted he hooked up with Cora, she would be over it by now. She can't look past the lying though. Not yet anyway.

There was a light knock on her door and Kate's heart stopped. What if it was Matt?

Kate smiled when she saw Judge Penny stick her head in. "Do you have a minute?"

"Sure," Kate responded. What was she going to say? No?

Judge Penny stood on the opposite side of Kate's desk. Kate offered her a chair, but Judge Penny refused.

"I have something important to discuss with you," Judge Penny said in her intense voice.

Hard telling what this was going to be about. "Alright," Kate replied.

"The Chief Judge in the Cincinnati Division wants me to transfer down there. Would you be interested in going with me?"

Kate stammered. Cincinnati? She didn't know a thing about Cincinnati aside from the few places she visited on family trips.

"When are you leaving?" Kate asked.

"In two weeks," Judge Penny said. "I want you to go with me because you are an excellent clerk. But if you don't want to go, I understand."

"Will I have a job if I don't go with you?"

"Yes. A new judge will be coming in to take my place. You would float between the other judges until the new judge starts."

"Can I have some time to think about it?"

Judge Penny nodded. "Of course. Let me know in the next couple of days. If you can't come with me, I'll need to hire someone."

Kate sat back in her chair after Judge Penny left her office. She was not expecting this at all. Kate liked Columbus and had no desire to move. At the same time, what if she got stuck working for a crappy judge? She could deal with Judge Penny. Could she deal with the new judge coming in?

And what about Matt? Yes things with them were awful at the moment, but the thought of moving two hours away from him seemed impossible. She needed to talk to someone about this.

Kate stood up from her desk and walked down the hallway to Judge's chambers.

"Hey sweetie!" Judge's secretary Judy said with a smile.

"Hi Judy. Is Judge in?"

"He sure is. He's in his office."

Kate paused right before she got to Matt's office. His door was closed, but she didn't hear him on the phone. Should she knock?

Before she could decide, Judge saw her from his desk. "Kate! Get your butt down here."

She sighed. Judge ignored all her lectures about acting professionally at the Courthouse.

"Hey Grandpa," she said before plopping down in one of the brown leather chairs in his office.

"What brings you my way?"

"Judge Penny is transferring."

Judge put down his pen. "I know. I couldn't give you a heads up. I'm sorry."

Kate shrugged. "I understand. No worries."

"What are you going to do?"

"I don't know. That's what I came to talk to you about."

"Do you like working for Judge Penny?"

Kate nodded. "I do. We get along well."

"Do you want to move to Cincinnati?"

"Not really," Kate admitted. "I love Columbus. Cincinnati isn't far away, but too far to come home for dinner."

"Matt's in Columbus," Judge pointed out.

Kate's face flushed. She and Judge never discussed her relationship with Matt, but the man wasn't blind.

"He is," Kate said. "But he's not the reason I would stay."

Judge raised an eyebrow. "No? You two seem serious to me."

Kate picked at the armrest of the chair. "We were."

"Ah, a lovers' quarrel."

"Gross. Don't use the word 'lovers'."

Judge let out one of his trademark belly laughs. "I forgot I'm an old man and you are my granddaughter."

Kate changed the subject. "Do you know who will be coming in? The new judge, I mean."

Judge shook his head. "Not yet. It's possible someone from Dayton will come here. Or it could be a new appointee. I won't know for a few weeks."

"And by that time Judge Penny will be gone," Kate concluded.

"Yes."

"What should I do?"

Judge sat back in his chair and stared out the window for a minute. When he straightened up, Kate knew his sage advice was coming.

"Go with Judge Penny for now. As soon as we get the new judge, come back."

"You think I should go?" Kate asked shocked. She was sure Judge would tell her to stay.

"If you like working with Judge Penny, then go. For now. As soon as we have the new judge in house, you can come back. You'll be bored if you stay here without an official assignment."

"True."

"It might be nice for you to get away for a while. May help you to resolve some of your issues." Judge wiggled his eyebrows.

Kate rolled her eyes. "You're the one with issues."

"I won't deny it."

Kate left Judge's office with a smile on her face. Per his usual, Judge had a good answer for her. Kate's happiness came to a halt when she saw Matt's door standing open. He would see her walk by. Should she stop in?

After some consideration, Kate decided to bite the bullet and stop in. Unfortunately, when she poked her head in Matt's office, he wasn't there.

I'll call him later, she told herself as she left Judge's chambers.

As Kate was walking back to her own office, Cora came out of the break room giggling with a group of law clerks.

Oy! Kate suppressed a groan and kept walking.

"Hey Kate!" Cora called out to her.

Kate couldn't blow Cora off because there were witnesses present. She plastered a grin on her face and looked over her shoulder without stopping. "Hey guys!"

Kate turned around, but Cora caught up with her.

"I heard you found my camera," Cora said with a fake smile. "Matt paid me back for it. Nice of him to do when you were the one who broke it, huh?"

Damn you Matt, Kate's head screamed. Why did you give her all the dirty details?

"He's a real gentleman," Kate responded, her sarcasm obvious.

"I'm sorry you guys broke up. But it's probably for the best."

Kate stopped in her tracks. Who said anything about breaking up? Did Matt tell Cora they broke up?

"Listen Cora. My personal life is none of your business. Don't talk to me about this again."

Cora feigned disappointment. "Gee Kate, I thought we were friends."

Kate bit back. "I don't hang out with slutty bitches. Try not to take it personally."

Cora's mouth dropped open in shock.

"Yeah, I have claws too Cora. Don't make me use them. I'll fuck you up." Kate smirked as she left Cora standing alone in the hallway.

Once back at her desk, Kate replayed the scene with Cora. Matt definitely told Cora all about his fight with Kate. How else would Cora know Kate broke her camera?

And what's the deal with the breaking up stuff? Did Matt think they broke up? Kate hadn't spoken with him because she was angry, but she didn't consider them officially over. She needed space. That's all.

Her mind kept coming back to Matt telling Cora about their fight. Why would he do that? Matt told Kate his fling with Cora was over. If that's true, why are they still friends? Plus, Matt had to know he was giving Cora ammunition to use against her. Where did his allegiance lie?

Kate pushed her thoughts about Matt and Cora to the back of her mind. She had to talk to Judge Penny.

*   *   *

Three days later, Kate was still ignoring Matt. She decided when she woke up this morning that today was the day she would talk to him. She had questions to ask him, although she wasn't sure Matt would tell her the truth. But she wasn't getting anywhere by blowing him off. It was time to face him and get some answers. One way or the other, their issues would be resolved.

Kate walked in to work with the intention of approaching Matt, but Judge Penny had ideas of her own. Kate was running around, making phone calls, and preparing last minute documents for Judge Penny all day. She didn't even have time to eat lunch.

At 3:30 p.m., Judge Penny called her.

"Kate, we have an impromptu meeting with Court personnel in half an hour. Judge Payne is announcing our relocation to Cincinnati."

Kate went into panic mode. She had to talk to Matt right away. She needed to explain her move. She dialed his extension without any hesitation.

"Come on, Matt. Answer!" she pleaded.

"This is Matt Sloan. I'm either away from my desk…" Matt's voicemail informed her.

Kate hung up before the message was over. She got out of her chair and walked to Matt's office. Just her luck, he wasn't there.

"Judy, do you know when Matt will be back?" she asked Judge's secretary.

Judy shook her head. "I don't. He's handling one of Judge's case management conferences at the moment."

Kate groaned.

"Do you want me to have him call you?" Judy asked.

"Yes, please."

Kate sat at her desk waiting for the phone to ring, but it didn't. When she walked into the personnel meeting, she was relieved to see Matt wasn't there.

Good, she thought. I'll be able to tell him myself.

Judge made the announcement quick and to the point. "Everyone, we called you together to let you know Judge Penny will be transferring to the Cincinnati Division."

There was some murmuring, but most of the law clerks didn't like Judge Penny and were probably happy to see her go.

"Kate will be going with her until we have a new judge in office here," Judge continued.

Kate blushed when all the law clerks turned to her.

"Please wish Judge Penny the best. Her last day will be next Friday." And with that, Judge walked out of the room.

Kate intended to leave right behind him, but she was cornered by a few of the law clerks. After answering their questions about how long she would be gone and if she was really coming back, Kate bolted for Matt's office.

"Matt's in his office," Judy told Kate when she walked into Judge's chambers, "but he has company."

"He does?"

Judy crinkled her nose. "Cora."

Kate tried to hide her anger. What the hell was Cora doing in Matt's office?

"Speak of the devil," Judy said before looking back at her computer screen.

Cora came floating down the hallway with a smug grin. "I'll miss you while you're gone Kate."

"I'm sure you will."

"I can't stand her," Judy said when Cora walked out. "She's a nasty thing."

Kate couldn't agree more. "Matt's door is closed, is he on the phone?"

Judy glanced over at her switchboard. "Nope. You're good."

"Thanks."

Kate's heart was pounding as she approached Matt's door. Here goes nothing, she thought as she knocked.

"Come in," Matt said from the opposite side.

Kate took a deep breath before turning the door handle and pushing the door open. "Hey, I need to talk to you."

Matt stood up. He was dressed in an all-black suit with a powder blue shirt underneath. She'd almost forgotten how attractive he was. Almost.

Matt's face was twisted in a scowl. "When were you planning on telling me you're moving?"

"I stopped by here earlier and you weren't in."

Matt shuffled papers around on his desk. "How long have you known?"

Kate gulped. "A few days."

Matt looked up at her in disbelief. "A few days Kate? A few days?"

"I'm sorry," Kate started. "I know I've acted…"

190

"Like a bitch?" Matt interrupted.

Kate was taken aback by his insult. "Excuse me?"

Matt walked toward her. "You don't speak with me for over two weeks and then you don't bother to tell me you're moving? Sounds pretty bitchy to me."

"First of all, I'm not moving. Second, don't call me a bitch. Let's not forget why I was upset in the first place. Which reminds me, what the fuck was that slut doing in your office?"

Matt crossed his arms. "She came to tell me that my girlfriend is moving."

"Well, isn't that special?! How did she know I broke her camera Matt?"

Matt was temporarily disarmed by her question, but quickly recovered. "I have to talk to someone."

Kate shook her head. "I don't believe this. You lie to me about screwing her, then you keep hanging around with her?"

Matt threw up his hands. "What am I supposed to do Kate? You aren't talking to me. I've reached out to you a hundred times. I'm not going to get on my knees and beg."

"At this point, it wouldn't help," Kate muttered. She started to leave, but Matt stopped her.

"What does that mean?"

"What do you think it means?" she shot back. "You're the one who already told slut-face we broke up."

Matt looked down at the floor. This was all the confirmation Kate needed.

"There you have it then," she said in the coldest tone she could summon.

Kate spun on her heels and walked toward the one place she knew Matt would never follow her – Judge's office.

*　　*　　*

191

Later that night, Kate told Theresa the whole sordid story as she sat on her bed.

"Can I be honest with you?" Theresa crossed the room and sat next to Kate on her bed. "You're my best friend and I don't want you to make a mistake."

Kate grunted. "Go for it."

"I think you and Matt need to sit down like mature adults and have a conversation. No nasty confrontations or springing bad news on each other. A calm and meaningful talk about where you want this relationship to go."

Kate smirked. "When did you become the relationship guru?"

Kate stood up from the bed and started packing her clothes into the cardboard boxes she lifted from the Courthouse. She would need enough clothes to get her through a few weeks. Her second cousin Lydia, who happened to have a spare bedroom in her condo in Cincinnati, offered to let Kate stay with her.

Theresa laughed. "I won't pretend to know anything about relationships. I've never been in one. I'm giving you an opinion as an outside observer. You and Matt are good together. That much I can see."

"Am I supposed to forget he slept with my arch nemesis? Or that he lied to me about it?"

"Give him a chance to explain himself Kate."

Kate's temperature was rising. "He made me look like a total idiot T. That bitch is home laughing at me right now. She's loving every minute of it. She ruined my relationship."

"She isn't ruining your relationship. You are."

Kate stopped what she was doing, holding crumbled up jeans in her hand. "So now this is my fault? It's my fault he hooked up with her? It's my fault he lied to me?"

Theresa put her hands up. "That's not what I meant. All I'm saying is he slept with her before he met you. As soon as he met

192

you, he stopped sleeping with her. It wasn't right for him to conveniently leave out his hookups with her, but he knows how much you hate her and didn't want to ruin things with you."

Kate was huffy. "He purposely didn't tell me something because he knew it would upset me. I get that. But do I want a partner who is going to hide the truth?"

Theresa sighed. "Let me ask you this Kate, if Matt told you about Cora when you first got serious, would you have been upset?"

"Yes!"

"Why?"

"Because I can't stand her!" Kate began her frantic packing again. "I don't want her sloppy seconds! And to think that they did things together, things Matt and I haven't done..." Kate stopped midsentence.

Theresa gave her a knowing look.

"Am I jealous?" Kate asked as she flopped on the bed.

Theresa patted her knee. "I think you are a little jealous. Matt did things with Cora he doesn't do with you. Sure it was sex fetish stuff, but it's still something he hasn't done with you."

"When I found the camera, my stomach sank. I couldn't believe he slept with her. She's so...bitchy and gross. And she had this over me the entire time. I felt like a fool."

"But Matt told you it's over, right?"

Kate nodded. "Yeah. He says it's been months."

"Do you believe him?"

"I don't know. They still talk with each other. She knew I broke her camera. She also ran to his office today to tell him I'm going to Cincy with Judge Penny."

"That is a little weird," Theresa acknowledged.

"It is. But maybe I'm overreacting."

193

"You're not going to know until you talk to him."

Kate fidgeted with the zipper on her hooded sweatshirt. "My image of him is broken. One minute he was the right guy for me, and then the next he didn't feel like the right guy anymore."

"No one's perfect Kate."

"I know."

"Do you?" Theresa pressed. "Because Matt is damn near perfect for you. If prior hookups with some skank are the worst thing about him, then I think you're good."

Kate teared up. "I've never felt this way about anyone T. Even angry with him, I wanted to call him, or stop by his apartment. I haven't been able to sleep or eat well since our fight."

Theresa stood up and grabbed a tissue from the box on Kate's nightstand.

Kate gave Theresa a grateful look. "Thanks."

The two women sat quietly for a minute before Theresa broke the silence. "Do you love him Kate?"

Kate looked at Theresa and finally admitted the truth. "I do."

Theresa pulled Kate up off the bed. "Then you know what you need to do."

*   *   *

Matt sat in his apartment with a beer in his hand, blankly watching the television screen. Alex left fifteen minutes earlier. Alex tried his damnedest to get Matt out of the house, but Matt refused.

"You can't wallow in your self-pity forever dude," Alex argued. "It's about time you got your ass out there again."

"I'm not in the mood," was Matt's repeated response to all of Alex's attempts.

Alex finally gave up. "Fine. Call me when you're ready to get some pussy."

Matt was lost in a daydream about Kate when his doorbell rang. He jumped up from the couch, hoping it was Kate.

He threw the door open and frowned. "Cora?"

Cora was standing in the hallway wearing a short skirt with pink high heels that laced up her calves. She had on a white halter top and a jean jacket.

"I thought you'd want some company tonight," she said as she pulled a bottle of Jim Beam from her oversized purse.

"I'm good," Matt said dryly before repeating his tag line, "I'm not in the mood."

Cora pouted. "I drove all the way over here Matt. The least you can do is take a few shots with me."

Matt considered his options. He should tell Cora to go the fuck home. She's the reason he and Kate broke up. On the other hand, he wouldn't mind getting shit wasted and forgetting about Kate for the night.

He opened the door further and walked away. Cora laughed as she shut the door behind her.

"That's my boy! Hook a girl up with a couple shot glasses."

Matt took two shot glasses out of his cabinet. One with a Hard Rock logo and the other with the block O for Ohio State. Cora filled the glasses to the brim.

"Bottoms up!" she exclaimed before tilting her head back and downing the shot.

Matt followed Cora's lead. The booze burned on the way down, but Matt welcomed the sensation. He needed this. He needed to get completely fucked up. He'd worry about Kate and how to fix things with her tomorrow.

A few shots later, he and Cora were snuggling on the couch.

"I messed up with Kate," Matt told Cora.

"My fault," Cora giggled. "I couldn't help myself. I hate that bitch."

Matt knew he was drunk, but couldn't stop his chatter. "Yeah, but you screwed me over too. I love her. Like, really love her."

"Why?" Cora asked. "What's so great about her?"

"She's funny. And smart. And pretty. She's everything."

Cora slid off the couch and onto her knees in front of Matt. She moved her hands up Matt's thighs and played with his zipper. "Oh yeah? Can she do this?"

*   *   *

Kate called Matt three times on the drive over to his place. She also sent him a text letting him know she was on her way. Matt didn't respond, but that didn't deter her. She was willing to wait outside his apartment if she had to. She found a decent parking spot outside his building and smiled when she saw his car.

She took the stairs to his floor and knocked on the door. Kate waited a minute, then knocked again. Nothing.

Maybe he's out with Alex, she thought.

Testing her luck, Kate turned the door handle. To her surprise, it was unlocked. Kate opened the door and peeked inside. The television was on, but Matt wasn't in the living room.

"Matt?" she called out. She didn't get a response.

Kate looked down the hallway toward Matt's room. The door was open and the light was on.

"Matt?"

And then she heard it.

Kate froze when she heard the moans. She turned her head and listened. She could hear two voices. One of them definitely Matt's, but the other was female. Kate's heart pounded as she tiptoed down the hallway, mentally preparing herself for what she was about to see.

Kate stood outside the door frame and momentarily squeezed her eyes shut. Did she really want to see this? Should she leave now, get in her car and not look back?

In the end, Kate's curiosity got the best of her. She opened her eyes, steeled her nerves, and looked into Matt's room.

There it was. Her worst fears realized.

The first thing she saw was Matt's ass. Oh how she used to admire that ass of his. Now, she felt vomit creeping up her throat as she watched it thrusting back and forth.

Matt was naked from the bottom down, but still had a grey t-shirt on. Kate suspected it was the OSU t-shirt she gave him a month or so ago.

Then Kate saw her. Cora. Laying on her back in Matt's bed. Her skirt and shoes thrown on the floor; her top pulled up high enough that Kate could see her electric pink bra. Kate would never buy any undergarments with neon pink on them again.

Only sluts wear hot pink, Kate would think while shopping at Victoria's Secret.

Cora's eyes were closed, her head tilted back, and her mouth open as she let out breathy gasps.

"No!"

Kate hadn't meant to yell. In fact, she put her hand over her mouth to keep herself from exploding. But the simple word had slipped off her tongue nonetheless.

Cora sat up and Matt stepped back, clumsily picking up his pants. Kate's head began to swim and she had to grab the door frame to stop herself from falling forward. She vaguely heard Matt say something, but she couldn't make it out. Through watery eyes, Kate saw Cora get up and pull her shirt down.

I have to get out of here, she thought desperately.

Kate turned and walked down the hallway as fast as she could. With each step, she was coming back to Earth.

"Kate! Stop! Please!" Matt yelled from behind her.

Kate started running through Matt's apartment and slammed the front door behind her. She flew down the stairs and out of the building's entrance. Because she parked close to Matt's building, she was standing next to her car door in seconds.

"Dammit!" Kate cursed as she fumbled to get the car keys out of her pocket.

Thank God for the key fob; she would not have been able to get a key in the door. As it was, she had a hard time getting the key into the ignition. She fired up her car and pulled away from the curb. As she passed Matt's apartment building, she saw him run out the door.

Kate didn't stop. Her tears were running down her cheeks in hot streaks and her hands were trembling. When she got far enough away, she pulled into a McDonald's parking lot and shifted the car into park.

Did that really happen? Was Matt really fucking Cora? Surely she imagined it all.

But it had been real.

Kate couldn't control the meltdown. She felt torn in two. Like someone cut her into pieces. She wanted to go back to Matt's and punch Cora in the face. She wanted to scream and yell at Matt until the veins in her neck exploded. She wanted to shake him and ask him what the hell was wrong with him.

Matt lied to her about his fling with Cora being over. They were probably hooking up the entire time she and Matt were together.

The bile rose in Kate's throat again. She threw open her car door and ran to the tree line in the parking lot. She bent over and threw up into the brown mulch. The taste was rancid and her nose was running.

From behind her, she heard a soft voice. "Honey? Are you alright?"

Kate looked up to see a woman dressed in pale pink slacks and a floral shirt. She had her gray hair pulled tight into a bun and was probably a very good grandmother.

Kate tried to smile. "I'm okay. Just not feeling well."

The woman frowned. "Do you need a ride?"

Kate shook her head. "No, I'll be fine."

The woman hesitated, but didn't press the issue. "Okay dear. Be safe getting home."

Kate waited until the woman walked away, then threw up what was left in her stomach.

* * *

Matt sat outside Kate's apartment for over an hour before he saw a car coming down the street that could be hers.

When Kate drove away from his apartment, he had to go back upstairs to get his car keys. He put on sneakers without bothering to tie the laces, and didn't wait for Cora to leave. Cora was crying, shaking as she put her ridiculous shoes back on. Matt didn't say a word to her. He pushed her away and ran out his front door when she tried talking to him.

He fucked up. Big time. He didn't know what else to do other than sit outside Kate's apartment and wait for her to come home. The last hour gave him time to come up with an apology worthy of Kate. Nothing short of begging was coming to mind. He told her earlier in the day he wouldn't get on his knees and beg, but that was a lie. He would crawl through glass if she demanded it.

Of all the times for Kate to come over, it had to be right then. He waited three weeks for Kate to call or stop by. Did she? No. She waited until he was hooking up with Cora to show up. Matt was so pissed at himself he could scream. Discovering he missed three calls from Kate before she stopped by his place made it even worse.

199

The biggest mystery of all – why was Kate at his apartment? Wasn't she moving to Cincinnati? Didn't she tell him it was over?

When Matt thought about the conversation they had at the Courthouse earlier in the day, the words, "we're over" never came out of Kate's mouth. It was implied, but not official. Matt took Kate's words to mean she was done with him. Moving to Cincinnati and not looking back.

Apparently, he was mistaken.

As the car approached Kate's building, Matt stood up to see if it was Kate. To his shock, it was.

Matt walked toward her parking spot, but Kate's red Jetta didn't stop. She hit the accelerator and her car roared past him.

"Kate! Stop!"

Kate's car did not slow down. Matt chased after it, screaming "Kate!" at the top of his lungs over and over again.

It was no use. Her car continued down the street and squealed as she took a right turn too fast. Matt ran for his car, but slowed to a defeated walk when he realized there was no way he could catch up with Kate.

What now?

I'll wait, he decided. I'll stay right here and wait for her.

Matt sat back down against the brick building and held his face in his hands as he cried.

Idiot, he yelled at himself. How could you be so stupid?! She's gone now. Gone. Forever.

The look of horror on Kate's face when she walked in his room will be burned in his mind for years to come. Her shock turned to complete fury before his eyes.

You will look back on this as the exact moment your life crumbled, he thought miserably.

He wanted to melt into the sidewalk. Matt heard a creak as the front door of Kate's apartment building opened. He didn't bother to see who it was. What was the point? He knew it wasn't Kate.

Suddenly, someone was standing above him. Matt looked up and saw Theresa.

After a second, he asked, "She isn't coming back, is she?"

Theresa's face was uncharacteristically soft. "No, she's not."

Matt put his face back in his hands and started weeping again. He didn't care he was crying in front of Theresa. He didn't care about anything.

Theresa sat down next to Matt and pulled his body toward hers. Matt leaned into her and cried on her shoulder. Theresa squeezed Matt and ran her hand through his hair, like his mother used to when he was young.

"Shhhh. It's okay Matty, Mommy's here," his mother would whisper. His mom's voice was the cure to all of Matt's ailments back then.

When Matt was cried out, he sat upright. There was a wet spot on Theresa's shirt where his face had been. Normally, he would have been embarrassed; but he didn't care if he looked like a wuss. His life was in tatters.

Matt leaned his head back against the brick wall. "I fucked up," he muttered matter-of-factly.

"Yeah, you did," Theresa said, voice still soft. No judgment, just sympathy.

"Did she tell you?" Matt asked, eyes still looking up at the sky.

"She did."

"She hates me, right?"

Theresa sighed. "Pretty much." And after a pause, "Can you blame her?"

Matt shook his head.

201

The two sat in silence for a while. Matt replaying the evening in his head over and over again. Eventually, Matt sat up and looked at Theresa, who was fiddling with her finger nail polish. It was clear she didn't know what to say, but he appreciated that she came down to see him.

"Why was Kate at my place Theresa? She didn't talk to me for weeks. Then she shows up in my bedroom."

Theresa stopped picking her finger nail polish and folded her hands in her lap. "You sure you want to know?"

Matt nodded. "Yes."

Theresa considered how much to say for a moment. "She was coming to have a grown up conversation with you."

"About what?"

Theresa's expression was filled with pity. "Kate realized she's in love with you."

Matt felt the tears welling up again, but he choked them back. "Fuck," was all he managed to say.

"Indeed," Theresa agreed with a frown.

Kate loved him. Matt let this sink in. Hope started blooming in Matt's chest. If Kate loved him, maybe begging for her forgiveness would work.

"Do you think she'll forgive me?" Matt asked with the slightest hint of optimism.

"Truth?"

Did Matt want the truth? "Truth."

"I doubt it."

Matt sighed. "That's what I figured." Matt's voice was raw from screaming for Kate and from the crying.

He had no idea what to do. Was it worth trying to track her down tonight? Should he wait until the morning? Matt asked Theresa what she thought.

"I'd give it some time Matt. Let her calm down."

"Is she coming back here?"

"No. Her mom is coming to get her stuff sometime in the next few days."

"She's moving out?" Matt asked in a panic.

"No. She needs her clothes for Cincinnati.

Matt relaxed a little.

Theresa stood up. "You want to come up for a drink? You can crash here tonight if you want."

Matt shook his head. "No. I'll get up in a minute and head home." Kate wasn't coming back to her place, so there was no point in waiting for her here.

"Okay." Theresa walked toward the building's entrance and pulled the door open. She paused before going in. "For the record, I was rooting for you Matt. You're a good guy."

Theresa went into the building and the door shut behind her.

He sure didn't feel like a good guy.

*   *   *

Matt went into work the next morning looking like shit. He didn't get back to his place until 2 a.m. and hadn't fallen asleep until at least 4:30. He managed to get a shower and put on some work appropriate clothes, but didn't bother to shave.

Matt had no idea if Kate told Judge about the prior evening's events. If Matt knew Kate, she didn't speak a word of it to Judge. Matt was still nervous though. Matt respected Judge and didn't want to get a reaming from him. Especially if the reaming involved the way Matt treated his granddaughter.

Matt avoided everyone on the way to his office. He wasn't in the mood to play nice. He shut his office door and sulked behind his desk. Images of Kate ran continuously through his mind on a loop. He was a man on the verge of a breakdown.

Matt sat up when he heard a loud knock on the door. Before Matt could respond, the door swung open. Matt's stomach flipped as Judge walked into his office and shut the door. Judge took a seat across from Matt's desk. Judge never sat in Matt's office. Ever.

Oh God. Here we go.

Matt started to speak, but Judge beat him to it.

"Matthew, I don't need to know the details, but I have a feeling you might know why my granddaughter called me at 6 a.m. this morning to tell me she is resigning her position."

Matt was shocked. "Kate? Resigning?"

Judge continued. "I don't make it a practice to meddle in the personal lives of my clerks or Court personnel. But this is my granddaughter."

Matt felt sick. "I can pack my things today, Sir."

Judge waved his hand. "Completely unnecessary Matthew. You are a good clerk. Probably one of the best. I don't want you to leave."

Relief washed over him. "Thank you."

Judge's words were kind and reassuring, but if Judge wasn't going to fire Matt, why was he bringing up Kate?

Judge didn't leave Matt in suspense. "The reason I'm having this uncomfortable conversation with you is I don't want you to make a terrible mistake."

Matt gulped. "Sir, I…"

Judge put up his hand. "Again, I don't need, or want, to know the details. I'm not the brightest man in the world, but I knew something was going on between you two before Kate admitted it to me. She was happier, lighter, a softer version of herself. And whether you knew it or not, so were you."

Matt smiled a little. He loved Kate. Of course it would show.

Judge went on. "Kate never walks away from confrontation or a challenge. For her to resign, to leave without any notice, it has to be bad."

Matt hung his head, ashamed of himself. He kept it together though. He would never be able to face Judge again if he broke down.

"If you listen to any piece of advice I ever give you Matthew, listen to this - don't let Kate be 'the one.'"

Matt looked up. "Huh?"

"Don't let Kate be the one who got away," Judge clarified.

"It's too late," Matt whispered.

"You're still breathing. It's not too late." Judge stood up. "Kate asked me to gather her personal items from her office."

Matt nodded.

Judge's eyes bore into his. "I'm going to pack the box now."

"Okay," Matt responded, not sure what Judge was trying to tell him.

"The box will be sitting on the conference room table until I get off the bench this afternoon. Just in case anyone wants to slip Kate a letter." Judge turned away from Matt and walked out of his office.

Matt exhaled a big breath of air. He wasn't getting fired. Judge had no idea what he'd done last night. Matt was grateful Kate hadn't spilled the beans.

But Kate wouldn't do that, would she? She was a classy woman who kept her business private. Kate could have easily thrown Matt under the bus and sought revenge. But she didn't.

Matt pulled out a yellow memo pad and a pen from his desk drawer. He sat rolling the pen between his fingers debating what he should say to Kate. Judge was giving him an opportunity to apologize, and Matt wanted to take advantage of it. This might be the only way he could get through to Kate and explain.

He started writing.

Kate,

You mean more to me than anyone in the world. My time with you has been the best time of my life. You own every piece of me. These few weeks without you have been Hell on Earth. I know I made a huge mistake last night, and it must look really bad. But I swear, I only hooked up with Cora because you told me it was over. I needed a distraction; something to dull the pain. I drank way too much and will regret it for the rest of my life. Please give me a chance. Please Kate, I don't think I can ever love another woman the way I love you.

Matt

Matt read the letter over and over again. Would it be enough?

Matt cradled his head in his hands and struggled with himself. His letter sounded so cliché. I drank too much…huge mistake… He couldn't let go of the thought that Kate would never forgive him.

"Fuck it," he said out loud before standing up. He crumpled the paper in a ball and threw it in his trash can. He grabbed his blazer off the back of his chair and stormed out of his office.

"Judy, tell Judge I went home sick," he said as he walked past Judge's secretary.

"Are you alright?" Judy asked with concern.

"No. I need to go home."

*　　*　　*

"Honey, are you going to tell me what's going on?" Kate's mom asked as they unloaded boxes of Kate's belongings from her mother's car.

Kate was moving out of her apartment with Theresa. She didn't plan on staying with her mom for long, but she couldn't stay at the apartment anymore. She wanted a fresh start.

"I don't want to talk about it Mom."

Kate's mother sighed. "Okay. I'm here when you're ready."

Kate brought the boxes into her old bedroom. It was exactly the same as it had been when Kate was in high school. Kate unpacked her clothes into her old dresser. It still had pink and purple My Little Pony stickers on it.

When her box was empty, Kate turned to her mom. "I'm going to the mall this afternoon. Do you want to go with me?"

"Sure. What are you shopping for?"

"I need to stop by the cell phone place. I want a new number."

Kate's mom stopped folding clothes that were tousled in the move. "A new number? Why?"

"No particular reason."

Her brow furrowed, Kate's mom asked, "Are you in trouble Kate? Is someone stalking you?"

Kate shook her head. "I'm avoiding someone. But he's not dangerous."

Kate told herself she wanted a new number so Matt couldn't call her. The truth was she didn't want Matt's number in her contact list. Calling him, despite what she saw last night, would be too tempting.

"What happened with Matt, Kate? I know you don't want to talk about it, but I'm worried about you. You quit your job; you moved out of your apartment with Theresa; and now you're talking about a new phone."

Kate sat down on her twin bed next to her mom. "He cheated on me Mom."

Her mother's mouth dropped open. "No!"

"Yep. And with the Courthouse bicycle."

Her mom tilted her head to the side. "The Courthouse bicycle?"

"Yeah, the Courthouse bicycle – everyone gets a ride."

Kate watched as understanding dawned in her mother's eyes. "Oh…"

"Yep."

Kate's mom rubbed her back. "I'm sorry Kate. I know you really liked him."

"I loved him Mom. Still do."

Kate's mom pulled her in tight. "It will fade. Give it time. You'll meet someone new. Someone who won't take rides on worn out bicycles."

Before leaving for the mall, Kate wrote down all the contact information she wanted to keep. When she got to Matt's number, she hit "delete." But when the prompt to confirm deletion came up, she backed out. She didn't have Matt's number committed to memory because it was stored in her phone. She never needed to dial it herself. Kate couldn't make herself delete Matt's number, but it would be gone after her trip to the cell phone store.

Kate and her mom shopped for a couple of hours. She got a new phone and a new pair of shoes. When Kate pulled into her mother's driveway, she saw Judge's car. They found him kicked back in the recliner watching TV.

"Hello ladies!"

Kate sat down on the couch. "Hey Grandpa."

Kate's mom leaned over to give Judge a kiss on the cheek. "Hi Dad. I see you let yourself in."

"I put the key back under the garden gnome. Where have you ladies been?"

"The mall," Kate answered.

"I brought your box from the Courthouse. I put it on the kitchen counter."

"Thanks."

"You want something to eat Dad?" Kate's mom asked.

"No, Grandma is making me a nice meal as we speak. A Diet Coke would be nice though."

"Sure thing," Kate's mom said before leaving the room.

Judge sat up in the recliner and closed the foot rest. He turned off the television and looked at Kate. "We need to talk about Matt."

Kate crossed her arms. "No, we don't."

"Okay. You sit and pout and *I'll* talk about Matt."

"There's nothing to talk about Grandpa. We broke up. End of story."

Judge didn't let up. "I don't think that's true. You two love each other."

Kate fought to maintain her composure. "I don't want to get into the nitty-gritty details with you. Trust me when I say if I told you the whole story, you would tell me to dump him."

"Tell me the whole story then."

Kate shook her head. "You and Matt work together Grandpa. It would be weird."

Judge shrugged. "So what? I talked with him about it earlier."

"You what?!"

"Yes. I sat down with him and told him to work things out with you."

Kate rubbed her temples. "Oh Grandpa. I wish you would stay out of it."

Kate's mom walked in and handed Judge a glass of Diet Coke. He took a long gulp then handed the glass back.

"I need to go before my dinner gets cold." He stood up and pointed a finger at Kate. "You think about this long and hard little miss. Love doesn't walk into your life every day."

Kate fumed as he walked out. "Mom, you better tell him to shut up about this. It's none of his business."

"You know how he is Kate. He makes everything his business."

A few minutes later, Kate opened the box Judge left for her. On top of the pile was a white envelope with her name on it. She recognized the handwriting immediately. She opened the envelope and pulled out a single sheet of paper.

> *Kate,*
>
> *I will miss you dearly. I wish you all the best. You know where to find me if you change your mind.*

"Who's that from?" Kate's mom asked as she walked in the kitchen.

"Judge Penny," Kate answered before dropping the note back in the box and closing the lid.

Chapter Eleven

Now

Kate stares at the ceiling above her bed in the Abraham Lincoln room. She walked around town for over two hours sorting out her thoughts.

Who is she really mad at? Judge? Or Matt?

She's incredibly disappointed to learn Judge had an affair. But if her grandmother forgave Judge, Kate should too. Her grandparents were madly in love with each other. When Kate's grandmother passed away four years ago, Judge was never the same. In his last days, Judge frequently mentioned being reunited with his wife.

"If there's a Heaven, she's in it Kate," he told her more than once.

"Give her a kiss for me," Kate responded each time.

"You can count on it. But I'm giving her a kiss from me first."

Kate rolls over and looks out the window. The third floor is high enough to see over the rooftops of the neighboring shops. In the distance, Kate can see the tall spire of a local church. Above it, the half-moon is shining in the clear sky.

Why does Judge want Kate to forgive Matt so badly? Did he really think Matt was her true love?

Judge acted as though he liked Scott. Clearly, he preferred Matt. Judge may not have known about Matt's wife, but he certainly knew about Scott. Maybe his intention wasn't to get Matt and Kate together, but to put the past where it belonged.

During her walk, Kate thought about what Matt said on the street. Kate never wanted to acknowledge the role she played in

211

their breakup. It was easier to blame Matt for everything than to admit she had a hand in it.

If she hadn't acted like an immature baby back then, would she and Matt be together now? If she had the conversation Theresa suggested instead of burying her head in the sand, her entire life would be different.

This is a hard pill for Kate to swallow. Finally, after all this time, she sees the big picture.

Kate sits up in bed and slides her feet into her ballet flats. She steps out of her room and knocks on Matt's door. A few seconds later, Matt pulls it open. He's wearing white and blue striped pajama pants and a white t-shirt. His black hair is disheveled from lying in bed.

"Sorry to wake you," Kate apologizes.

"You didn't. I'm having trouble sleeping. Want to come in?"

Kate hesitates, but accepts the invitation. Matt steps to the side to let her in. She walks over to the desk and takes a seat in the wooden chair. Matt sits at the foot of his bed.

"What's up?" he asks her.

"I've done a lot of thinking tonight. About Judge. About us. And I want to make amends with you."

"Okay," Matt says.

"I realize the part I played ten years ago. I understand why you thought we were over. I was cold hearted and acted like I didn't care. For that, I'm sorry."

Matt rubs his hands on his pajama pants. "Why didn't you reach out to me after that night? I waited years for you to come around Kate. You never gave me the chance to explain myself or to apologize."

"I couldn't get the image of you with Cora out of my head Matt," Kate admits. "Every time I thought of you, I thought of her."

Matt gets up and stands next to his window. His face illuminated by the street light outside. "You don't know how many times I've wondered what my life would be like if those few minutes never happened." He turns back to look at Kate. "I would give anything, anything, to erase what I did."

"I wish it never happened too. But it did. We both screwed up and we need to accept it. I think that's why Judge brought us together."

Matt nods. "You think he knew what happened?"

"He had to know somehow. Why else would he have Jack tell us the story about his affair?"

"Maybe Judge thought what he did was much worse than what happened with us. Sort of a 'if she could forgive me, you can forgive each other' kind of thing."

"Yeah, maybe." But Kate isn't convinced. Judge wouldn't want his dirty laundry aired unless he felt it was truly necessary. "Do you think Cora told him?"

"Why would she do that?"

"To get you fired."

Matt considers this a moment. "Nah. She had no reason to tell Judge. She quit a few weeks after you left. She got a job at a big law firm."

"Do you know where she is now?"

"No. We spoke before she left. I know you find it hard to believe, but she felt bad about what happened. She said she needed to get her life in order."

"Really?" Kate is shocked. She figured Cora was thrilled with how things played out.

"Cora told me she didn't recognize herself anymore. It was sad, actually."

"Huh," Kate says. "I hope she did it then. I hope she turned her life around. I hated her with a passion, but if she was truly remorseful, I wish her the best."

Matt smiles at her. "Look at you. Acting all mature."

Kate groans. "Being an adult sucks."

"Yes, it does," Matt agrees.

Kate chews her bottom lip. "Cora didn't tell Judge. T didn't tell him, and I swore my mom to secrecy. How could he have known?"

They contemplate the options until Matt chuckles.

"What?" Kate asks.

"I know how he found out."

"How?"

"I wrote you a letter. Judge told me he was bringing a box of your stuff home from the Courthouse. I was going to put the letter in the box."

Kate flashes back to the moment when she opened her box from Judge. She got a letter, but it wasn't from Matt. "I never got your letter. Do you think Judge took it?"

Matt frowns. "I never put it in the box. I wussed out and threw it in my trash can. He must have found it. I went home sick that day. He had full access to my office."

"As nosey as Judge was, he'd totally go through your trash," Kate surmises.

"Agreed."

She can't help but ask the question burning in her mind. "What did the letter say Matt?"

Matt glances at her, the moonlight streaming across his face. "It doesn't matter now."

"Yes it does," she responds in a near whisper.

Matt steps away from the window and walks over to Kate. He kneels down in front of her.

Kate sits straight up. "Matt, what are you doing?"

He takes her hands in his and stares into her eyes. "I am sorry for what I did back then. I'm sorry you had to hear an awful story about Judge because of me." Matt chokes up, then clears his throat. "I'm sorry I didn't fight harder for us."

She softens. "You did fight for us Matt. I'm the one who quit."

"No. I knew you were afraid of commitment. I knew you were latching on to the camera thing to give yourself a reason to back out. I thought giving you space was the answer, but I was wrong. I should have been at your door every single night begging for your forgiveness."

"Don't blame yourself Matt. I ignored your calls and messages. Then, when we finally talked about it, I said things I didn't mean. I gave you the wrong impression. I see it now."

Matt squeezes her hands and she squeezes back. They stare into each other's eyes before Matt stands up and sits down on the bed. He covers his face with his hands, then rests them under his chin.

"I got the next clue from Jack."

Happy for the subject change, Kate says, "Oh, good. I was worried he didn't leave it. What did it say?"

"I don't remember it verbatim, but it was something like: Drive where the autumn leaves put on their show. Go to the Ranger's Station, he'll tell you what you need to know."

"Hocking Hills," Kate says without hesitation. "Judge camped there for a week every year in late October. He loved the fall foliage. He'd come home with a million pictures and bust out the projector."

"Sounds exciting."

215

Kate chuckles. "The pictures were beautiful, but you can only look at so many pictures of leaves before you get bored."

"I guess we're going camping."

"Indeed," Kate agrees. She stands up and stretches her arms. "I'm heading to bed. I'll see you at breakfast in the morning."

Matt watches her walk to the door. "Good night Kate."

She smiles at him. "You know, I never thought I'd be able to be in the same room with you again. Yet here I am, looking right at you and not wanting to punch you in the face."

Matt puts his hand on his cheek. "Good. I'm too old to take a hit now."

"Good night Matt," Kate says as she walks out the door.

Once back in her own room, Kate stares at the moon from her window.

"You did it old man. I forgive him."

*   *   *

The drive to Hocking Hills is a long one. Kate heads north on I-71 toward Columbus. She would love to get off the exit for her own house and forget about the rest of the scavenger hunt. But she's come this far, why stop now?

Kate pulls into the Ranger's Station a few minutes after 1 p.m. She and Matt both stretch their arms and legs when they get out of the car. The trip was comfortable, she and Matt held a decent conversation. They discussed politics, jobs and their new favorite pastimes. It was a light chat, nothing too personal.

The Ranger's Station is exactly what Kate envisioned. It is a wood cabin made of dark brown logs. Rocking chairs adorn the front porch and wind chimes play a soft melody. The front door creaks as Kate pushes it open.

Inside the cabin are various stuffed animals, as in animals that were once alive. Kate does her best not to cringe. She doesn't understand hunting as a hobby. She questions people who kill for sport. Judge used to hunt deer, but he ate all of the meat after it was processed.

Kate looks past a stuffed owl and sees a small office.

"Hello?" she calls out as she heads toward the door.

She hears an office chair roll and a tall man wearing an all khaki outfit appears in the doorway. "Yes?"

"Hi. I'm Kate Marshall," she turns toward Matt, "and this is Matt Sloan. We were told to come here for the next stop on a scavenger hunt."

The man, who is probably in his late forties, eyes her suspiciously. "Scavenger hunt?"

"Um, yes. You see, my grandfather..." she starts to explain.

The man laughs. "I'm teasing. I've been expecting you." The park ranger shakes Kate's hand. "Roy Timmons. Pleasure to meet you."

After shaking Matt's hand as well, Roy waves them into his office. It is small and sterile looking. The walls are bright white and fluorescent lights buzz overhead. Posters from the State of Ohio Department of Parks and Wildlife are the only decorations in the room. The desk is fake wood and metal. Two grey folding chairs sit against the wall opposite the desk.

Roy takes the seat behind the desk. "Pardon the office. I'm hardly ever in here."

"No problem," Matt says as he and Kate sit in the metal chairs.

"I knew Judge well. He stopped in every year to see me when he camped. I was sorry to hear of his passing."

Kate smiles. "Thank you Roy. He loved coming here."

"Judge sent me a letter a few months back. Said he wanted to set up a scavenger hunt for his granddaughter and her friend. We spoke on the phone and we came up with something for you guys.

217

Your uncle Jack called me yesterday to say you two would be up here sometime this afternoon."

Kate shifts in her chair. "What do you have in store for us?"

"Nothing too crazy," Roy says with a grin. "We want you to see the best of what Hocking Hills has to offer. It's a shame it's not fall though. We're at our best in the fall."

Roy opens a desk drawer and pulls out a pamphlet. He unfolds it on the desktop. "This is a map of the surrounding area. I've circled several locations with a red marker."

Kate and Matt lean over to peer at the map. Kate counts ten locations.

"Safe to assume you want us to visit each location?" Matt asks.

Roy nods. "Yes. I need you to take a photograph of each spot. It can be on your camera phone, but I need to see proof you visited the sites. There's a few rules. You must have a photo at sunrise and two have to be at sunset."

"So we need to stay for at least two nights," Kate concludes.

"That's right. You also have to camp in the location I selected for you."

Kate sits back in the chair. Two nights? She wants to go home. And this isn't the last stop on their scavenger hunt. They still have one more place after this.

Matt examines the map. "Is the campsite on here?"

Roy points to a spot on the map. "Yes, it's the red star."

Kate looks at the red star and groans. It's in the middle of stick figure trees, which means she'll be spending the next couple of nights in the woods.

"Don't you worry, there are trails leading right to it. You won't have to make your own way," Roy explains.

This does not make Kate feel any better.

"Did you two bring camping gear with you?" Roy asks.

218

Kate and Matt shake their heads.

"There's a few stores near the highway that will have what you need. At a minimum, you should get a cooler with ice and a few food items, a tent, some sleeping bags, and a lighter."

Roy gives Kate and Matt the map, along with additional pamphlets about the park. He walks with them to Kate's car and holds the door open for her.

"You two have fun. Stop back if you need anything."

"Thank you," Kate says as Roy closes her car door.

"Certainly."

Kate pulls away from the Ranger's Station and waves good-bye to Roy.

"I haven't been camping since I was a kid," Matt tells her as he sorts through pamphlets.

"Me neither."

"It looks like our location is within walking distance to the public showers and bathrooms."

Kate hadn't thought about bathrooms. "Thank God. I would hate to get poison ivy squatting in the forest."

Matt laughs.

They spend the car ride making a list of items to buy at the store.

"Bug spray, don't forget bug spray," Kate says. "Oh, and pillows."

When they are near the highway, Matt points out a hotel. "We could stay there. Roy wouldn't know any different."

Kate considers this, but thinks better of it. "I'm sure he'll check in on us. No way he'll take our word for it. He's making us bring pictures of the locations because he doesn't trust us."

"You're probably right. Hey, you want to grab a bite to eat before we go shopping? It might be our last chance for a hot meal."

Twenty minutes later, they're sitting in a booth of a chain restaurant waiting on their food. Matt is reading over their shopping list in his phone to make sure they aren't forgetting something. Kate watches with amusement as Matt's mouth moves as he reads.

One of the many things I forgot about him, she thinks to herself. All those weird idiosyncrasies I immediately recognize as being a part of Matt that I stored away somewhere.

"I think we've covered everything," Matt says as he puts his phone down.

"If not, no big deal. The campsite isn't too far away."

The waitress sets down their drinks and tells them their food should be out shortly.

"You haven't said much about what you've been doing the last ten years," Matt says before taking a sip of his soda.

"What do you want to know?"

Matt shrugs. "Give me the summary in two minutes or less."

"Let's see...I moved to the Cleveland area and got my Master's Degree in Education. I was a professor at a law school up there for a few years, and now I'm back in Columbus."

Matt waits for her to say more, but she doesn't.

"Wow. You took all of twenty seconds."

Kate laughs. "I don't know what to say! How do you sum up ten years?"

Matt plays with his straw wrapper. "What's the game where one person gets to ask a set number of questions and the other person has to answer them?"

"You want to play twenty questions?" Kate asks with a grin. "Yeah, I guess we can do that. But you get five questions."

"Only five?" Matt protests. "It's been ten years! One question for every two years doesn't seem fair."

"It is what it is. Choose your questions wisely."

Matt's eyebrows furrow, deep in thought. After taking a sip of his drink, he asks, "Why didn't you marry the guy you were engaged to about seven years ago?"

Kate grimaces. Quinton is not a topic she likes discussing. "Anything else you want to ask?"

"There's all kinds of questions I want to ask you, but this is the one I asked first."

"Can I defer the question until later?"

"Sure. I'll make it the last question."

"Okay," Kate agrees wearily. At least she'll have time to formulate her answer.

"New first question, why didn't you tell Judge about Cora?"

This question brings up some bad memories too.

"Can't you ask me some lighter questions? Like my favorite TV show or something?"

Matt laughs. "Fine. What is your favorite TV show?"

"*Younger*," Kate answers before he can change his mind about the question.

"Don't know it."

"It's great!" Kate exclaims. "A woman in her forties pretends to be twenty-six. She gets to live her twenties all over again."

Matt's eyes gleam. "I'd love to live my twenties over again."

A strange feeling rises in Kate's stomach as she meets Matt's eyes. They'd been together when they were in their twenties. So full of life and energy, even after a sleepless night wrapped in each other's arms.

"Of course, I'd change a few things." Matt shifts his gaze and breaks the spell. "The food's here."

The waitress sets out their plates – a chef salad with grilled chicken for Kate and a chicken quesadilla for Matt.

As they both start digging into their food, Kate tries to put visions of the steamy nights she and Matt spent together out of her mind. Matt was the only man she'd never faked it with. Not once. He knew how to press her buttons. Kate shivers as she remembers a particular evening in Matt's office.

"Chilly?" Matt asks. "I have a sweatshirt in the car."

Kate shakes her head, praying she isn't blushing. "Um, no. I'm alright."

After a few bites, Matt moves on to his second question. "What's been your best vacation since the last time we saw each other, and who did you go with?"

Another easy one.

"Maui. By far. It's absolutely beautiful there. Scott and I went there for our second anniversary."

Remembering the trip makes Kate smile. The ocean was a surreal blue. No matter how far out you swam, you could see your feet. She squealed with joy when she saw sea turtles swimming five feet away from her. It was the ultimate vacation. Even if she had to diet for three months to fit into her red bikini.

"Hmmm, let me see, so many options," Matt strums his fingers against the table as he ponders his next question. "I'll give you one more easy one."

Kate waves her hand as if to say, "Proceed."

"Did Judge ever talk to you about me?"

Kate resists the urge to gulp. This isn't an easy one at all.

222

She tells the truth. "He tried."

Matt raises an eyebrow.

"And I told him to stop," Kate concludes. "I, uh, didn't want to hear about you."

Kate can say more, but she doesn't. Thankfully, Matt doesn't press her for more information.

"Well then, I guess that brings us back to why you didn't tell Judge about that night."

Kate considers a smartass response, but decides to give a straight answer. "I didn't want to ruin his relationship with you."

"What did you tell him?" Matt asks.

"Is that your fifth and final question?"

"No. It's subpart B to question four."

Kate smirks. "Damn lawyers. I should have stipulated no subparts allowed."

The waitress removes their plates and leaves the bill. Kate snatches it up and pulls money out of the stash Judge gave them.

"Well," Matt says, waiting on Kate's response.

"I told him it was none of his business."

Matt's eyes get big. "Did you really?"

"Yep."

"I bet he loved that!" Matt laughs.

"Oh, I'm pretty sure it was killing him."

Matt rubs his hands together. "Fifth and final question. Tell me about your first fiancé."

Kate sighs. "Quinton was a great guy. A good boyfriend. Smart, funny, and he helped me get my first teaching job at Case Western."

"And…"

223

"There were a lot of obstacles. In the end, I think it got to be too much."

"What kind of obstacles?"

"Well, to start, he was African American and I'm obviously not. You wouldn't think it would be such a big deal anymore, but it was. It was shocking."

"Really? That sucks. You see more and more interracial couples, I was hoping the walls were coming down."

Kate nods. "I know what you mean, but they're still there. My family didn't have an issue with it, but his did. Especially his mom."

"She didn't like you?"

"It had nothing to do with me in particular. Her philosophy is that strong African American males should marry an African American woman to better the community."

Matt shakes his head. "It's a shame she couldn't see how wonderful you are."

"I understand where she is coming from. I learned a lot about oppression and the continuing struggle to better the African American community. And a part of me felt guilty for taking such an amazing person away from that community."

"You would never try to keep him from his family and community."

"I know. I think he knew it too. But it was hard. It was like people were one of two extremes. Bending over backwards to tell us how okay they were with us being together, or glaring at us and telling us it was wrong. Either way, it was constantly in our face. We weren't Kate and Quinton, we were an interracial couple. Period."

"Is that why you broke it off?"

Kate thinks for a minute. She loved Quinton. When she was with Quinton, she saw a future with him. But she also saw how the tension with his family was breaking Quinton. His family was important to him. Still, it wasn't the straw that broke the camel's back.

"No. I think it contributed to the breakup, but it wasn't the only reason."

"Elaborate please," Matt says.

"I want kids. He doesn't. It's a deal breaker."

"Yeah, kids are a big deal."

"Do you like being a dad?" Kate asks, hoping to get the focus away from her love life.

Matt's eyes light up. "Love it! My kids are amazing. They keep me moving every day."

"Do you have any pictures?"

"Of course!" Matt pulls out his phone.

After searching for a minute, he turns his phone around to show Kate a picture of two dark-haired children sitting together on a picnic blanket.

Kate takes Matt's phone to get a closer look. The little girl, Carlie, has a big smile on her face that reaches her hazel eyes. Kate knows those eyes well, they're Matt's. The little boy, Noah, is sticking out his tongue and holding a half-eaten piece of watermelon. Like his sister, Noah has bright, hazel eyes.

They could be my children…

Kate has no idea where the thought came from, but it sucker punches her. She hands Matt his phone before he can notice her trembling hands.

Stop…stop…stop, she keeps telling herself.

But she can't get the thought out of her mind. If she and Matt had stayed together, if things hadn't gone to shit, she could very well be the mother of those two beautiful children.

Kate distantly hears Matt talking. "...and Noah is such a smart aleck. I have no idea where he gets it from. Kate?"

Kate blinks and shakes the crazy thoughts out of her head. She puts on a smile. "Sorry. I think I zoned out for a second."

"It's okay. I tend to go on and on about my kids."

"No, you're fine. I love hearing about your kids."

Matt checks his watch. "We better get a move on. We have a lot of shopping to do and we need to get a picture done tonight."

Kate slides out of the booth. "Speaking of pictures, we may want to buy a camera."

"Why? Roy said we can use our phones."

"True. But where are we going to charge our phones?"

Matt's groans. "Duh! I didn't even think of that."

Kate taps the side of her head. "Always thinking."

"I better call home today before we head to the campsite. I have to let Naomi know I will be in the middle of nowhere and may not be able to call for a couple of days."

They thank the hostess on the way out of the restaurant. The sun is high in the sky and the humidity makes the air sticky.

"I need to call Scott too. Otherwise, he'll send out a search party."

"My kids are going to be so jealous," Matt says as he gets in the passenger seat. "They've been asking me to take them camping."

"Why don't you?"

"Let me tell you a secret," Matt drops his voice to a whisper, "I hate camping."

Kate laughs. "Find your big boy pants Matt. It's going to be an exciting two days."

Chapter Twelve

Seven Years Ago

Matt hung up the phone and fell onto his couch.

Kate is getting married.

Matt didn't know what to do with the bombshell Judge just dropped on him.

"Now is the time Matthew," Judge urged. "Don't let her walk down the aisle without telling her how you feel about her. You'll regret it. I promise you."

Judge was right. He had to get in touch with Kate. He thought of no one but her for the past three years. Matt fantasized about begging for her forgiveness and sweeping Kate off of her feet every day.

Fear always held him back though. Kate might tell him to go fuck himself. Matt didn't think he could handle Kate's rejection again. Once had been enough. More than enough. It had been catastrophic.

Matt was embarrassed to admit he still held out hope he and Kate would get back together. He told himself time would numb Kate's anger and she would love him again. He was giving her space and letting things calm down.

Judge tried on a few occasions to push him along, but Matt didn't want to rush it. He was waiting for the right moment; some sign from the universe that it was the perfect time to make his move.

Judge mentioned Kate's new boyfriend in previous conversations, but Matt didn't worry about it. Let her have fun. Let her meet new guys. She'll see the love she had with Matt was something unique, something special.

Hell, Matt had even gone out with a few girls. But he never took it seriously. He was merely biding his time until he was ready to seek Kate out.

Now, he was in full panic mode. Kate was engaged!

What did this mean? Was this his sign from the universe to swoop in? Stop her before things got too far? Or did it mean he waited too long? Had he let the opportunity pass him by?

Matt sat on his couch with his head in his hands. He couldn't believe Kate said "yes" when this guy proposed. Kate had no issue turning down a proposal. Yet, she accepted this man's ring. Did she love him?

Matt debated whether to get up and pack. If he was going to fly back to Ohio and win Kate over, he couldn't wait another minute. But something Judge said kept him from getting off the couch.

Matt had asked a simple question, "Is she happy?"

There was a pause before Judge answered. "She seems to be."

Matt leaned back into his couch.

Kate is happy. I can't ruin it for her, he thought.

Matt was beside himself and could feel the tears welling in his eyes. And then, as fate would have it, his phone rang.

"Hello?" he answered without looking to see who it was.

"Matt? Is that you?"

Matt recognized the voice. It was Naomi, his girlfriend of about four months.

Matt liked Naomi, a lot. She was fun, witty and beautiful. The type of woman any man would be proud to bring home to mom. Her only flaw – she wasn't Kate.

Matt cleared his throat. "Yeah, it's me."

"You sound funny. Everything okay?"

Matt suddenly had the craziest idea he'd ever had in his life. Instead of stopping himself from making a huge mistake, his warped mind propelled him forward.

"I was thinking you and I should go to Vegas tonight."

"What?" Naomi sounded surprised.

"Yeah. You, me, Vegas, a drive thru wedding chapel…"

Naomi laughed. "Did you go out drinking after work again?"

"No, I'm stone cold sober. What do you think?"

"Are you serious?" The laughter was gone from Naomi's voice.

"Absolutely."

"You're asking me to marry you? Tonight?"

"I suppose I am."

"Oh my God Matt!" Naomi squealed into the phone. "You know I'm head over heels for you! If you're serious, I'll start packing."

"Get out your suitcase. I'll be at your place in half an hour."

Matt hung up the phone before he could change his mind.

What the hell are you doing?! You've lost it, the rational part of his brain yelled.

Matt responded out loud, "I'm moving on."

Three months later, Matt found out Kate called off the wedding. By that time, he was married and Naomi was six weeks pregnant.

Chapter Thirteen

Now

"We'll be in separate tents," Kate explains to a distraught Scott.

"This is getting borderline insane Kate."

Kate has never heard Scott like this. He's usually easy going and relaxed. He's flat out flustered and Kate doesn't know how to handle it.

"I know Scott. I promise you, you have nothing to worry about."

Scott sighs. "I probably sound like a lunatic."

"No, you don't. I would say the exact same thing if the situation were reversed."

Silence fills the line.

"What can I do to make this better?" Kate asks.

"Nothing. I can't tell you to come home because your family will kill me. I can't start off on the wrong foot with them."

Kate leans up against her car. She's in the parking lot of a Walmart. Matt is fifty feet away consoling his own partner.

"If you want me to stop this, I will. Right now. You're more important to me than any potential inheritance. My family can wait."

"As much as I'd love to have you on the other side of the bed tonight, I won't ask you to do that. I'm sorry for being paranoid. If you were up to something, you wouldn't tell me what was going on. You'd lie and say you're in Hocking Hills and he's in Saskatchewan."

Kate laughs, relieved to hear Scott crack a joke. "Separate tents. On opposite sides of the fire. Deal?"

231

"Deal," Scott agrees. "Make a s'more for me."

"Will do baby. I love you."

"Love you too."

Kate ends the call and glances over her shoulder at Matt. He's standing with his cell phone up to his ear and his free hand wedged in his hair. From the look on his face, things aren't going well.

While she waits, Kate goes through their receipt once more to make sure they have everything they need. Her car is filled with camping equipment. They bought two of almost every item in the sporting goods section.

Satisfied with their purchases, Kate gets in her car. Bored, she calls Theresa.

"Camping? Yuck," is T's reaction.

"Agreed."

"Are you staying in a cabin?"

"Nope. In a tent, in the middle of the woods."

"Oh, hell no!" Theresa exclaims. "You couldn't pay my ass to do that shit."

"You should join us."

"And be the third wheel on your lovers' getaway? No thanks."

"It's not like that T!" Kate protests.

"Sure. Whatever. How are you two getting along?"

"Fine. We've had a few conversations and I think I've finally forgiven him."

"Well, I'll be damned! It only took you ten years and about three years of therapy in the interim."

"Two years of therapy, thank you very much," Kate says.

"My bad. Two years."

"I feel like a weight has been lifted off my chest."

"Uh-oh."

"What?" Kate asks. "What uh-oh?"

"I know I've teased you endlessly about this, but don't get caught up in the moment." T sounds uneasy.

"Don't be ridiculous T."

"I mean it Kate."

Kate is surprised by the sudden turn in Theresa's tone. "I'm not going to get myself in any trouble. I've forgiven Matt, but I'm not sharing a sleeping bag with him anytime soon."

"Do what you want Kate. You'll get no judgment from me. I've slept with married men. But I know how you are."

Kate huffs. "And how am I?"

"You can't handle an affair. You're not made for it. You'll feel guilty about it the rest of your life."

"I'm not having an affair."

"Yet," Theresa notes.

Kate leans her head against the driver side window. "I'm not having an affair," she repeats.

"Good. Let that be your mantra for the next couple of days. Being alone in the woods with a man you used to be in love with, and who you admit is great in bed, is a recipe for disaster. For you anyway. For me it would be a porno in the making."

Kate rolls her eyes, but chuckles. "I love you T. You're messed up, but I love you."

"I love you too bestie. Whatever happens, I want details." A second later, Theresa amends her statement. "I take that back. If nothing happens, I don't want details."

Kate ends the call with Theresa and is a little annoyed to see Matt is still on the phone. She wants to set up camp as soon as possible so they can get at least one location out of the way. Plus, she's wasting gas sitting here with the AC on.

233

She scrolls through the radio stations and stops on a Mumford and Sons song. She recognizes it immediately as "I Will Wait." Kate turns it up, she loves this song.

Kate is singing along when she's struck by the lyrics. A man pouring his heart out, telling a woman that he loves her so much, he'll wait for her. She steals a glance at Matt, who is approaching the car. He has a wry smile on his face. She knows the look well.

For a moment, all the love she once felt for him comes flooding back. The crazy, overwhelming, breath stealing love that crippled her when it came to an end.

Theresa's joke about therapy was based on truth. Kate went to therapy sessions to deal with the pain of losing Matt. Endless discussions dissecting the ins and outs of the relationship. The therapist giving her advice about how to deal with the breakup and different coping mechanisms.

The real reason she didn't marry Quincy? She'd be officially off the market if she got married. She'd be sealing the deal. A crazy part of her wanted Matt to seek her out and beg for forgiveness. Tell her he couldn't live without her.

But he never showed up.

Kate realized almost too late that she didn't love Quincy at all. She loved the idea of him. A good man with attributes similar to Matt, but not the real deal.

After her breakup with Quincy, she came to terms with the fact that she needed to move on. She went to more counseling sessions, ones she didn't tell Theresa about. Her therapist told Kate how to put Matt behind her and how to invest in another relationship.

Then she met Scott. Wonderful, amazing and loveable Scott. She loves him. Everything about him. Scott made her forget about Matt. Which is why she agreed to marry him. If Scott could make Matt ancient history, then he was the one. Matt was no longer the standard because he didn't exist to her anymore.

Until he showed up in her office.

Matt opens the car door and shuts it behind him. Without saying a word, he puts on his seatbelt.

Kate shifts out of park and reverses out of her parking spot. "Your talk went as well as mine, huh?"

Matt groans. "It wasn't pretty."

"Scott wasn't too happy either."

"I don't blame them. Really, I don't. I wouldn't like Naomi camping in the wilderness with an ex."

"I thought she didn't know about me."

Matt smiles. "She doesn't. I can't imagine what she would do if she did."

Kate stops at a traffic light. "Not to be conceited or anything, but why didn't you tell her about me? Wasn't there a conversation about former lovers before you tied the knot?"

"No. We got married on a whim."

This surprises Kate. Matt could be impulsive, but she never imagined he'd rush into marriage.

"How long were you together before you got hitched?"

"Four months."

"Oh," Kate says simply. "No big wedding then?"

Matt shakes his head. "We went to Vegas with a group of friends and got married in a small chapel on the strip."

"Sounds fun."

"It was fine, but it was..." Matt stops himself.

"What? It was what?"

He shakes his head. "Nothing."

Kate's curious about what Matt isn't saying, but she doesn't push him. "I considered a destination wedding. I wanted to go somewhere in the Caribbean, or maybe Hawaii again."

"Why don't you do it?"

"I want the fairy tale," Kate admits. She blushes as Matt stares at her. "What?"

"I didn't peg you for the Cinderella type. That's all."

"No one is more shocked than me. I told my mom no frills, nothing fancy. But when we started looking at the invitations and wedding dresses, it hit me. I want a big, obnoxious wedding that I'll spend way too much money on."

Matt asks her about every detail of the wedding, from the cake flavor to the music selection. Kate gets caught up in the conversation and they are pulling into the parking area for their campsite in no time.

"We're here," Kate announces as she takes a spot near the edge of the woods. She's about to get out of the car when Matt stops her.

"Do you have a picture of yourself in your wedding dress?"

Kate is stupefied by Matt's question. Why does he want to see her wedding dress?

Getting herself together she replies, "Sure. I have some in my phone. Judge was too sick to go dress shopping with me."

She wonders what Matt looked like on his wedding day. If he wore a suit, or if he was casual. She doesn't ask because a part of her doesn't want to know. She doesn't want to hear him talk about how great the day was.

She rummages through her bag and pulls her phone out. She searches through the pictures while Matt waits.

"Here you go," she hands Matt the phone. "There are several, but I'm sure you don't want to look at all of them."

236

Matt stares at the picture of Kate. She's standing on a short platform with her back to three mirrors, wearing the dress she will get married in. The lace top is sleeveless with a sweetheart neckline that shows off her décolletage. The dress fits close to her body until mid-thigh, where it begins to flare out. The shop owner told Kate it was a "fit and flare." Kate didn't care what the dress was called, she loved it.

Her hair is pulled back in a sloppy bun on top of her head and she's laughing. When Kate's mom took the picture, Theresa had just walked out of the fitting room in the most hideous dress Kate had ever seen.

Matt scrolls to the next picture and studies it. In this one, Kate has a more serious look on her face. Matt scrolls to the next photo of the shop owner pinning a veil in Kate's hair. The next picture is Kate facing the camera wearing her full wedding attire.

Matt stares at this one the longest. He is lost in another world. After a moment, he turns his head away as he hands Kate her phone back.

"Very good choice. Scott will love it."

"Thank you," Kate says before putting her phone back in the bag.

"Well, we better get moving," Matt responds as he opens the car door.

Kate sits in her seat a little longer. She stares out the windshield at the tree line.

What was he thinking about, she wonders. Was he imagining being on the opposite end of the aisle when the church doors open? Does he think about how I could be walking toward him if we hadn't messed things up?

"You coming?" Matt asks as he pulls items out of the backseat.

Kate blinks her eyes. "Yep."

For the next several minutes, they try to figure out how they are going to get everything they bought to the campsite.

"Here, throw the small items into the cooler, and then we'll each carry an end," Matt suggests.

They squish what they can in the cooler and the rest in the packs they bought.

"How far away is the site?" Kate asks.

"About half a mile."

"Let's get what we can now and come back for our sleeping bags. There's no way we'll be able to carry all of this stuff in one trip."

Matt moves things around for a few more minutes before giving up. "You're right. We'll have to make two trips."

"You know what we should do," Kate says, "we'll get our tents set up, then come back and drive to the furthest location for our sunset picture. Make it worth the walk back."

"Good idea."

The pair start walking down the dirt trail juggling the cooler between them. It's filled to the brim with ice and camping equipment. Kate's hand hurts after a few minutes. She and Matt switch sides to give her left hand a break.

The trail is relatively flat and the brush on both sides has been cut back recently. As they get further into the woods, the summer sun gets lost in the leaves above them. Kate welcomes the cooler temperature.

"Hopefully there is a good spot for us to put our tents," Matt says.

"I'm sure there will be. Roy knows we're novices."

Matt isn't as sure. "If Roy is anything like Judge, he put us in the worst spot possible. Our tents will have to balance on tree limbs."

"We can always make a trip into town for a saw," Kate jokes.

Luckily, there is a clearing up ahead.

"This has to be it," Matt says as they set down the cooler. He takes the map out of his back pocket. "Yep, we're here."

"How can you tell?"

"There's only one clearing on the map."

Kate is relieved to see there is plenty of space for two tents and a fire. They unload their equipment and decide how they want to place everything. Kate brings her tent over to her designated area and unzips the bag it came in. How a tent fits in a bag the size of a baseball bat is beyond Kate's comprehension.

A few yards away, Matt opens his own tent. "Wanna race?"

Kate snickers. "Men. You're so competitive."

"This is going to suck. A friendly competition may make it more interesting."

"Fine. Don't cry when I'm done first."

Matt puffs out his chest. "I am man. I better than woman," he says in a caveman voice.

Kate giggles, then gets to work. She reads the instructions thoroughly to get an idea of what she'll be doing. Next, she lays out all the pieces in the order she'll need them.

"You going to start sometime today?" Matt calls from behind her.

Kate glances over her shoulder and sees Matt has begun construction. "Stop worrying about what I'm doing and worry about your own tent."

She could tell Matt he put pole "E" where pole "B" should go, but what would be the fun in that?

Kate reads over the first few steps again before getting to work. Her back is to Matt, so she has no idea how he's progressing. She focuses on her project and is in the zone.

There are a few times a pole doesn't want to cooperate with her, but she keeps her cool in front of Matt. She doesn't want to give him anything to use against her. Every now and then, Kate hears Matt mumbling obscenities to himself, which makes her smile.

Kate has her tent completely built thirty minutes later and is ready to put down the spikes.

"Did we bring the hammer?" she asks before turning around for the first time. She bites her lip to stifle her laughter.

Matt is standing with his hands on his hips staring at his half constructed tent. It looks like a deranged beetle laying on its back; poles sticking out at odd angles.

Kate walks over to stand beside him. "Need some help?"

Matt hangs his head. "Yes."

"What was it you were saying earlier about men being better than women?"

"Yours was easier than mine."

"They are exactly the same!"

Matt narrows his eyes. "Sure they are."

With Kate's assistance, Matt's tent is done within fifteen minutes. They hammer the spikes in for their tents, then step back to admire their work. After unloading the rest of their supplies, they walk back to the parking lot.

"Which spot is the furthest away?" Kate asks when they get to the car.

Matt pulls out the map and lays it on the hood. "This one. But there's a notation that it's a tricky hike. We may not want to do it at night. It will be dark as hell."

Kate nods. "You're right. I'm clumsy enough as it is." Kate looks over the map. "How about this one?" Kate asks as she points to another location.

"Works for me."

"You know what," Kate says as she looks at her watch, "we may have time for two spots. There's one just up the road."

Matt picks up the map and starts folding. "Let's do this."

*   *   *

"This sucks," Kate mutters under her breath as she tries not to fall over.

It's dark and Kate can hardly see where she's going. The beam of light from her flashlight dances across the path as she and Matt make their way back to the campsite.

They went to two locations and got their first sunset photograph. Two down, eight to go. The first location was a beautiful pond surrounded by cattails on its edges. Small fish swam along the shoreline hoping tourists would throw them a crumb or two.

Their sunset location was a peak overlooking the forest. It was beautiful, but it will be breathtaking in the fall. There weren't many people there, but the number of parking spaces indicated it is a popular location once the leaves start painting the tree line.

"We're almost there," Matt says from behind her.

"Are you sure?"

"We have to be close. We've been walking for a while now."

Kate shifts the box in her hand. She insisted on buying herself a battery powered air mattress, but questions the decision now. The box is heavy and cutting into her arms.

"I hope so. I may have to ditch this," Kate says as she shifts the weight of the box to her left arm.

Matt catches up to her. "Give it to me. I'll take it."

Kate accepts Matt's offer and hands Matt the box. Her arms scream with relief as she shakes them out. "Thanks."

"No problem," Matt says as he walks on in front of her.

241

A few minutes later, they make it to the campsite. Kate sets up the starter logs for a fire while Matt finds some downed tree limbs. Between the starter logs and a lighter, they have a fire in minutes.

Kate sits on her rolled up sleeping bag and admires the flames. The branches and twigs crackle as they succumb to the heat. Pieces of charred leaves blow up into the air, then disintegrate before her eyes.

"Want a hot dog?" Matt asks from behind her.

"Sure, I'm starving."

Using the skewers they bought at the store, Kate holds her hot dog over the fire and watches the skin slowly turn from light tan to a leathery brown.

"You like yours well done I see."

Kate nods. "Yep. I like them burnt beyond recognition. Gives me a false sense of hope that whatever crap they put in here has been burned off."

Matt laughs. "I don't think anything will kill what they put in a hot dog."

The two enjoy their makeshift dinner as the crickets chirp and the stars gleam overhead.

"It is nice out here," Matt observes. "You don't see stars like this in a city."

"No, you don't." Kate stands up and brushes off her shorts. "I'm going to set up my bed. I'm tired."

"Me too."

Kate heads to her tent and lays out the air mattress. She cringes when she turns on the motor for the air pump. It sounds like an airplane is taking off.

"I think you've scared off any woodland critters," Matt jokes.

"At least we won't have to worry about wolf attacks."

Matt squints toward the dark tree line. "Are there wolves out here?"

Kate shrugs. "Not anymore."

"Do you want to walk back to the public bathrooms?" Matt asks her. "I can use a tree, but I'll walk over there with you if you want the company."

"Thank you. I was terrified of walking there by myself. I've seen too many horror movies."

As they make their way to the bathrooms, leaves and twigs crack under their feet. There is a faint rustling in the brush next to them and Matt stops.

"What was that?" Matt asks.

Kate's heart is pounding. "I don't know. Let's keep moving."

They pick up their pace, but whatever is in the brush stays with them. The branches move and shake as their stalker walks parallel to them. Matt stops again and shines his light in the direction of their company.

Kate is terrified. She stands behind Matt with her body pressed against his. She hides her head between his shoulder blades, but peers over his shoulder when Matt yells, "Get out of here!"

They pause for a moment to listen for movement. When there is none, they start walking again. Kate stays close to Matt.

"Do I make a good human body shield?" Matt asks her.

"We'll find out."

Matt laughs. "You know what they say, you only have to outrun one person."

"I'm not above tripping you."

Kate is trying to stay lighthearted, but she's scared. If an animal attacks them, there is no one around to help. She was teasing Matt about the wolves earlier, but for all she knows, they live in these woods.

"There," Matt points, "you see the lights?"

Kate looks and sees two small, white orbs of light. "Thank God!"

She picks up her pace, grateful to see the bathrooms. But as she does, the rustling in the brush starts up again.

Matt walks faster alongside her. "We're so close. Whatever this thing is, it won't want to step out into the lights."

"How do you know?" Kate asks, winded from their pace.

Matt glances her way. "I don't. Worst case scenario, lock yourself in the bathroom."

"If I make it to the bathroom…"

They're within yards of the bathing facilities, but whatever is chasing them hasn't relented.

"I'm running for it," she yells to Matt before sprinting toward the bathroom.

Matt follows suit. Kate can hear the rapid beat of her heart in her ears. It reverberates through her entire body.

You're almost there, you're almost there, she repeats to herself.

Matt's feet pound the ground beside her. His breath is quick and steady. When her feet hit the gravel surrounding the bathing facilities, she's thrown off balance. Matt reaches out his hand and steadies her.

Her temporary stumble affords her the chance to look behind her. What she sees freezes her in place. Their pursuer has made an appearance. Matt skids to a halt beside her.

"What are you…" Matt stops midsentence when he sees what Kate is staring at. "For the love…"

Kate bursts out laughing.

244

"A raccoon, really?" Matt says in disbelief.

A large, black and grey raccoon with small, beady eyes gazes back at them. It stares them down for a minute, then saunters over to the trash can outside the bathrooms. It climbs up the side of the bin, gives them one last glance, and then disappears through the swinging lid.

Kate puts her hand over her heart. "That scared the hell out of me!" she exclaims between laughs.

"No shit!" Matt says. "I was sure Sasquatch was chasing us down."

No longer concerned about being ambushed, Kate turns toward the building behind them. It is made of dirty, white cinderblocks with cracks scattered throughout. Wood beams bolted to the top row of blocks hold up a flimsy metal roof. Moths and bugs swarm the yellow lights atop the poles on either side of the building.

"These bathrooms are creepy," Kate says with a frown.

Matt isn't impressed either. "Smell awful too."

"Wish me luck," Kate tells Matt before walking through the heavy, brown metal door marked with a "Women's Bath House" sign.

The inside of the bathroom makes Kate's unease worse. Cobwebs fill the corners and the faucets are rusted out. Streaks of brown run down the sides of the once white sinks. More moths fly around the exposed light bulbs and a foul stench fills the air.

Kate hesitantly pulls open one of the wooden doors for a stall, afraid of what she might find. She recoils. The toilet seat is off kilter and chunks of the plastic are missing. The water is pale yellow and flies take turns landing on the metal piping coming out of the wall. Kate wishes she had antibacterial wipes with her, but two layers of toilet paper will have to do.

"You okay in there?" Matt yells from outside.

"No!"

Kate hears Matt chuckle, then the crunch of gravel as he steps away from the building.

Men have it so easy, she thinks as she compels her body to go to the bathroom as quickly as possible.

"I may have been better off with the tree," she tells Matt when she walks outside.

"The showers in the men's bathroom are terrifying. You know how they told us to wear flip-flops in the shower at college? I think I'm going to need steel-toed boots for this place."

"I didn't even look at the shower stalls," Kate says. "I'm sure they'll be awful too."

The walk back to their campsite is uneventful. The fire is still going, but the flames have calmed.

"Do you want any marshmallows?" Matt asks as he picks up the bag from their pile of food.

"No thanks. I'm tired."

"Alright," Matt says as he sits down. "I'll see you in the morning."

Kate unzips her tent and throws her sleeping bag inside. Her full-size air mattress takes up nearly every inch of her tent and she struggles to get herself undressed. Once she's in her pajama shorts and t-shirt, Kate opens her sleeping bag so it is a blanket instead of a cocoon. She takes the plastic wrapper off her new pillow and lays down.

Kate listens to the crackling of the fire and the sounds of nature. Being out in the woods scares her a bit, but she's comforted knowing Matt is right outside her tent. He'll wake her if something happens. She drifts off to sleep within a few minutes, her mind and body exhausted from the day.

An odd sound wakes Kate a while later. Kate doesn't know how long she's been asleep, but it seems too soon for Matt to be waking her up to get a sunrise picture. When the noise continues, there's no mistaking it's the zipper on her tent.

Kate leans up on her elbows and screams when she sees a dark figure hovering near the opening of her tent.

"Shh! It's just me."

Kate relaxes for a second when she realizes it's Matt.

Wait...Matt?

"What are you doing?" she asks, her blood rushing through her body.

"I'm getting in your bed. I can't lay on the hard ground anymore. I'm too old for that shit."

"What?! No!" Kate protests. "You can't sleep in here!"

Matt sighs. "Don't worry. I'm not going to feel you up or anything. My back is kinked and if I don't sleep in here, I won't be able to walk in the morning."

Kate shifts to one side of the bed as Matt crawls in her tent. He zips it shut, then lays down underneath his own sleeping bag. Kate feels uneasy, but she doesn't know what to do. Should she leave and sleep in his tent?

Forget that, a voice inside her mind says. Do you want to sleep on the ground? This is your bed, and you're sleeping in it.

"We'll go to the store tomorrow and get you an air mattress," Kate tells Matt as she stays as far away from him as possible, the side of her body pressed against the canvas of the tent.

"Sounds good," Matt says with a yawn.

Kate rolls to her side with her back to Matt. "Never speak a word of this to anyone."

She doesn't get a response. Matt is already asleep.

*   *   *

Kate groans when her battery powered alarm clock goes off at 5:00 a.m. She curses as she struggles to find the silly thing. She locates it wedged between the foot of the bed and the tent. She flops backward onto the air mattress and creates a wave that lifts Matt up in the air an inch or two.

"Good Lord woman! Calm down over there." Matt sits up and stretches his arms. His white t-shirt is wrinkled and his hair is askew.

It's been a long time since Kate laid eyes on Matt first thing in the morning. He looks so damn cute with bedhead and sleep in his eyes.

"It's my bed. I can do as I please," Kate retorts. She has her sleeping bag pulled up to her chin.

"Thanks for having pity on me," Matt says as he gathers up his sleeping bag. "I was going to walk back to the car if you refused to share."

Matt crawls to the door and unzips the opening.

"I'm walking to the bathrooms," Kate tells him. "I need a quick shower, and then I'll be ready."

"Same here. I'll go get my stuff."

Kate throws off her blanket when Matt is gone. She lets out a breath, relieved they are no longer sharing confined quarters. Scott would die if he found out Matt shared a tent with her last night.

He'll never know, Kate thinks to herself as she slips on her sneakers. And there's no point in telling him. Matt stayed on his side of the tent, and I stayed on mine. If I tell Scott we shared an air mattress, he'll never believe nothing happened.

After she grabs her travel bag, she joins Matt by their extinguished fire.

"You ready?" he asks her.

Kate nods her head in response.

It's still dark on the path, but the horizon is showing a sliver of light. Kate quickens her step.

"We need to get a move on or we'll miss the sunrise."

"We'll be fine," Matt assures her. "Roy didn't say the picture has to be taken at the first sign of the sun."

Kate hustles into the ladies' room and ignores her natural instinct to cringe as she shuffles past the toilets toward the showers. When she reaches the showers, she grins. They look brand new. A silver plaque on the wall reads, "Renovations possible by the generosity of the Women of Hocking Hills Society." Evidently, the women of Hocking Hills wanted clean showers.

Too bad they didn't pony up the dough for new toilets when renovations were underway, Kate muses.

Kate starts the water and sighs when the warmth covers her skin. She allows herself a moment to rejuvenate, but then gets her butt in gear. She has a limited amount of time to clean up.

Kate washes her hair at a frenzied pace and soaps up her body while the conditioner sets in. She grabs her razor and starts to put it down after she shaves under her arms. But something stops her. Kate feels compelled to shave her legs. She shaved them yesterday, but they have a hint of stubble.

Why bother? You don't have the time, she thinks.

The devil on her left shoulder speaks up – you don't want Matt seeing any stubble. Do you?

Kate has a thirty second internal debate before she lathers up her legs.

Just a quick shave, she tells herself.

Kate dries off as best she can before getting dressed. She hates the way her clothes cling to her damp body in places, but she has to go with it. She rolls her wet hair up into a big clip. She takes a

249

peek at herself in the mirror above the sinks, but her reflection is muddled in the dingy, cracked glass.

"Oh well," she mumbles. "It is what it is."

When she walks outside, Matt is waiting for her. His hair is wet, but combed into its usual style. He's in khaki cargo shorts and a navy blue t-shirt.

"Ready?"

"Yep," she replies. She glances over at the horizon and sees fresh yellow and pink hues spreading across the Eastern sky. "The location is only five minutes away, right?"

"Yes, ma'am. We'll make it."

The walk to the car takes about ten minutes. After putting their bags in the trunk, Kate jumps in the driver seat and starts the car. Matt barely has his door shut when Kate backs out of the spot.

"Whoa there speed racer!"

Kate grins. "Better put your seatbelt on."

There is a huge parking lot for their first location of the day. Several of the spaces are full. A couple of people walk by with professional grade cameras and tripods.

"This must be a popular spot," Matt observes.

Kate sees a sign reading, "Old Man's Cave." The name rings a bell.

"Judge talked about this place a lot. He loved it."

Once out of the car, Kate and Matt follow the small crowd of people. Soon, they reach the cusp of the cave.

"Wow," Matt says with awe in his eyes.

That's an understatement. Standing at the top of the trailhead, Kate looks down into the natural rock formation. Kate was expecting a dark and dank cave. But this looks like someone took a giant knife, cut into the ground, and exposed everything that was once hidden.

"Pictures don't do this place justice," Kate tells Matt before they start their descent into the basin.

The natural dirt path takes them by jagged rock formations and trees that have managed to take root and thrive. The voices of the people around them echo off the rock walls.

The pair stand at the bottom of the trail near a waterfall. Because it's a bit chilly, Kate huddles close to Matt as they wait for the sun to make a full appearance. Around them, other would-be photographers position their cameras. Everyone is silent as they wait for Mother Nature to put on a show.

As the sun appears over the top of the rock ledge, Kate hears the rapid fire click of the cameras. Matt is holding their newly purchased camera and takes a few pictures.

"Got it," he tells Kate in a hushed voice.

They move away from the waterfall to allow others to have a chance to witness the spectacular view. When they're far enough away from the group to talk comfortably, Matt pulls the map out of his back pocket.

"The trail is a loop about three miles long. If we take the trail, we'll pass two more locations and end back here. I say we walk it."

Kate takes the map from Matt and looks it over. "We might as well. Driving to each of the spots would take as long as walking the trail will."

Matt nods. "Agreed."

They start down the trail. They don't talk much as they stroll along. There's no need for conversation, nature is doing all the talking. Occasionally, as they make room for other hikers, their hands will brush against each other. Kate is on high alert when this happens.

At one point, Matt puts his hand on the small of Kate's back to gently move her out of the way of a couple coming up quickly behind them. Kate's entire body warms. She turns to look at Matt, but he is smiling and greeting the couple walking passed them. As soon as the couple passes, Matt continues along the trail as if nothing odd happened.

A simple pat on the back and I'm on fire, Kate thinks as she follows behind him. I really need to get it together.

The second and third locations are pretty, but not as stunning as Old Man's Cave. Matt takes a few pictures of each spot, then they continue on. They finish the trail and walk back to Kate's car.

"I'm starving," Matt says as they buckle up.

"Me too."

Matt reaches into his backpack. "After you went to bed last night, I made peanut butter sandwiches for us. Want one?"

"Look at you!" Kate says with a smile. "I didn't know I was camping with June Cleaver."

Matt laughs. "I figured we would have a quick lunch, and then go into town for dinner later."

"Sounds good to me," Kate replies as she pulls out of her parking spot. "We need to go to town to get you an air mattress anyway."

"Oh yeah, I forgot about that."

I haven't, Kate thinks to herself.

Nor has she forgotten the comfort she felt in her bones last night sleeping next to Matt. A comfort she hasn't felt in years. Ten years to be exact.

Chapter Fourteen

Now

"Fifth stop of the day," Kate announces as they park in a small parking area for Rock Bridge. "If we get done with this one quick enough, we may have time for two more locations.

Matt looks at the clock on Kate's console. It's four o'clock.

"This trail is listed as one of the more rigorous trails Kate. It says to allot at least two hours to complete it."

Kate shrugs. "We'll be done by six. We can squeeze another one in before the sunset photo. The sun doesn't go down until after eight."

Matt nods his head in agreement, although he wouldn't mind dragging this out. After Hocking Hills, they only have one more stop on Judge's crazy scavenger hunt. Soon his time with Kate will be at an end.

Matt has Kate all to himself, and he wants it to stay that way for as long as possible. Matt misses his wife and children, but his longing for Kate has taken over.

The wall Kate put up between them has come down. He is seeing the real Kate again. Not the "I hate Matt more than life" Kate; the Kate he fell in love with years ago. There are times when they are talking that he forgets ten years has passed. It's like they've never skipped a beat.

Being in the middle of nowhere with her only intensifies the feeling. Everyone they know is far away. No one is interfering with their time together. They are in a bubble of sorts, and he doesn't want to pop it.

He is wracked with guilt. He doesn't want to feel this way. Matt wishes he could see Kate as a friend, not his former lover. But he can't help it. He knows it's wrong, but he can't stop it.

253

You know how to stop it, Matt thinks as he watches Kate put on a backpack filled with Clif bars and water bottles. You stop flirting with her. You stop thinking about how good that kiss felt after skydiving. The least you can do is stop making excuses to share a bed with her.

It was amazing lying next to Kate last night. Their bodies weren't touching, but knowing Kate was there was satisfying enough. He just wanted to be close to her. He has a burning compulsion to be near Kate that he can't quiet.

"This doesn't seem so bad," Kate says when they are five minutes into the trail. "It's relatively flat."

"It will get worse, trust me."

"Such a party pooper."

Matt snickers. "I'm warning you, that's all. I saw the elevation changes on this trail. Trust me when I say it will not be flat the entire time."

"Where is everyone?" Kate asks a few minutes later. "We haven't seen a single person since we got here."

Matt noticed this too. At all of the other locations they've visited, there were groups of people with them. Not huge crowds, but at least a handful of other tourists.

"I don't know. Maybe the trail's difficulty rating scared them off."

Kate looks over her shoulder at him. A wisp of hair has come free from her hair clip and it blows across her face. "This isn't any harder than the other trails we've done."

Matt smirks. "Okay Bear Grylls. Tell me how you feel about it when we're done."

A few minutes later, they walk up to a steep hill leading into the woods. The path is riddled with exposed tree roots. Matt has to watch every step he takes. Kate has slowed significantly and is no longer running her mouth.

"How are you doing?" he asks when he sees sweat beading near her hairline.

"Fine," she answers.

"Do you want to take a break?"

Kate shakes her head. "No, I'm good."

The trail flattens out for a few yards and Matt stops to get a water bottle out of his backpack. He looks around and realizes they are completely surrounded by trees. There's no way he's walking off the trail. If he did, he would get lost and never find his way back out.

Kate is also scanning their surroundings. "Kind of freaky out here, isn't it?"

"Yes. This is *Deliverance* shit out here. Crazy locals could kidnap us and no one would ever know."

Matt sees Kate shiver. "Don't say that!"

"We're fine. People walk this trail every day. Roy wouldn't send us out here if it was dangerous," he says to comfort her.

Kate relaxes. "You're right. Roy knows this area like the back of his hand. If he thinks we can do it, we can."

They take another break fifteen minutes later. Matt is sweating and worries he smells disgusting. Kate, on the other hand, makes walking in the heat look glamorous. Her face is glistening and her clothes hug her body in all the right places.

"You weren't kidding Matt. This trail sucks."

He smiles, but doesn't say, "I told you so." He knows all too well Kate hates being taunted.

After more treacherous terrain and a few more breaks, they begin the descent to the Rock Bridge. Going down is easier than walking up the inclines, but it's scarier. Matt's shoes slide on the dirt trail and he is on high alert in case he stumbles.

255

Matt, who is behind Kate, sees her struggling to maintain her balance.

"You alright?" he asks her a few times.

"I think this would be easier if I sat on my butt and slid down."

Matt can't argue with her.

Their hard work is worth it when they reach Rock Bridge.

"Wow!" Kate says as she looks across the rock formation. "It is literally a rock bridge."

Matt laughs. "What did you think it would be?"

"I don't know, but not this."

The bridge is approximately ten feet wide and about a hundred feet across. It connects the hillside Matt and Kate are standing on to another hillside across a large ravine. At the center, it is probably thirty feet high. A fall from the bridge could mean a broken leg, or much worse, depending on what you land on.

"It's hard to believe this is a natural formation and not man-made." Matt takes a few steps out onto the bridge. He turns back to Kate. "You coming?"

She shakes her head vigorously. "I don't think so."

Matt walks back toward her and extends his hand. "I won't let you fall."

Kate hesitates, but then takes his hand. His heart skips a beat as her fingers entwine with his. It feels good to have Kate's trust again.

"We'll go slowly," he tells Kate as he takes the first step.

"Okay," she responds in a hushed voice.

Kate squeezes his hand and stays right next to him. He loves having her so close. They creep across the bridge and Matt pauses in the middle.

"What are you doing?" Kate asks with wide eyes. "Why are you stopping?"

Matt uses his free hand to take the camera out of the pocket of his cargo shorts. "We need to get a picture of this place. What better spot is there?"

Kate wraps her arms around his waist and bear hugs him as he lets go of her hand to take a picture.

Matt chuckles. "You jumped out of a plane a few days ago. This should be easy."

"I had a parachute on when I jumped out of the plane," Kate mumbles into his shirt.

As much as he enjoys being Kate's human teddy bear, Matt puts the camera away and takes her hand. "Come on, let's go."

They cross to the other side and Kate sits on the hillside. "Oh, thank God! Solid ground."

Matt sits beside her. "Can I steal one of the Clif bars out of your bag?"

"Sure." Kate takes her backpack off and hands it to Matt.

Matt rummages through the choices and decides on the chocolate chip flavor. "Want one?" he asks Kate.

"Yeah, I better. It's a long walk back."

They sit on the hillside and take in the view of the bridge. Matt has seen some spectacular places in his life, but the Rock Bridge is truly impressive.

"Are you up for walking across it again? We can go back a different way, but it will take longer."

Kate groans. "I don't want to go back across, but I don't want to go the new route either. At least I know what I'm in for if we go back the way we came. Who knows what the other trail is like."

"You prefer the devil you know."

"Exactly."

Matt doesn't argue. He looks forward to holding Kate's hand again. The pair sit quietly for a few minutes as they eat their snack and finish off their bottles of water.

Out of nowhere, Kate asks, "Have you ever wondered what life would be like for us?"

He doesn't know what to say. Of course he has. Every day. But does he want to admit it?

When he doesn't answer right away, Kate starts talking again. "I used to tell myself we never would have made it. Brushed it off by thinking we would have broken up anyway. But I think I told myself that because I was so hurt. You know what I mean?"

Matt finds his voice. "Yes, I know what you mean."

Kate is looking out over Rock Bridge. "We were really good, weren't we?"

Matt watches her as he says, "We were great."

Kate flushes and glances over at him. "Can I confess something to you?"

"Of course," Matt says, his heart in a frenzy.

"I've never loved anyone the way I loved you Matt. I don't think I ever will." Kate holds his eyes.

Matt's mind whirls as he gazes back at her. He always questioned how she felt. Theresa said Kate loved him, but Kate never said the words herself. To hear Kate say she loved him back then is almost as great as if she said she loves him now.

Without thinking, Matt leans forward and cradles Kate's face in his hand. He expects her to pull back, but she doesn't. Instead, she closes her eyes and rests her cheek on his palm. Emboldened by Kate's response, Matt lowers his head and brings it within an inch of her lips. Matt takes his time, giving Kate every opportunity to back out.

Just as his lips graze Kate's mouth, the sound of laughter breaks the spell. Matt looks up to see a group of teenagers approaching the bridge.

"Shit," Matt mutters as he and Kate pull away from each other.

Kate stands up and grabs her backpack. "I'm ready to go."

She is flustered, her movements rapid and jerky. She steps away from him and makes her way to the bridge.

Matt picks up his own bag and slips his arms inside the shoulder straps. He's disappointed. They were so close. Why, oh why, did these bratty kids have to show up?

The teenagers are huddled in a group on the other side of the bridge and are throwing stones down into a puddle below. From what Matt can gather, they are trying to see who can get closest to hitting a log in the water.

Matt's heart plummets when Kate crosses the bridge on her own. Her hands are gripping the straps of her backpack and she is looking straight ahead. She's upset with him. She has every right to be too. Kate is a good woman. She doesn't skirt the line between right and wrong. She is squarely on the side of right in moral dilemmas.

Once they cross the bridge, the pair start back the way they came. Neither says a word. Kate is holding her head high with her chin jutting forward, looking like a stereotypical stuck up woman.

Matt knows better though. This is Kate's warrior stance. When she's feeling weak or intimidated, she holds herself in this way. Matt wonders if Kate even realizes she does it, or if it happens naturally.

After a few minutes of silence, Matt catches up to Kate and gently touches her arm.

"Stop. Please? Let's talk about this."

Kate looks at her feet instead of up at him. Matt reaches out and tilts her chin upwards. There are tears in her eyes.

"Don't do that. Don't cry. We didn't do anything wrong."

"We would have though," she protests. "If those kids hadn't shown up, we would have."

Matt nods. "But we didn't. You don't need to feel guilty."

"I can't help it," she admits before closing her eyes.

Matt pulls Kate in for a hug and tucks her head under his chin. "Nothing happened. You did nothing wrong."

Kate whispers, "I don't feel guilty because we almost kissed."

Matt steps back. "What is it then? Why are you so upset?"

She stands silent for a moment, then tries to turn away. "It's nothing. We have to keep going."

Matt holds on to her arm. "No. We're going to talk about this. I refuse to make the same mistakes we did ten years ago. I'm not going to hold everything in, and I'm not going to let you do it either."

Kate sets her jaw and Matt prepares for her to rip him a new one. She does the opposite. "I want to hold your hand; I want to kiss you; and I want to feel the way I did back then. That's what I feel guilty about."

Matt's jaw drops open.

"Happy now?" Kate asks, her eyes ablaze.

"You have no idea," he says before swooping in on her.

Kate lets out a little "eep" as he pulls her in tight against him. He doesn't hesitate this time as he brings his mouth to hers. Her lips feel so comfortable, like he's home. She wraps her arms around him and everything they've held back erupts.

This kiss is as intense as the day Kate ambushed him after they went skydiving. Matt chalked it up to adrenaline, but now he remembers – kissing Kate always felt like this. His body is on fire and he wants to lay her down on the dirt trail and take her right there. Make Kate his again.

Too soon, Kate pulls away. She rests her forehead on his, both taking deep breaths.

"No more," Kate says in between pants. "We can't do this again."

Before Matt can dissent, Kate steps away. She walks down the trail without another word. There's nothing Matt can do but follow her.

*   *   *

The rest of the day is awkward. Neither tries to make conversation. Their exchanges are limited to their hike and where they are heading next.

"We need to get a sunset picture," Kate tells him. "If we don't, we'll have to stay another night."

Matt wants to ask her if that would be so bad, but he remains quiet. She made it clear their dalliance is over. They are going to behave now.

As he walks along, Matt goes back and forth between joy and remorse. Shouldn't he feel bad about kissing Kate? Shouldn't guilt be crushing him right now? He is married! And he has two beautiful children.

Thinking of his kids does garner a twinge of self-hate. He heard Dr. Phil say once that when you cheat on your spouse, you cheat on your children too. It would destroy him to disappoint his family, to know he caused them pain.

Matt doesn't want to think of his kids right now. Or the fact that he will be home with them in a few days. He's in bubble world with Kate. His kids exist outside of bubble world.

My family will never know about the kiss, he reminds himself. No one will ever know. Kate won't tell anyone, and I'm certainly not telling anyone. This trip will be my secret. I can lock it away and keep it for rainy nights. What happens here isn't real. This is a reprieve from my everyday life.

Living in a temporary fantasy world with Kate has much more appeal than being a good guy. He loves Naomi, but in the "she's the mother of my children" way. Not the Kate way.

Matt removes himself from his internal dilemma as they approach Kate's car.

"We driving into town?"

"We don't have time," Kate says as she throws her pack in the backseat. "We won't make it to the store and back before sunset."

"Gotcha."

Matt gives Kate directions to the next location. It's a relatively easy spot. Once parked, it's a short walk to a wood carved bear. The bear stands ten feet tall and has a fish in its mouth.

"Why in the world would Judge want us to come here?" Matt asks.

Kate shakes her head. "No idea."

They sit on a park bench waiting for the sun to set. Both pretending to watch the small group of people milling around the statue. Bored, Matt takes the camera out of his pocket and scrolls through the pictures he's taken so far. He's got a few good shots.

"I want to see," Kate says as she scoots closer to him.

When she leans in close, Matt can smell her unique "Kate" scent. It sends a longing through his body he's never felt before. Matt needs to get away. If he doesn't, he'll try to kiss Kate again.

"Here." Matt hands her the camera and stands up. "I'm going to use the men's room."

"Oh, okay," she says before looking down at the camera screen.

After he uses the bathroom, Matt walks around for a few minutes. When the sun is low enough in the sky to be considered

262

a sunset picture, he walks back to Kate. She is standing in front of the bear and angling the camera for a picture.

"Did you get one?" he asks.

"Yep. We're good," Kate says with a smile.

She seems different than she did ten minutes ago. Lighter, maybe. She isn't scowling at him and her walk is peppy.

What got into her, he wonders.

"A few more pictures and we're done!" Kate exclaims as she gets in the car.

Oh, that's why she's in a good mood, Matt realizes. We're closer to being done.

He feigns happiness. "Yep, we're in the home stretch."

"Are you up for another hot dog dinner?" Kate asks.

"That's fine with me."

"I'm tired and I need a shower. I was thinking we could head back to the campsite, eat, and then walk to the bathrooms to clean up."

"Sounds good," Matt answers, hoping he doesn't sound as miserable as he feels.

Then he remembers something. They need to go to town for a reason other than dinner – the air mattress. Kate has forgotten about it. Matt's about to remind Kate, but he shuts his mouth.

What are you doing, his conscious asks. Remember the talk we had earlier? You know, the one about doing the right thing? Start doing the right thing!

But he can't bring himself to do it. If they don't get the air mattress, he may be able to finagle himself into Kate's tent again tonight. He wants another night in bed with her. He won't make a move, he'll merely enjoy his proximity to her.

Yes, that's it. He can sleep in her tent, but that's all. Sleep.

Walking back to the campsite is as difficult as it was the night before, but not as scary. Matt knows what to expect and feels less on edge.

They scarf down a couple hot dogs and some potato chips before heading to the bathrooms. Their banter is light, but it's not uncomfortable. They talk about their locations for tomorrow, and guess what their last stop on the scavenger hunt will be.

"What if Judge sends us to Paris, Kentucky?" Kate asks. "When I told him I wanted to go to Paris, France, he told me Paris, Kentucky is practically the same thing."

Matt laughs. "I have a feeling we're in store for another death-defying feat."

"Like what?"

"Maybe he'll have us go bungee jumping. Or deer hunting," Matt guesses as he leads them to the bathrooms.

"I'm not doing either one of those."

"Yes, you would. You haven't come this far to quit on the last challenge."

"Bungee jumping, maybe. Killing an animal, never."

"You were ready to kill that raccoon last night," Matt quips.

"I was not. I was ready to let *him* kill *you* last night."

Matt laughs. "Gee, thanks."

"No problem."

Matt can't see Kate's face, but he'd bet money she is smiling.

Matt takes the quickest shower possible. Unlike Kate's facilities, his were not recently remodeled. In fact, it looks like they've never been remodeled. When he's done, he sits on the ground outside and leans back against the cinderblock building.

As lucky as he felt earlier when Kate forgot about the air mattress, he now feels concerned. She's not upset with him anymore and he doesn't want her angry again. He wants to finish off their trip on a good foot. If he does, maybe Kate will stay in contact with him. It would be amazing to have her in his life in some way. Even if it's friendship.

Kate comes out of the bathroom, her hair wet and dripping down the back of her blue t-shirt. She's wearing a pair of men's boxers, blue with white polka dots. She looks so damn cute.

"Sorry to keep you waiting," she says with a smile.

Matt stands up. "I haven't been out here long."

Kate walks toward the trail, but Matt stops her.

"Kate, wait."

Kate turns to look at him. "What's up?"

"I have a confession to make."

She tilts her head to the side. "Okay..."

Matt shifts his weight to his other leg. "The thing is, you forgot to get an air mattress for me."

Kate smirks as she raises an eyebrow. "Who says I forgot?"

Without further explanation, she turns on her heels and starts walking. Matt stands stupefied for a moment.

Kate looks over her shoulder, "You coming?"

Matt steps to it and catches up with her.

There are so many questions running through his mind. If Kate didn't forget the air mattress, why didn't she drive to town?

Is she only saying she didn't forget because she doesn't want to look silly?

What is her plan?

Will she sleep on the ground in his tent?

Or does she want him to share a tent?

If she does want to share a tent, what does that mean?

"You're overthinking it," Kate says from in front of him.

"Overthinking what?"

"You know what," she answers coyly.

What the hell does *that* mean? This woman still knows how to torment him.

When they get back to camp, Matt's about to ask what the arrangements will be. Before he can start the conversation, Kate walks over to her tent and unzips it.

"I'm going to sleep. You're welcome to join me whenever you're ready."

Matt's groin twitches at the invitation.

Calm down, he tells himself. She's offering her bed, not her body.

"I'll be there in a second," he calls back to her. "I have to put the fire out." Literally and figuratively.

Matt pours water from water bottles over the fire and watches it fizzle out. White smoke fills the air as he douses the flames.

He's so confused. What is the source of Kate's sudden change of heart? She was upset earlier, near tears. Now she's playfully inviting him into her tent.

Or is he imagining the flirting? That has to be it. His ego seeing a temptress when Kate is merely being nice.

When the fire is completely out, and Matt has promised himself a hundred times that he will behave, he squats down and crawls into Kate's tent. It's dark inside, with nothing but the moonlight to illuminate the space. He crawls in, then turns around to close the zipper.

Kate is laying down with her sleeping bag on top of her like a blanket. He slowly crawls to his side of the bed on his hands and knees, trying not to rock the bed too much. Kate is quiet and he wonders if she fell asleep. In a lot of ways, it would be better if she did.

Like Kate, he uses his sleeping bag as a blanket and lays on his back. He stares at the dome shaped ceiling of the tent and listens to Kate's steady breathing. He wants to reach out and touch her hand, but resists the urge. He closes his eyes and repeats the day in his mind. He immediately flashes back to their kiss on the trail.

Matt's eyes fly open when Kate whispers, "I keep thinking about it."

"About what?"

"The trail."

Matt swallows the lump in his throat. "Me too."

"We shouldn't have done it."

"No. It was wrong."

Matt's eyes have adjusted to the darkness and he can see Kate laying on her side, her back to him.

"Do you regret it?" she asks.

"No," he answers immediately.

"Neither do I," Kate admits. She rolls onto her back. "I guess that makes me a bad person."

Matt chuckles grimly. "Then so am I."

The pair lay quietly side by side, their arms inches from each other. The sleeping bags rustle gently as Kate slides her hand to his. He takes it and squeezes it with his own.

"I missed you," Kate says in a soft voice. "I didn't want to, but I did."

Matt turns his head to the side. Kate is gazing at him from her side of the bed.

"I miss you every single day Kate. I wonder what you are doing and if you are happy. I think about you all the time."

"Why didn't you come after me?" she asks. "Why didn't you show up on my doorstep?"

"I wanted to, but I didn't think you would forgive me."

Kate's eyes are filled with tears. "I played tough Matt. I understand why you thought I would do that."

"Would you have turned me away?"

Kate's answer destroys him. "No. I waited for you. But I realize my pride played a huge part in this. I should have found you. I should have chased you down instead of expecting you to do all the work."

Kate starts crying softly.

Matt rolls over and hugs her to his chest. "Shhh. It's alright."

"No it's not. Everything is so fucked up. We're too far gone now," Kate whimpers into his shirt.

Tears form in Matt's eyes. "We're together now. At least you don't hate me anymore."

Matt strokes Kate's still damp hair as she leans against him. She calms down and they lay together in their embrace.

If this is all I get, it's enough, Matt thinks. Just to be here with her. To be able to hold her like this.

Kate pulls away and Matt worries she will roll over on her side of the bed again. Instead, she looks up at Matt.

"You're a good man Matt."

Kate's statement reminds Matt of his conversation with Theresa all those years ago while they sat outside Kate's apartment building. He didn't feel like a good man then, and he doesn't feel like a good man now.

"No, I'm not."

"Yes, you are. Which is exactly why I'm making the first move."

Before he knows what's happening, Kate's mouth is on his. Despite the promise he made to himself by the fire, he doesn't try to stop the train. He welcomes it. Burns with it.

He puts his hand in Kate's hair and holds her head in place. He doesn't want her to pull back. Soft moans escape from her mouth when he slides his tongue between her lips.

Matt rolls on his back and Kate's body is on top of his. Her hair cascades around his face as he runs his hand down her back and over her backside. Kate sits up and straddles his lap. She playfully licks her lips before pulling the t-shirt up over her head. The look on her face is pure lust and his body can't handle it.

Matt tucks Kate into him as he lifts himself up and rolls her onto her back. Kate giggles as their bodies create waves in the air mattress. Matt takes off his own shirt before covering her mouth with his. Kate gasps as Matt slides his pelvis between her legs.

His hands roam Kate's body. The landscape is familiar, yet exhilarating. How many times has he fantasized about this? Her skin under his fingertips puts all those fantasies to shame.

As Matt's hand travels south and touches the top of Kate's pajama shorts, he knows he's about to cross into dangerous territory. He won't be able to turn back if he goes beyond this point.

Kate's whispered words send heat down the length of his body. "Did I ask you to stop?"

Chapter Fifteen

Now

Kate opens her eyes to a fair amount of sunshine. She sits up and holds the sleeping bag to her chest. She blinks the sleep out of her eyes. Judging by the amount of light hitting the tent, she guesses it's around 7:30 a.m.

As she wakes up, Kate looks around the tent. Matt is still asleep, his naked body covered to his waist by the other sleeping bag. Seeing Matt dozing peacefully without a shirt on causes reality to hit Kate square in the jaw.

Oh...my...God! I slept with Matt!

Kate puts her hand over her mouth. I had sex with a married man!

And I'm engaged!

Oh no...Scott...

A kaleidoscope of thoughts swirl in her mind in a nonsensical pattern. Images of last night collide with memories of her last night with Scott. Worse, the pictures of Matt's children make an appearance. She needs to get out of the tent. Now!

Kate wraps herself in the sleeping bag and unzips the tent. She steps out into the humid morning air. She takes deep breaths in through her nose and out her mouth. It's a breathing technique Judge showed her long ago for running. But it helps in stressful situations too.

Calm down. It's okay, she tells herself.

No, it's not okay, screams a voice in the back of her head. You fucked Matt last night! What the hell are you doing?! You're going to screw up everything! What are you going to tell Scott? What is Matt going to tell his wife?

271

This is all her fault. She instigated it. Despite telling Matt on the trail there would be no more hanky panky, she purposely didn't go to town. She didn't want another air mattress. Not having one gave her the perfect excuse to let him sleep in her tent.

And then the flirting. What had that been about?

Kate can't pinpoint the exact moment she decided to go for it. Maybe it was when she was sitting alone staring at the ridiculous bear carving. She realized Matt was going to be out of her life again. Probably for good this time. She's getting married in a few months, and he's going home to his wife and kids. As much as she can't stand the thought of betraying Scott, she hated the thought of letting Matt slip through her fingers even more.

You're a slut, she thinks to herself. Plain and simple.

Warm tears run down her cheeks. What the hell is she going to do now? Go back in the tent, get dressed and act like nothing happened? How will she ever look Scott in the eyes again?

The worst thought of all filters through the chaos of her mind: I'm still in love with Matt.

Kate hears a rustling noise behind her, and then Matt's husky morning voice.

"Hey," he says sheepishly.

Kate wipes the tears away with her hand and then turns to him. "Hey."

Matt climbs out of the tent in his blue plaid pajama pants. His hair is tousled and he has a short beard growing in. He's handsome as ever.

Matt motions toward the tent. "Come back in."

Kate shakes her head. "I can't."

"Are you going to wear a sleeping bag all day?"

Kate looks down at herself and the red sleeping bag draped on her body. He has a point.

Kate walks back toward the tent and ducks inside. Matt follows her in, then zips the closure shut. Kate lays back down on the air mattress and stares up at the tent's ceiling. Matt lays beside her and snuggles in close.

"Are you okay?" he asks.

Kate doesn't know how to answer, so she doesn't say anything.

Matt props himself up on his elbow. "I'm sorry if you're upset. We got caught up in a moment last night."

Kate looks over at him. He doesn't seem as conflicted as she is.

"Caught up in a moment?" she says with a smidge of venom. "Really? That's how you are going to describe what we did?"

Matt frowns. "Sorry. I was trying to help."

Kate turns her head away. "I feel awful."

"No one is going to know what happened."

"I'll know Matt."

Matt skims his fingertips over her arm. "I should feel awful, but I don't. I've wanted you for so long, and you're finally here."

"This is all fleeting Matt. None of this is real."

"I know," Matt says with a note of sadness.

They lay together, Matt softly stroking her skin.

"Do you want to leave?" he asks her.

"I don't know what I want right now."

Matt wraps his arms around her and kisses her forehead. "It will be okay."

Kate pulls away from Matt and sits up. "How can you be so calm about this?! You just cheated on your wife! You just cheated on your beautiful children! And for what? One night with an ex you haven't seen in ten years? I'm not worth it Matt!"

Kate is hysterical now. Guilt fills every corner of her body.

"Not worth it?" Matt responds. "I don't regret what I did last night for a second. You might, but I don't. And yes, I know it's shitty. I should be begging God for forgiveness. But truth be told, I feel fucking amazing. I spent the night making love to the woman I love. And if that makes me a selfish bastard, then so be it. I would do it again in a second and not think twice about it."

Kate is stunned by Matt's raw honesty. More shocking is how true his words ring in her heart. Any guilt she feels has more to do with how much she enjoyed last night, not genuine regret.

"Will you please say something?" Matt pleads. "Don't make me feel like the asshole here."

Kate stammers. "I'm sorry. My brain is on overload."

Matt moves toward her and touches her shoulders. "I love you Kate. I have loved you since that night on the bench across from Nationwide Arena. I have loved you every single day since then, and I am going to love you for the rest of my life."

"I love you too," Kate says before pressing her forehead to his.

Without another word, Matt tilts her head up with his finger and kisses her softly on the lips. Their kiss becomes more heated with every passing second. Kate lets the sleeping bag slip out of her hand and they fall back onto the bed together.

*   *   *

An hour later, Kate is in her pajamas and walking with Matt to the bathrooms. They are hand in hand instead of one in front of the other. They didn't break down the tents. They decided they will visit the final two locations on the map, stop by the Ranger's Station, and then come back to clean up the campsite.

Kate knows they are delaying the inevitable, but she isn't ready to go yet. Once those tents come down, their tryst will be over. They'll move on to the last stop of the scavenger hunt and have no reason to be together anymore.

As the hot water cascades over her body, Kate wishes she could wash her conscious clean too. Will she be able to walk away from this unscathed? She doubts it.

After putting on shorts and a t-shirt, Kate looks at her reflection in the dingy bathroom mirror. Who is this woman? Two weeks ago, she hated Matt with a passion. Now, she wonders how she'll let him go.

She meets Matt outside and they walk to the car. Their discussion of the final pictures is a reserved one. Neither is excited about moving forward with this mission anymore.

But they do what they're supposed to do. They get the final two pictures and drive to the Ranger's Station.

"Good afternoon!" Roy says in a booming voice as they walk in the door. "I was beginning to wonder about you two."

Kate can't help but smile at his energy. "We got 'em! All ten pictures."

Matt stands next to Roy and flips through the pictures on the camera.

"Looks like ten pictures to me. Two sunsets and a sunrise included." Roy walks toward his office. "Did you two have a nice time?"

Kate and Matt exchange a glance.

"Yes, a very nice time," Matt answers.

Kate tries not to smirk.

"Good. Glad to hear it," Roy calls from his office. He walks out a moment later holding a white envelope. "I believe this is yours," he says as he hands it to Kate.

"Clue #6" is scribbled across the front in Judge's handwriting.

Kate opens the envelope and a small key falls into her hand. It is brass and has no distinctive markings. Kate pulls out a small sheet of paper from the envelope that says, "My bank in Columbus. Box 256."

"What does it say?" Matt asks.

"We're going to his bank in Columbus."

"His bank?"

Kate nods. "Yes. He must have a safe deposit box there."

Matt looks at the clock on the wall above Roy's office. "It's already 4:30 p.m., no way we'll make it to the bank before it closes."

Kate watches as a smile creeps across Matt's face. She doesn't have to ask him if they are thinking the same thing – another night in the woods together. Not taking down the tents turned out to be an excellent decision.

"Thank you for your time Roy," Kate says before giving him another handshake. "It's beautiful out here."

"I'll miss seeing your grandfather every fall. He and I always went to the diner up the street for a meal."

"There's a diner up the street?" Matt asks.

"Yes, sir. They make the world's best biscuits and gravy. Serve it all day long too."

"We should check it out," Matt says to Kate. "We're here because of Judge. Might as well eat at his favorite diner."

They get directions from Roy, then head out. As promised, they see a sign for "Margie's Diner" a few miles up the road. The diner is actually a small wood cabin Kate would have driven right by if she wasn't looking for it.

"Are they open?" Kate asks as she looks at the cabin through her windshield.

"Only one way to find out." Matt gets out of the car and walks toward the entrance. He climbs the wood porch's three steps, then pulls on the handle for the glass door. It opens.

276

Kate is greeted by the smell of pancakes as she walks inside the diner. Immediately at the entrance is the cash register. It is sitting on a glass display case filled with delicious looking desserts. Lemon meringue pie, red velvet cake and apple pie catch Kate's attention.

A woman in a blue and white checkerboard apron comes out of the kitchen. She's wearing jeans and a white t-shirt under her apron and a pair of Keds. Her red, curly hair is held back by a simple brown headband. She looks to be around fifty, but a well-maintained fifty.

"Good afternoon. Welcome to Margie's. You want a booth or a table?"

"A booth please," Kate answers.

Their waitress grabs two menus and two sets of silverware. She leads them past three booths before they reach the corner booth. Kate surveys the restaurant as she takes the seat backing up to the wall. There are four booths on the opposite side of the restaurant as well. There are eight tables with four chairs a piece filling the center of the room. A stone fireplace takes up the bulk of the back wall and the front wall is reserved for walking space to the kitchen.

There are no other customers. Not one.

"Are you getting ready to close?" Kate asks. "We don't want to impose."

"No hon. We're open until seven. This is just an off time for us. The dinner crowd will start rolling in about twenty minutes from now. I survive on my regulars."

"I bet you're busy in the fall," Matt says.

"Oh yes," she agrees. "We have a wait an hour long once the leaves start turning."

The waitress tries giving them menus, but Kate stops her. "I don't need a menu. Roy told us your biscuits and gravy are world famous."

277

The woman chuckles. "You've been talking to the Ranger, huh?

Kate smiles. "Yes, we just came from there."

"You may know her grandfather," Matt says. "Judge Payne."

The waitress's eyes twinkle as her smile widens. "You're Judge Payne's granddaughter?"

"Yes, I am."

She touches her hand to her heart. "I adored that man. Sweet as can be. I was so sorry to hear he passed."

"Thank you. He loved coming out here."

"And we loved having him. Judge was the life of the party."

Kate and Matt both laugh.

"One time, he came in here swearing he saw a bear. Had a tall tale about it. None of us believed him. Well, later that night, one of the guys who was giving him grief walked out to his car and came running back in here screaming and raising Cain. He said something attacked him in the parking lot. Turns out, it was your grandfather in a bear suit!"

"No he didn't!" Kate exclaims.

The waitress laughs. "I swear on my life! Old Stan about had a stroke."

"Yep, that sounds like Judge," Matt chuckles.

"Oh honey," the waitress says when she sees the look on Kate's face. "Stan deserved it. He's a real asshole."

This makes Matt laugh even harder.

The waitress brings their drinks a few minutes later. Kate catches her before she walks away again.

"I didn't get your name."

"I'm Margie."

278

Kate smiles. "I figured as much, but wanted to be sure."

They exchange more stories about Judge before there's a holler from the kitchen.

"That's my husband," Margie explains. "Your food is ready."

Kate and Matt eat their meal and talk about mundane things. They are avoiding the elephant in the room. They have one more night together. Reality can wait a little while longer.

The biscuits and gravy are good, but Kate thinks her grandmother's were better. The dinner crowd trickles in and a second waitress comes in to help Margie. Margie tells a few of the regulars that Judge's granddaughter is present and they come over to visit. They all say their condolences and each has a Judge story to share, many of which Kate has never heard.

Before they leave, Kate orders a slice of red velvet cake to go. "It was Judge's favorite," she tells Matt. "I have to get a slice."

"Of course you do," Matt says with a smirk.

On the drive back to the campground, Kate's body tingles. As soon as they get in the tent, all hell is going to break loose. She can hardly control herself.

The electricity between them crackles as they start down the path for their campsite. Matt sticks out his hand and Kate takes it without hesitation. She can feel his heartbeat in his palm. They both start walking quicker, anxious to get to their destination.

About half way there, Matt stops and pulls her off the path. He leans her against a tree.

"What are you doing?"

Matt puts his hands on the tree on either side of her shoulders. "I can't wait any longer."

Matt lowers his mouth to hers and presses Kate against the tree with his body. A moan escapes her lips when he moves his mouth away to kiss her neck.

"You taste so good," he murmurs. Matt puts his hand up Kate's shirt and cups her breast through her bra.

Kate is about to unbuckle his shorts when the snap of a twig nearby stops her cold. She pushes Matt back.

"Did you hear that?"

"What?" he asks looking around.

"I heard something."

They both pause and listen to their surroundings. Sure enough, Kate hears more noise coming from behind them.

"Someone's coming up the path," Matt tells her as he looks over her shoulder. He bends down and pretends to tie his shoe.

Kate leans against the tree casually as she waits for the group to pass. She hears soft laughter as the group gets closer and closer. Matt stands up when the group draws near. He raises a hand to acknowledge them. Four men carrying full camping packs on their backs each say a quick "hello" as they pass. Kate nods her head at them, then slumps against the tree when they're out of sight.

"That was close," she mumbles.

Matt shrugs. "So what if they caught us? They don't know us from Adam."

"True," Kate admits. "Still embarrassing though."

Matt grins. "It's been a while since I got busted making out in public."

They get back on the path and begin the trek to their campsite again. Almost being caught tempers Kate's hormones. For now.

"Will you be able to lie to Scott?" Matt asks her out of the blue. "If he asks you if anything happened between us?"

Kate kicks a rock. "I'll have to, won't I?"

Matt nods. "Yes. Will he buy it?"

Kate is wondering the same thing. "I don't want to think about going back home Matt."

"I understand."

She stops and wraps her arms around him. "I want to enjoy this moment with you. Let's pretend the world doesn't exist. It's just us."

Matt smiles down at her. "Sounds good to me."

*   *   *

The next morning is rough on Kate. After another great night lost in Matt, it's time to go. They take their time breaking down the tents and gathering all of their supplies. Kate struggles to get her tent back into its carry bag.

"Can I just leave it here?"

Matt chuckles. "If it was still standing, someone would see it as a nice gesture. Crumpled up in a ball, it's littering."

Kate sighs. "Okay."

They struggle to arrange all of their equipment in a way that will allow them to make only one trip to the car, but it's impossible. They take a load to the car, then head back for the rest of their stuff. Seeing the campsite taken apart breaks Kate's heart.

Matt comes up and puts his arm around her. "I guess this is it, huh?"

Kate frowns. "It appears so."

She rests her head on his shoulder and they stare at what's left of their private getaway. Matt kisses her forehead. Kate could have stood like this forever if a family didn't walk up behind them.

Kate turns to see their new company. A couple in their thirties or forties walks up with two young girls in tow behind them.

"Hello," the woman says, her blonde hair tucked under her cap. "We must be in the wrong spot."

281

Matt drops his arm. "No, you're probably where you're supposed to be."

"We're leaving," Kate explains.

The woman smiles. "Thank goodness! I don't think I can walk any further with this giant backpack!"

Her husband steps up beside her. "I think she brought our entire house."

"We're going to be here a week," the wife defends herself.

Kate can't help but be envious of this family. They get to spend a week in this spot. Her fantasy world for the last couple of days.

"We'll get out of your way." As Kate bends down to pick up her tent, she looks up at the family. "Do you guys want our tents?"

The couple exchanges a glance.

"Are you sure?" the wife asks.

"Yes," Matt answers. "We don't need them."

The woman smiles. "That's awfully nice of you. Now the girls can each have their own tent."

The girls, who both appear to be under ten, break out in wide grins. "My own tent!" one of them exclaims. "Awesome!"

Matt and Kate exit the happy scene. Kate glances over her shoulder for one last look at her hideaway. The new family is moving in. This is their spot now. Kate turns back toward the trail. With each step, her mood darkens.

*   *   *

The drive to Columbus isn't long enough. Matt keeps his warm hand on her thigh the entire ride. They listen to the radio and Kate hums along to a few of the songs. Many of them bring their situation to mind, probably because she can't think of anything else.

They pull into the bank around 1:30 p.m.

"What do you think is in the box?" Matt asks her.

"The key to your new car," Kate guesses.

"Me too."

"If it is, you won't have to fly home. You'll get to ride home in style."

Matt smiles. "If the car runs."

"It does," Kate tells him as she opens the front door to the bank. "At least it did the last time Judge took it for a spin."

The bank is your standard banking facility. White tile floors and cherry countertops protecting three bank tellers. A man sitting at a desk to their right greets them.

Kate walks over to him. "Hi. We need to get into a safe deposit box, please."

After exchanging basic information and showing the man her I.D., he walks them to the room with the safe deposit boxes.

"Wait here a moment. I'll be right back with your box."

Kate and Matt stop at a wooden table outside one of the vaults. The banker comes back with a long, silver rectangular box. "Your grandfather left instructions for us."

"He did?" Kate asks.

"Yes. I'll never forget it. He provided us with your name and said I could not give you the box unless a tall gentleman with black hair came in with you."

Kate exchanges a smile with Matt. "Good ole Judge. Always on top of things."

The banker sets the metal deposit box on the table in front of Kate. She puts the brass key in the key hole and turns it. She lifts the lid on the box and peers inside.

There are two small, white gift boxes labeled #2 and #3 in black ink. The only other item in the safe deposit box is a DVD inside a plastic case. A sheet of paper is taped to the outside of the clear case. The paper is labeled #1. Kate removes the items from the safe deposit box and the banker puts it back into the vault.

"I'll give you two some privacy," he says before walking away.

Kate takes the sheet of paper off the DVD case and unfolds it.

Kate and Matt:

If you're reading this – Congratulations! You've made it to the last stop. Please watch the enclosed DVD before opening the boxes. Of course, I can't stop you if you jump the gun.

Love always,

Grandpa/Judge

Kate flips the paper over, but the back is blank. She was expecting an epic letter from Judge. In fact, she was longing for one. A lasting message that she can cherish for the rest of her life. Instead, she gets a few quick lines in his barely legible writing.

"This is it?" Matt asks after he reads the note.

"Appears so."

"Where do you want to watch the DVD?"

Kate picks it up. "I don't know. I'm not ready to go back to my place."

Or my life...

Matt thinks about their options. "I need a hotel for the night and most hotels have DVD players. If not, we can buy one for ten bucks."

Kate nods. "Good idea."

She puts the DVD and the small boxes in her purse. They thank the banker for his time and walk out to Kate's car.

"Where do you want to stay tonight?" Kate asks Matt.

"Doesn't matter to me."

Kate pulls out of the bank parking lot and drives a few blocks before she spots a hotel. "How about the Hampton Inn?"

"That'll work."

Kate sits in the car debating whether she should call Scott while she waits on Matt to check into the hotel. He's probably worried sick about her. She hasn't spoken to him in three days.

She turns on her phone and waits for the worst. And there it is – ten missed calls from Scott. All from yesterday, the day she was supposed to leave Hocking Hills. She has two voicemail messages. Despite the alarm bells going off in her brain, she listens to them.

Scott's voice on the first message makes her wince.

"Hey Babe, it's me. I've been trying to reach you all day. I guess things took longer than expected. Please call me when you can. I love you."

Kate saves the message and waits for the next one.

"Hey lady. It's Theresa. Scott called to ask me if I've heard from you. Now he's got me worried. Call me when you make it out of the wilderness."

Kate's hand is shaking when she takes the phone from her ear. She doesn't have the nerve to call either one of them back. Instead, she resorts to a text message. She sends them both the same thing:

> *Hey! Finally out of the woods. Judge had us going here, there and everywhere. At the last stop of the scavenger hunt now. Should be done soon. I'll call you later.*

There. She reads it again, despite having already sent it. She's fairly sure it sounds like a normal message.

A few minutes later, Matt comes back out to the car.

"Good news. They have DVD players." Matt's smile falters. "What's going on?"

285

"Scott called."

Matt's face drops. "Oh. How did it go?"

"I didn't talk to him. He left a voicemail and I sent him a text."

Matt takes a seat in the car, but leaves the passenger door open. "I should probably check my phone too." He takes his cell phone out of his pocket and turns it on.

Kate watches his face as he listens to his messages. He seems as crestfallen as she feels.

"Naomi?" Kate asks when Matt hangs up his phone.

"Yep. Three messages. Each one more urgent than the last."

"Call her."

Matt groans. "I don't want to."

"You have to," Kate urges softly. "She doesn't deserve to worry."

Matt gives Kate a sideways glance, then steps out of the car. He walks a few feet away and puts his cell phone to his ear. He turns his back to Kate as he starts talking and she can't make out what he's saying.

I shouldn't have checked my cell phone, Kate thinks. I've just immersed us in the real world.

When Matt ends his call, Kate gets out of the car. "How did it go?"

Matt frowns. "Awful. She was really worried about me. She didn't seem happy with my explanation."

"I'm sorry."

Matt puts his phone back in the side pocket of his cargo shorts. "She'll get over it. Eventually."

Kate holds up the DVD. "Ready to watch?"

"I'm dying to watch!" Matt says while grabbing his bag from the back of Kate's car.

286

They take the elevator to his room on the fourth floor and Matt swipes the key card to let them into room 432. The room is nice, but like any other hotel room Kate has seen. There's a queen size bed with a tan colored down comforter and six white pillows. A small desk with a chair occupies a corner near the window, and an entertainment center sits against the wall facing the bed. Nothing too exciting.

Matt turns on the TV and takes the DVD from Kate. He slides it into the machine and they both wait like eager children on Christmas morning for the video to start. Kate gasps when Judge's faces comes on the screen.

Judge looks ill in the video, but not as sick as he was during the last few weeks of his life. He is wearing his favorite pair of red flannel pajamas and smiling at her from the TV. Kate covers her mouth with her hand to hold back her shock.

Matt pauses the video. "Are you okay?"

She was hoping it would be Judge on the DVD. But she was still unnerved when she saw his face.

"I need a minute," Kate says when she can catch her breath. She stands up and walks over to the window. She looks down on the city streets below until she's composed.

Kate walks back over to the end of the bed and sits next to Matt. "I'm ready. Start it up."

Matt rubs her back. "You sure?"

Kate nods. "Yes." Matt hits the "play" button, then takes her hand in his.

Judge reappears on the screen. This time, Kate is ready for him.

"By this time, you two have likely figured out why I sent you out on this venture..." Judge pauses for drama, "because I'm a cranky bastard!"

Kate can't help but laugh with Judge.

287

Judge clears his throat. "Kate, I'm sure you were mad as hell. Matt, I'm sure you weren't happy either.

Matt gives Kate's hand a little squeeze and she smiles at him.

"I hope you two have found a way to forgive each other. Whether you wanted to admit it or not, you were both harboring ill will. I wanted the two of you to talk about your past and put it behind you. Life is too short. Too short."

Judge looks down at his hands for a moment, then back at the camera. "I'm not going to lie and say I wasn't partially motivated by the thought of getting you two back together. But I know it might not be possible.

"Kate, I don't want you to take this as a sign that I don't like Scott. Because I do, very much. He's a good man and will make an excellent husband. My only concern, if I have one at all, is you don't have the light in your eyes like you did when you were with Matt. But maybe it was because Matt was your first real love."

Kate doesn't know what to think. What would Judge have said if he knew Matt was married?

"And Matthew,"

Matt sits up straighter when he hears his name.

"If you haven't won her over yet, do so now. Tell her you're sorry. Get on your knees and beg if you have to."

Matt and Kate chuckle at Judge's tone of voice.

"I want the two of you to build a bridge and get over your past. If you've both moved on to other loved ones, so be it. But at least you won't look back on your time together with such disdain.

"Now, about those two boxes..."

Kate lets go of Matt's hand and dashes over to her purse to grab the two boxes.

"Box #2 is for Matt. It's the key to your new car. Enjoy it my friend! I know you'll take care of her."

Kate hands the box to Matt and he slides the lid off. Sure enough, a silver key on a tiny steering wheel keychain sits inside.

"Box #3," Judge continues from the video, "is for you Kate." Judge puts his hand up, "Don't open it just yet."

Kate stops herself from opening the box and puts it back down on her lap.

"I know your mom and your aunt are going to be upset with me for giving you what's in the box, but I don't care. I'm dead, remember?"

Judge's smile slips before he opens his mouth again. He starts choking up, which makes tears immediately spring to Kate's eyes.

"I have loved you like my own daughter Kate, maybe more so. I have a bond with you that I cherish from the bottom of my heart. You mean the world to me. I want nothing but your absolute happiness. I can't be with you on your wedding day. I won't be able to walk you down the aisle, and it kills me."

Judge stops to wipe a tear from his eye with the cuff of his flannel pajama top. "It's the one thing I wish I could be around to do. Obstacle courses, skydiving, camping, they're all exciting. But to see you on your wedding day, in your beautiful dress…that's what I regret most."

Tears slide down Kate's cheeks. She's thought many times about how she will walk down the aisle without Judge. Her wedding will feel empty without him.

"I want you to open the box now," Judge instructs, then pauses to give Kate time.

Kate opens the box and gasps when she sees her grandmother's diamond ring. "No way," she murmurs.

"Wear it on your wedding day. It will be a reminder of your grandmother and me. We will be with you always sweetheart."

Kate slips the ring on her finger and a tear splashes her hand.

"I don't care which guy you choose to marry Kate, but I do hope you pick the right one. Think about who will make you happy and who will be a good father to your children. Family is everything."

Kate looks back up at the television and Judge is walking toward the camera.

"Time for me to go. You and your mother will be here soon. Can't look too suspicious. I love you."

And then the screen goes black.

Kate and Matt sit in silence, soaking it all in. The part that keeps playing in Kate's mind is "Family is everything." Judge is right; family is everything.

"Is your mom going to be upset about the ring?" Matt asks.

"No." Kate glances at him. "But my aunt will be. I think she's been dreaming about how it will look on her finger for the last few years."

Matt jingles the key in his hand. "I have the key. No idea where the car is though."

"I'm sure Phil knows where it is."

They lapse back into silence. Kate doesn't know what to say. Their scavenger hunt is over. Mission accomplished. They have no legitimate reason to be together anymore.

Kate stares at the blank television. Not sure what to do. Matt reaches out and puts his hand on her thigh.

"I don't want you to go. Not yet," he tells her.

Kate turns to look at him. His face a mirror of her sadness. "I have to leave eventually."

"Do you? Can't we figure something out?"

"Like what Matt? Are we going to run away together? Leave everyone behind?"

Matt stands up and runs his hand through his hair. "No. Yes. I don't know. But I can't lose you again." He gets down on his knees in front of her. His eyes are glassy and his tone is desperate. "I can't live without you Kate. I've done it once. And it was awful. Please."

"Matt, I don't know what you want me to say."

"Say you'll be in my life. Say we'll make something happen."

Kate closes her eyes. "I can't."

Matt's hands fall from her legs. When she opens her eyes, his shoulders are slumped and he's giving her puppy dog eyes.

"You have kids Matt. Two beautiful children who need a father. I can't give them my childhood."

"I can still be in my children's lives Kate."

"So you're going to get divorced? Leave your wife for me? That will destroy your children. And they'll blame me. They'll hate me."

Matt shakes his head. "No they won't. You're thinking the worst. We can make this work Kate. I know we can."

Kate feels like she's running, although she's not moving. Can she take the leap with Matt? Can she ask him to leave his wife? She won't let Matt move to Ohio, he has to be near his children. Which means she would have to move to Colorado.

And what about Scott? She loves him. She does. Enough to marry him without hesitation. What if this time with Matt has been a fantasy? They've been in their own world for days. If they are together for real, so many obstacles will present themselves. Jobs, homes, marriages, children...

Can she handle that? Can she ask Matt to blow up his life? She knows Matt won't do what her dad did. Matt will be involved in his kids' lives, but what about her? She wants children of her own. She would be a great step-mom, or at least she'd try to be. But she wants a baby. She wants to be pregnant and have the

291

"mom" experience from day one. Would Matt be willing to do that with her?

Kate thinks about Judge and what his advice would be in this situation. If Judge knew Matt was married, he never would have set this up. He would have considered Matt off limits and any reconciliation between them impossible. Kate decides to make the "right" decision as opposed to the decision she wants.

Kate slides down onto her knees in front of Matt. She lifts his chin so he's looking her in the eyes.

"I love you Matt. I always will."

"But you're leaving, aren't you?"

She nods. "It's the right thing to do. You know it too."

Matt leans forward and wraps her in an embrace. She squeezes back, knowing this might be the last time she ever holds Matt in her arms.

He whispers in her ear, "I will wake up every morning the rest of my life wishing I was waking up next to you."

"So will I."

Matt kisses her cheek. "You are the love of my life Kate. No one will compare to you. Ever."

Her heart is breaking, it will never be the same. She needs to leave before she loses her gumption.

Kate holds Matt's chin in her hand and gives him one last soft kiss. She stands up and Matt holds onto her hand until she's too far away. His fingertips slip off the bottom of hers with a finality that takes her breath away.

She didn't think she would ever feel as devastated as she did ten years ago, but she was wrong. The tidal wave of despair is almost upon her. Kate stands at the hotel door and takes a final glance at Matt. He's leaning with his back against the hotel bed gazing back at her.

"I love you Matt," she tells him before turning away and opening the hotel door.

She gets out of the room as fast as she can. Once the door shuts behind her, she leans against it for a second. She wants nothing more than to go right back in there.

Move, a voice inside her head yells. Her conscience knows she's on the verge of wussing out.

Kate pushes away from the door and scrambles for the elevator. She hits the down button repeatedly.

"Come on! Come on!" she demands, as if her talking to the elevator will make it go any faster.

She looks around and sees the door for the stairwell. She takes off for the stairs, trying to fight off the sobs that want to explode from inside of her.

Kate throws open the door for the stairs and jogs down them. She's going so fast, she feels a bit dizzy. When she sees the door marked, "Lobby" she pulls it open and speed walks toward the exit. She slows her pace when she enters the revolving door and tries to return the smile of the elderly woman on the other side of the glass.

Finally outside, Kate takes a deep breath. She needs a game plan, right now. Kate pulls out her cell phone and calls T as she walks to her car.

After three rings, Theresa picks up. "What's up biotch?"

"Where are you?" Kate asks breathlessly.

"I'm at the office. Where the hell are you? You sound terrible."

"I'm coming to see you."

Before Kate hangs up, she hears T say, "Kate? What's…"

Theresa's office is only a few blocks over from Matt's hotel, but Kate doesn't want to leave her car behind. It would give her an excuse to return to the hotel. If Kate comes back, she won't be able to stop herself from seeing Matt.

Kate parks her car in the parking garage under Theresa's office building. She curses to herself as she waits for the underground elevator to take her up to the fourteenth floor.

Just a little longer, just a little longer, she repeats in her head.

When the elevator doors open, Kate waves at the receptionist without stopping to say "hi" like she usually does. The receptionist gives Kate an odd look, but doesn't stop her from going down the hall. Theresa's door is open and Kate can see Theresa sitting behind her desk, the city skyline at her back.

Kate closes the door to T's office and leans back against it. Relieved to be in a safe place.

Theresa puts down her pen and stands up. "Kate, what is going on?"

Kate opens her mouth to explain, but instead of words, the floodgate of emotions she's been holding back come out in a pained moan.

"Oh my God!" Theresa exclaims and rushes over to Kate.

Theresa pulls Kate into a tight hug as Kate cries uncontrollably. Theresa doesn't need to ask what happened. She doesn't offer solace or advice. She just holds on to Kate for dear life.

Because that's what best friends do.

Epilogue

Twenty-three years later

Matt's heart flutters as he walks up to the law school. He smiles when he thinks of the last time he was here. The shocked expression on Kate's face as he burst through the door, like a deer in headlights. He frequently thinks of that day and the scavenger hunt. Their time together was something he cherished through the years. A secret place only he knew about.

After Kate left him at the hotel, he stayed another night in Columbus. He needed to unload the emotional baggage before he went home to face his wife and kids.

Matt put on a show when he got home. Feigning the excitement a man who just inherited the muscle car of his dreams would have. When no one was looking, his smile fell. He was consumed by his fate to be without the love of his life.

Matt filled his emptiness with activities and obligations. He volunteered to be the coach for his son's little league team; he joined a church softball league; he was secretary of the local bar association; and he made a point to take Naomi on a romantic date every month.

Despite his hectic schedule, there were times when he had nothing better to do than sit and think. Inevitably, those thoughts turned to Kate.

A couple of months after the scavenger hunt ended, Matt took a chance. He sent a "friend" request to Theresa on Facebook. Matt tossed and turned that night. Did he make a mistake? What if Theresa declined his request? Worse, what if she accepted and he spent the rest of his life obsessed with her page?

The next morning, Matt was elated to see Theresa accepted his request. His happiness was cut short when he scrolled through Theresa's page and saw photographs of Kate's wedding. Matt's heart plummeted when he saw the smile on Kate's face as Scott slid the golden band on her left ring finger. She was wearing the dress he saw in her cell phone pictures. The same one she wore in his dreams of their fantasy wedding.

Matt never wanted to be another man so much in his life. He was filled with a sudden and strong jealousy of Scott. This was the man who would wake up next to Kate every morning. The man who would hold Kate in his arms when she needed comforting. The man who may be the father of her children.

Matt was in a particularly foul mood for the rest of the day.

At one point, Naomi turned to him, a sour look on her face, "What the hell is your problem today?"

Matt apologized for his behavior and planted a fake smile on his face. He sent Naomi two dozen pink roses the next day, her favorite.

Matt limited how often he checked Theresa's Facebook page. Tuesday night was his designated Facebook night. He looked forward to Tuesday night all week. Matt knew this was neurotic, but he wanted to feel connected to Kate in some way. Even if it was from a distance.

At times, it seemed Theresa was well aware of the reason Matt sent her the friend request. She included comments in her posts that specifically addressed Kate and what she was up to. Like the day Theresa made a post on Facebook about Kate's health:

> *Sending good mojo to my friend Kate who has been under the weather lately. Hopefully her doctor appointment tomorrow goes well.*

Matt panicked when he saw this. What if Kate's illness was serious? He would rush to her side, discretion be damned.

Thankfully, Theresa followed up the next day:

> *All my worry was for naught - my bestie is pregnant with her first child! She is due in the beginning of November.*

Matt was relieved and sad at the same time. Kate was okay! But she was having someone else's child. The jealousy of Scott reared its ugly head again.

There was another reason for Matt's melancholy. He had a dream, a secret dream he could never tell anyone about. As his children grew and made their way toward adulthood, Matt envisioned himself heading back to Columbus. Once his kids were off to college, he was free to pursue Kate again.

Matt loved Carlie and Noah, and would never change the choices he made. They were his greatest contribution to the world. Wonderful children he knew would grow up to be amazing people.

But in the back of his mind, Matt was counting down the years until they would be out of the house. Not because he wanted rid of them, but because he wanted Kate. Kate having a child of her own meant Matt would have to wait even longer for her.

After the initial upset, Matt felt happiness. Kate wanted children and she would be a wonderful mom. She would know the love only a mother knows.

Theresa posted pictures online of Kate and her baby girl the day the baby was born. The smile on Kate's face and the sparkle in her eyes made Matt tear up.

"Enjoy her Kate," he said out loud to no one but himself.

Two years later, Kate had a baby boy. Matt again felt the twinge of disappointment. This pushed his ridiculous dream even further back.

In the meantime, Matt was the best father he could be. His children adored him and he enjoyed watching them grow immensely.

Being a good husband was much harder. He loved Naomi, but not the way he loved Kate. Matt tried to forget about Kate and focus on his relationship with Naomi, but it was difficult. There were times he felt like he was walking through life in someone else's body.

Given the way he treated Naomi, he was not surprised when she asked for a divorce.

They were walking in the door from dropping Noah off at college when she said, "Well, our work here is complete. When do you want to see a lawyer?"

Matt gave her a weary look.

Naomi's eyes were soft. "Matt, I'm not stupid. And please don't act like this isn't what you want."

Matt sat down on their brown leather couch and sighed. "I'm sorry Naomi."

Naomi sat beside him and leaned her head on his shoulder. Matt instinctively put his arm around her.

"I wish you loved me Matt," she told him.

"I do love you."

"I know. But not like you love her."

Matt closed his eyes. "How did you know?"

"You were never the same after you came home from Columbus."

"Why didn't you say something?"

Naomi sat up and looked Matt in the eyes. "Because I'm in love with you." A tear dropped from Naomi's eye. "And I wanted us to be together. But we're both selling ourselves short here. I deserve better. I deserve someone who loves me more than anyone else."

Matt wiped the tear with his thumb. "I tried Naomi. I really did. I wish I could be the man you deserve."

"I know you tried. And that's why I'm not angry anymore. You were so great with Carlie and Noah. I couldn't have asked for a better father for them. Truly. But they're going their own way now. And I need to find my own way too."

The dissolution was final less than a year later. The kids were shocked and angry at first, but as they say, time heals all wounds.

Matt moved into a small condo in Colorado after he and Naomi sold their house. He continued his regular job and his community activities. He even went on a few dates. There was never a spark.

Matt watched Kate's life unfold via social media. Theresa did an excellent job documenting Kate and her family. Kate's daughter was a dead ringer for her mother and Kate's son had her eyes. Matt noticed Scott was rarely in the pictures. He didn't know if Theresa did that for his benefit, or if Scott wasn't present for the events.

When Kate's son celebrated his eighteenth birthday, Matt started getting anxious. Could he really go back for her? Could he interject himself into her life again? He witnessed the beautiful life she built for herself. How vain was he to believe that Kate would want him back? Maybe their time together all those years ago was merely a fling. Something Kate needed to get out of her system before settling down with Scott.

Just when Matt decided to leave Kate alone, he read a post from Theresa that he couldn't help but think was meant for him. It was posted underneath a picture of Kate and her son in his new dorm room.

> *So proud of Camden! Kate and I got him all moved in. Camden is super excited about starting college and I know he will do fantastic. Congratulations to Kate and Scott for raising such a wonderful boy. And good luck to Kate on the next phase of her life. I know she is looking to pursue new passions, as well as old ones. Children can temporarily keep us from the things in life we really want.*

To everyone else, the last few sentences of Theresa's post may have sounded cold. A few would chalk it up to Theresa never having children.

"Tsk, tsk," they would say, "Theresa thinks children are an aggravation. How sad is that?"

To Matt, the post meant something else entirely. Matt wanted to call Theresa, but he didn't have her number. He considered sending her a message through the social media site. He didn't though. He wasn't brave enough to flat out ask Theresa if he was the "old passion" Theresa referenced in her post

In the end, he decided to find out for himself.

Matt booked a flight to Columbus. It was impulsive and ridiculous, but he couldn't sit back any longer. He bought a roundtrip ticket in case he was reading into something that wasn't really there.

Now, here he is, standing outside the law school wondering what the hell he's doing.

Matt swallows hard and walks through the entrance of the school. He catches a glimpse of his reflection in the glass door and frowns. His hair is grayer and the lines on his face have deepened since the last time he saw Kate.

Matt is also wearing glasses now. Naomi told him the glasses make him look distinguished, but Matt isn't so sure. He feels old in them.

Matt walks through the hallways and up the stairs to Kate's office. Except when he gets there, the placard on the door reads, "Professor Beau Jeffries". He was so preoccupied, he never stopped to consider Kate would be in a different office.

Matt turns away from the door, intending to go back downstairs to the information desk. But he doesn't need to.

Kate is standing behind him, multi-colored folders in her arms and a shocked expression on her face. Like him, time has worked its magic on her face and hair, but Kate is still stunningly beautiful.

She takes a step toward him.

Matt is terrified. She is about to tell him to get lost. He soaks in all he can, confident this is the last time he'll see her in person.

Matt's heart skips a beat as Kate smiles warmly. "What took you so long?"

Acknowledgements

I would be nowhere without my friends and family. They have made everything in my life possible. My guinea pig readers are the best; you know who you are. My husband and son have put up with me stowing away in my office for hours at a time and my crankiness when I stay up way too late writing. My sister is my social media guru; I'd be lost without her.

Right before I finished editing this book, I went on a trip to Las Vegas with my fantasy football league – Finkle's Laces Out League. So a special shout out to them. My sister-in-law and mother-in-law joined me on the trip and showed me things in Vegas I can never unsee. Love you guys!

I love to hear from my readers. You can follow me on Facebook or on Instagram - @Neva_Bell_Books. You can also reach me via email at NevaBellBooks@gmail.com. I will try to return any inquiries promptly. Check out my other books and leave a review – if you feel so inclined.